**"All right, look," Captain Kira Nerys
said as the alternate Winn Adami
moved in to confiscate their phasers.
"We're not who you think we are."**

Opaka laughed. "Oh, I'm quite certain of who you are,
young woman. I knew it the moment I saw *him*." She
pointed a finger at Vaughn. "What I demand to know
is why you've come here, and why you're posing as the
Intendant."

Kira grinned involuntarily, a nervous rictus catalyzed
by the sheer absurdity of seeing Opaka Sulan as the gun-
slinging master of a labor camp, and Winn Adami as her
lieutenant.

Vaughn, for his part, seemed preoccupied studying
the faces around him. What he expected to learn from
doing so, Kira had no clue. They'd spoken little during
the two hours it had taken them to walk here from
Akorem's Rock—after Nog had successfully beamed
them across the dimensional gulf from Deep Space 9—
pausing in their journey only to snatch some indigenous
clothing from a vacant farmhouse in order to conceal
their uniforms as they continued toward Vekobet.

"I came here because of Iliana Ghemor," Kira told
their captor.

THE NEW ADVENTURES OF
STAR TREK: DEEP SPACE NINE®

The Lives of Dax by various authors

A Stitch in Time by Andrew J. Robinson

Avatar, Book One & Book Two by S. D. Perry

Section 31: Abyss by David Weddle & Jeffrey Lang

Gateways: Demons of Air and Darkness by Keith R.A. DeCandido

"Horn and Ivory" by Keith R.A. DeCandido from
Gateways: What Lay Beyond

Mission: Gamma, Book One—Twilight by David R. George III

Mission: Gamma, Book Two—This Gray Spirit by Heather Jarman

Mission: Gamma, Book Three—Cathedral
by Michael A. Martin & Andy Mangels

Mission: Gamma, Book Four—Lesser Evil by Robert Simpson

Rising Son by S. D. Perry

The Left Hand of Destiny, Book One & Book Two
by J. G. Hertzler & Jeffrey Lang

Unity by S. D. Perry

Worlds of Star Trek: Deep Space Nine, Volume One
by various authors

Worlds of Star Trek: Deep Space Nine, Volume Two
by various authors

Worlds of Star Trek: Deep Space Nine, Volume Three
by various authors

Warpath by David Mack

Fearful Symmetry by Olivia Woods

COLLECTIONS

Twist of Faith
by S. D. Perry; David Weddle & Jeffrey Lang;
Keith R.A. DeCandido

These Haunted Seas
by David R. George III and Heather Jarman

STAR TREK
DEEP SPACE NINE®

THE SOUL KEY

OLIVIA WOODS

Based upon *Star Trek*®
created by Gene Roddenberry
and
Star Trek: Deep Space Nine
created by Rick Berman & Michael Piller

POCKET BOOKS
New York London Toronto Sydney

Pocket Books
A Division of Simon & Schuster, Inc.
1230 Avenue of the Americas
New York, NY 10020

This book is a work of fiction. Names, characters, places, and incidents either are products of the author's imagination or are used fictitiously. Any resemblance to actual events or locales or persons, living or dead, is entirely coincidental.

First Pocket Books paperback edition August 2009

POCKET and colophon are registered trademarks of Simon & Schuster, Inc.

For information about special discounts for bulk purchases, please contact Simon & Schuster Special Sales at 1-866-506-1949 or business@simonandschuster.com.

The Simon & Schuster Speakers Bureau can bring authors to your live event. For more information or to book an event, contact the Simon & Schuster Speakers Bureau at 1-866-248-3049 or visit our website at www.simonspeakers.com.

Cover art and design by Alan Dingman

Manufactured in the United States of America

10 9 8 7 6 5 4 3 2 1

ISBN 978-1-4391-0792-8
ISBN 978-1-4391-2343-0 (ebook)

For my daughter Valerie

"Destiny is not a matter of chance; it is a matter of choice."

—William Jennings Bryan

You can either make your own decisions . . . or you can let these prophecies make them for you.

—Jadzia Dax
"Destiny" *Star Trek: Deep Space Nine*
written by
David S. Cohen & Martin A. Winer

PROLOGUE

"The fact is, Miles, the situation out there isn't good . . . and it's getting worse by the day."

Miles O'Brien scowled as he lowered himself into his chair in the station commander's office. The last thing he needed was for his visitor to belabor the obvious. Michael Eddington was a pragmatist; he generally didn't mince words and he had a useful knack for zeroing in on the essence of any issue, free of emotion. As such, Eddington's role as one of O'Brien's closest advisers—not to mention as a leader of the Terran Rebellion in his own right—was usually invaluable.

Today was a notable exception.

"I don't need to be reminded how bad it is," O'Brien snapped. "What I'm waiting to hear is how your meeting with the Autarch's representatives went."

"Well then," Eddington said, "the first thing you need to know is that I was never allowed to meet with his representatives. I met with the *representatives* of his representatives—a bunch of Mizarians who showed up just so they could tell us to get lost. The short version is this: we shouldn't expect any help from the Tzen-kethi."

O'Brien scoffed. "Damn fools," he muttered. "They've got a helluva lot more to lose than we do, and still they refuse to see how vulnerable they are."

Eddington shrugged. "We knew it was a long shot. Quite honestly, I was surprised they agreed to speak to us at all, even through a third party. The Autarch has no love for the Alliance, but he won't risk antagonizing them by giving our people safe haven—or providing us with weapons and matériel. To his way of thinking, he's playing it safe."

"He thinks he's safe now, but the détente between the Tzenkethi Coalition and the Alliance isn't going to last forever," O'Brien said. "The Cardassians have been itch-ing to annex their worlds for years. Eventually they're going to find an excuse to attack, and when that happens, the Autarch is going to wish he'd partnered up with us. And by then it'll be too damn late!" He pounded his fist on the desk, managing to strike the spot that was starting to turn into a well-formed depression in the gleaming black surface.

"Maybe Leeta will have better luck with the Talar-ians," Eddington said. "Has there been any word from her?"

O'Brien shook his head. "*Defiant*'s on silent running. With the Alliance getting more determined—especially the way they came after us in the Badlands—I didn't want to take any chances."

Muttering curses, O'Brien turned away from his desk and sought the calm he sometimes found gazing out the office's great picture window. Terok Nor's axial rotation had once again brought Bajor into view. The teal-and-white orb was nearly in half-phase, swaddled in darkness. From this vantage point, it looked peaceful, betraying nothing of the tension that had gripped it these last four years—ever since O'Brien and his followers had captured Terok Nor and issued their threat to bombard the planet from orbit should the Klingon-Cardassian Alliance ever make the slightest move against the station. For four years that gambit had kept them relatively safe; Bajor was too important to the Alliance for them to risk it over Terok Nor. But what, other than achieving mere survival, had the rebellion actually accomplished in those four years?

From O'Brien's perspective, it amounted to two words: *Damned little.*

"Do you ever wonder if we're just kidding ourselves?" O'Brien asked aloud, watching as a storm vortex crept over Bajor's terminator.

"No, I don't," Eddington said emphatically. There was an edge in his voice—a note of warning that O'Brien knew was meant to tamp down any further discouraging talk.

O'Brien didn't care. "I do," he admitted.

"Then I'll pretend I didn't hear that."

O'Brien snorted and turned to look his friend in the eye. "That's not like you, Michael."

"The alternative would be to relieve you of command, and my job is complicated enough already, thank you very much," Eddington replied with equanimity. He paused, and a look of understanding softened his hard stare. "Look, Miles, we both knew this was never going to be easy. And yes, we've had a bad year."

O'Brien barely resisted chuckling out loud at Eddington's gift for understatement, which rivaled that of his own Irish countrymen. Characterizing the past year as "bad" was on a par with describing the Emerald Isle's ancient history of brutal, bloody struggle—both against the British and each other—as "the Troubles."

"Between the debacle at Empok Nor and the setbacks we've suffered since then," Eddington continued, "there's no question that the Alliance is stepping up the pressure—thanks in no small part to Kira's return to grace as Bajor's Intendant."

O'Brien nodded. "She always did seem to take the rebellion personally, didn't she?"

"A rebellion that you and Sisko started," Eddington said, placing both hands on O'Brien's desk as he leaned forward. The edge in his voice returned abruptly. "You are one of the fathers of the rebellion, Miles. Never forget that. It means that you don't get to have doubts, or regrets. You can't afford the luxury of wondering whether all of this was a colossal mistake. You just *don't*."

O'Brien sighed and nodded, acknowledging the bitter yet inescapable truth underlying Eddington's words, though he wished to hell he could have denied it. He knew he didn't really have a choice in the matter—not if he wanted to be the human being he believed himself capable of becoming. Born to a race that had lived as slaves since the Klingons and Cardassians had conquered the corrupt and brutal Terran Empire during the previous century—a star-spanning imperium that once had dominated this part of the galaxy—O'Brien had known nothing but toil, penury, misery, and indignity.

But that had changed more than six years ago, after a visitation by the natives of a parallel universe helped him and Ben Sisko imagine that humankind might be destined for something else, something better than the extremes of human history. Something nobler than the commonplace cruelties and casual atrocities that the human species had once inflicted upon others, and now endured almost as a kind of collective penance.

The rebellion against the Klingon-Cardassian Alliance had been born out of that accidental interdimensional encounter, with Sisko leading the charge, O'Brien at his side, and a motley band of ex-slaves who'd stood little chance of surviving that first day, much less changing anything for themselves or anyone else. But survive they had, and in time they had drawn others to their cause, both humans and members of other species who had been oppressed by the Klingon-Cardassian Alliance.

And when Sisko had ceased to be part of the equation, O'Brien had, in time, found the leader inside himself to keep the rebellion going, because he still clung to the belief that a better life was possible. If humanity was indeed capable of taking charge of its collective destiny, then Miles Edward O'Brien could certainly steer his own. Believing that kept him going.

At least most of the time.

"You're right, Michael," O'Brien said at last. "It won't happen again."

The other man's hands came off the desk, his posture relaxing. "Good. Now, regardless of whether or not

Leeta makes any inroads with the Talarians, you may want to consider—" Eddington broke off as the office doors abruptly parted, and the weathered face of Luther Sloan appeared on the threshold.

"You two had better get out here. Tigan's got something."

O'Brien nearly leaped over his desk in his haste to get to ops. Tigan was at the situation table, shaking her head at what she was seeing displayed on its surface.

"What's going on, Ezri?"

"Beats the hell out of me," Tigan said, strands of her shaggy black hair partially obscuring her right eye as she studied a comm console. "According to this, there's a subspace transmission coming in, but I can't tell where it's coming *from*."

O'Brien glanced over her shoulder. "That *is* odd."

"Maybe our friends on Bajor have come up with a new way to avoid having their signals traced," Sloan suggested from the tactical station.

"Could be," O'Brien mused. If so, it would be a real breakthrough for the rebellion. No more clandestine shuttle flights down to the planet for meetings with the religious enclaves. They might even be able to adapt the system to the transporter.

Steady there, Miles. Best not to get ahead of yourself.

"I'd say it's an audio-video transmission, judging from the bandwidth it's using," he noted aloud. "Put it on the screen."

Tigan complied, but the only thing that appeared in the main holoframe was a snowstorm-like curtain of static.

O'Brien scowled. "Ezri, keep trying to trace the signal . . . and try talking to them, whoever they are. Michael, come with me. Let's see if we can boost our gain."

As he and Eddington moved to the communications station on the upper level, O'Brien could hear Tigan saying, "Hello? Who is this? Please identify yourself."

Eddington tried reconfiguring the subspace antennae while O'Brien took a harder look at the transmission that was struggling to get through. The waveform was beginning to look familiar to him.

"Oh, shite. I think I know what this is."

"Signal looks like it's clearing up," Eddington said.

O'Brien sighed and watched as the static on the holoframe slowly dissipated. "We may end up wishing it hadn't."

The images of four people gradually resolved into being. Two humans and two Ferengi.

Eddington's mouth dropped open in shock. "Is—is that Bashir on the left?"

"It is," O'Brien said grimly, "and it isn't." In point of fact, the four individuals on the screen were all people O'Brien knew to be dead—at least in *this* universe: Bashir, Sisko, Nog, and Quark. They were standing in an exact duplicate of ops, right in front of the station commander's office.

O'Brien leaned toward Eddington and whispered, "Get Keiko up here. Now."

"Oh, no," Ezri said in evident dismay. "Not you."

Nog, the younger of the two Ferengi, turned to the older one, who was smiling into the camera. *"She doesn't look too happy to see you."*

"Shows what you know," Quark told him. *"She and I have a rapport . . . . Don't we, my dear . . . ?"*

"Quark!" someone snapped from off camera.

"This is a trick," Tigan said.

"It's not a trick," O'Brien whispered, too softly for anyone else to hear.

"I realize this comes as a shock," Sisko assured Tigan. *"We've been on the receiving end of them from your side enough times to know the feeling. But I can assure you we're exactly who you think we are."*

"Yeah, you'd have to be, wouldn't you?" Tigan mumbled. She looked up at O'Brien. "You want to get in on this?"

O'Brien sighed and made his way back down the steps to rejoin Tigan at the situation table. "Hello, Captain Sisko. Doctor Bashir. It's good to see you both . . . but this does raise a lot of questions."

"It's good to see you, too . . . Smiley," Sisko said. *"I'm glad we don't have to waste a lot of time trying to prove to you who we are."*

"I recognized the carrier wave you're using. Clever idea, adapting my dimensional transport module for communication between our universes," O'Brien said, noticing that Nog seemed to stand up a little straighter after hearing that. "And I have to admit, using a bunch of people we know to be dead on this side was a nice touch." For some reason, the comment prompted Quark's counterpart to roll his eyes.

In the same moment, O'Brien's first officer emerged from one of the turbolifts. Along with Eddington, Keiko Ishikawa had become one his closest confidants since she'd led a shipload of liberated slaves from Korvat to Terok Nor almost two years ago. More than that, he and Keiko had become lovers, and at the sight of her long black hair tied back from her lovely face, O'Brien felt himself relaxing at once. She stared in fascination at the holoframe as she joined him at the situation table, followed by Eddington and Sloan.

O'Brien made some quick introductions, and Sisko did the same as more people gathered next to him: Tigan's counterpart, the Intendant's, even Iliana Ghemor's.

"Smiley, it's me," Ghemor said.

O'Brien frowned. "Excuse me?"

Ghemor sighed. *"The morning I left the station to go to Bajor, you were on very little sleep—voles in the bulkheads kept you up half the night, you told me."* Before O'Brien could respond, the Cardassian turned to Tigan. *"By the way, Ezri, how did Leeta like that little 'surprise' you planned on giving her for her birthday?"*

"Hey!" Tigan complained.

"Iliana," O'Brien said, needing no further convincing, "what the hell are you doing over there?"

Luther Sloan tried not to show it, but he was enjoying himself immensely. Everything he knew about the alternate universe he had learned from O'Brien and Tigan, the only people left on Terok Nor who'd had any direct experience with that parallel continuum. And while he found it difficult to believe that any version of Julian Bashir wasn't a complete jerk, he felt an irrepressible thrill at seeing the people who had inspired O'Brien and Ben Sisko into starting the Terran Rebellion.

But the wonder of the moment threatened to dissipate as Iliana Ghemor began to tell them what was, in Sloan's estimation, a preposterous tale.

If pressed, Sloan would be forced to admit that Ghemor had worried him from the start. She wasn't the first Cardassian to have sided with them against the Alliance, but she seemed an unlikely traitor. She was the daughter of its former director and had been an agent of the Obsidian Order before fleeing her people under extremely suspicious circumstances some months ago. Of course, similar doubts had once been cast upon Ishikawa, especially after she'd started sleeping with General O'Brien, but in both circumstances, the rebellion's leader had stood by his decision to accept the women who had joined their cause. And to her credit, the information Ghemor shared with them on Alliance security had been directly responsible for the success of a number of strikes the rebels had launched against military targets in Klingon-Cardassian territory.

Then, just two weeks ago, Ghemor had disappeared without explanation.

One of the rebellion's most carefully concealed successes was the relationship it had cultivated with a growing underground dissident movement on Bajor. This movement, led by a cabal of mystics who wanted to kick the Alliance out so that Bajor could reclaim its lost spiritual heritage, could claim secret supporters at all levels of Bajoran society. Whether or not one bought into all the mumbo-jumbo they espoused, a partnership with a network of Terran sympathizers operating on one of the Alliance's most valued planets simply wasn't a resource O'Brien could refuse after their representatives had come secretly to Terok Nor to make their proposal, not so very long after the rebels had first taken over the station.

The two groups immediately began hatching plans to coordinate their goals and efforts and their tactics and strategies, though contact between the station and the religious enclaves was by necessity limited in order to minimize the risk of exposure to either group. No comm signals passed between the two groups, ever. Information was sent back and forth by messenger, and only when it was determined that travel to and from the surface could be accomplished without detection.

Iliana Ghemor had seemed perfect for the job. *Maybe too perfect*, Sloan had thought when O'Brien decided to bring her into the loop. She knew how to bypass the security systems that Bajor employed, she was an expert at covert ops, and she was Cardassian—one of only two species besides the Bajorans who could walk the planet unchallenged. When rumors began to spread that Intendant Kira was returning to Bajor to meet with its ruling political body, O'Brien chose Ghemor to see if the rumors were true—and if they were, to amass the intelligence she needed to make sure Kira never left Bajor alive.

Ghemor had embarked on her mission to Bajor, but had never returned.

She had been expected back in five days' time. By the second week, it was clear that something must have gone wrong. Of course, it was always possible that the delay had been unavoidable; Ghemor might still be looking for a window of opportunity get back to Terok Nor without being noticed by the Alliance's ever-vigilant forces. But Sloan had never trusted her entirely, and he suspected that O'Brien's mood these last several days might have stemmed, at least in part, from his own growing doubts about the Cardassian. But with no way to contact the enclaves without jeopardizing their safety, all the rebels could do was bide their time and wait.

And now here they were, listening to Ghemor as she spoke to them from the alternate universe, warning them about a threat she seemed to think surpassed anything the rebellion had yet confronted. Sloan couldn't help but notice her conspicuous avoidance of the exact circumstances that had led up to her decision. And she seemed entirely less than clear about what she thought was at stake.

"Emissary of who now?" O'Brien asked.

"*Emissary of the Prophets,*" Ghemor repeated. "*Look, it's complicated, but what you need to know is this: the same wormhole, the same aliens, that exist in this universe also exist in ours. They just haven't been discovered yet. But the act of finding them is something that the Bajoran people will recognize on a primal level, whether they still keep their old faith or not. The person who succeeds in opening that door and making contact with the beings on the other side—that individual will be known to the Bajoran people as a religious icon with tremendous influence, much the way it happened here. And what I'm telling you, O'Brien, is that the person who is actively seeking to fulfill that role right now is the deranged Iliana Ghemor of this universe, in the guise of Kira Nerys. If she succeeds in finding that wormhole, she'll be like a demigod to Bajor, and you don't want to know what she's capable of if she gets the chance to wield that kind of power."*

Ghemor paused before continuing. *"I know I should have come to you before I crossed over. I let myself become emotionally involved because of who she is, and I thought I could stop her on my own. I was wrong."*

"Iliana, I'm not sure how much of this I can believe," O'Brien said, scratching the back of his head. "You're telling me that the Intendant may already be dead, but not really because your own counterpart may have taken her place in order to fulfill some Bajoran religious prediction?"

"I realize it's a lot to take in," Ghemor said, *"and I'm sorry that it's taken me this long to report back. But you have to understand that I was trying to combat an outside threat not just to the rebellion, but to the entire balance of power in our universe. If this woman succeeds in doing what she intends, Bajor will follow her like some kind of messiah. She could even start a damn holy war within the Alliance."*

"You make that sound like a bad thing," Tigan said laconically.

"It would be," Ishikawa said. "A war like that would devastate the region. People like us would be its first victims."

"The faithful versus the infidels," Eddington agreed. "With a madwoman calling the shots."

"You see now why we felt the need to warn you," the Intendant's counterpart said. *"General O'Brien, I also have a stake in seeing this woman stopped. She's proved herself a threat on our side as well as yours. My people and I stand ready to assist you."*

"I appreciate the offer, Captain," O'Brien said. "And I accept. You can start by explaining exactly where . . . What the bloody hell—?"

Sloan was running back to his station before O'Brien could finish cursing. The loud, dull tones that had interrupted his conversation sent everyone present into action; something had tripped Terok Nor's long-range proximity sensors.

"We've got multiple warp signatures on approach vectors," Ishikawa reported. "Looks like Klingons. ETA, two minutes."

"Raise shields," O'Brien ordered. "Charge all weapons and prepare for planetary bombardment. I want a torpedo lock on Ashalla in the next thirty seconds."

Sloan's hands danced rapidly over his tactical console, executing the well-practiced moves that gave O'Brien the results he demanded.

"General, what are you doing?" The question had come from the alternate Kira.

"What I warned them I'd do, Captain."

"You can't attack Bajor," Kira said. *"Millions of innocent lives—"*

"Captain, exactly how do you think we've managed to hold Terok Nor all this time?" O'Brien asked. "It's by convincing the Alliance that if they pushed me too far, Bajor would suffer the consequences of their actions."

A new curtain of static was falling across the holo-screen. *"Nog . . . aking up!"* Kira was shouting. *"Do someth . . . !"*

". . . rying . . . terfering with . . . ignal lock, overri—"

The comlink to the other universe went dead.

"We've lost their signal," Eddington reported, reading data off his side of the situation table. "Something cut into it."

"From the Klingons?" O'Brien asked.

"Maybe," Eddington said, beads of sweat forming below his receding hairline. "You think they picked up the transmission?"

"I think I don't give a damn. Luther, where's that torpedo lock?"

"Target acquired," Sloan announced, an almost surreal calm settling over his soul as battle, and perhaps death, approached. "Weapons charged and ready."

"Enemy ships entering firing range in . . . one minute," Ishikawa said.

Eddington shook his head. "If only *Defiant* were here. . . ."

"How many ships are you reading?" O'Brien asked Ishikawa.

"Twelve," she answered. "Including the *Negh'Var*."

O'Brien offered her a mirthless grin. "Pretty good odds, then, even without *Defiant*."

"That's not funny, Miles. . . . What if they *do* force you to attack Bajor?"

"It won't come to that."

"But—"

"Keiko, trust me," Smiley said, his gaze reassuring. "It won't come to that."

Standing on the uppermost platform of the observation tower, Opaka Sulan looked out over her labor camp, noting the regimented discipline of the workforce and its taskmasters, and was satisfied to see the ordered, mechanical efficiency she had cultivated here since taking operational command of the mine three years ago. On the northern side of the camp, huge excavated rectangles descended into Bajor like steps leading into some mythic underworld.

True, the recently discovered new veins of raw uridium now required them to delve far deeper into her planet's already-ravaged crust than ever before, but Bajor had come to know unprecedented economic prosperity since becoming the Alliance's primary supplier of the vital metal. Bajor's political capital had likewise risen exponentially since the dark days of Imperial Terra, before Bajorans had learned how to influence the quadrant's great and mighty, and Bajor's value as a power broker had elevated its status from that of a mere subject world to that of a respected ally.

Now Terrans and their former associates served Bajorans, performing the backbreaking menial work that kept Bajor—and, by extension, the Alliance—prosperous. One day, perhaps sooner than those in power were willing to acknowledge, the highly coveted resources of Opaka's world would be gone, exhausted. She hoped she would not live to see it. But then, sadly, there was much she had hoped never to see that had already come to pass.

How the times do change.

"What are you thinking about?" her companion asked.

Opaka continued to survey her domain from the ramparts. "I was thinking about the past," she admitted, and a chuckle escaped her lips in spite of herself. "And the present . . . and the future."

"Really?" the other woman asked. "You know, there are times when I suspect you're actually *proud* of this place."

Opaka scowled and looked at her friend, but if Winn Adami had intended her comment as a rebuke, no trace of it was apparent in her smile. "You're teasing me now."

Winn shrugged, a motion that was almost lost under the padded armor that covered her upper body. "Maybe a little."

Opaka shook her head and returned to her overview of the camp. East of the mine, several cargo skimmers were being filled with raw uridium ore in preparation for its transport to the processing center in Ilvia. "Don't you have anything better to do than rattle my cage?"

"You *need* rattling from time to time," Winn opined. "If only to keep you on your toes."

"I've managed this long."

"True. But when you first came here, you weren't nearly so sure of yourself."

"Things were different then," Opaka said. "*I* was different."

"My point exactly," said Winn. "You were caught unawares by the unexpected, and it changed *everything*. You need to tread carefully, lest the *next* change be less to your liking."

Opaka was growing impatient. "If you have bad news to deliver, Adami, then out with it! I'm becoming too old to put up with your little tactic of 'preparing' me for the latest unpleasantness. Let's have it."

"Terok Nor is under attack."

Opaka nodded, somehow not surprised. "I take it you wouldn't be telling me this if it hadn't been confirmed."

"Your daughter has been monitoring the comnet—"

"I wish you'd stop calling her that! She isn't my daughter."

"She may as well be," Winn said. "She certainly looks to you as—"

"Finish that sentence, Adami, and I swear I'll push you off this tower."

Winn shrugged again. "Fine, have it your way. The fact remains that the battle for Terok Nor is finally upon us, and we need to be ready for the outcome of—" She interrupted herself, apparently distracted by something happening out at the camp's perimeter. "What's going on down there?"

Opaka heard shouts coming from somewhere below. The two women followed the voices to the south rail of the observation platform, from which they could see a flurry of activity around the main guard tower. Outside the fenced perimeter of the camp, a pair of figures were emerging from the wilderness, walking toward the main gate.

"Who the *kosst* are they?" Opaka wondered.

"I have no idea," Winn said, squinting at the unexpected visitors. "But we won't find out by remaining up here."

Opaka cursed again and went to the lift. Winn followed her, and both women checked their sidearms as they made their rapid descent from the top of the watchtower. Once on the ground, Winn discreetly snapped off orders to her overseers as she and Opaka hurried to the gate, which to her shock and anger her own security people were already pulling open to admit the travelers.

The chief of the guards ran toward her, looking pale.

"What's the meaning of this?" Opaka demanded. "Why did you open the gate without my authorization?"

"Mistress, it's . . . it's the Intendant," the chief said.

Opaka's eyes narrowed as the visitors strode toward her. The shorter of the two was clearly Kira Nerys, but she wore none of the trappings of her office. Instead she was dressed in drab, baggy clothing of the type that Opaka had seen on the peasants who lived in the valley's agricultural townships. Her taller companion was similarly dressed, except that he also wore a hood. Although he stood behind Kira and kept his head down, Opaka could see that he was an old human with a close-cropped gray beard.

This unannounced visit and the attack on Terok Nor cannot be a coincidence, she thought, and her anxiety grew both steadily and insistently.

"You know who I am, I take it?" Kira asked without preamble, her smile dripping with smugness.

"Of course, Intendant," Opaka said, bowing deeply. "Welcome to Vekobet. I am this facility's administrator, Opaka Sulan. And this is my chief overseer, Winn Adami. Your presence honors us. I regret that I wasn't informed that you were planning to pay us a visit today. I would have prepared a proper reception, had I known."

"Naturally," Kira said. "But you weren't *meant* to know of my coming. My servant and I have been traveling in secret."

"May I inquire as to what brings you here?"

Still smiling, the other woman leaned in and whispered conspiratorially. "My purpose isn't for the ears of the rabble serving under you. Is there some place where we can speak privately?"

"Of course. Please follow me." Opaka nodded to Winn, who dropped back, and then Opaka led her two visitors toward the cluster of sturdy old buildings along the camp's eastern fence—it was all that remained of the thriving rural community that had occupied this site since long before the Council of Ministers had seized the land for mining operations on the Alliance's behalf.

As they crossed the empty intersection at the center of the camp, Opaka offered up a brief history of Vekobet, pointing out its key features, expounding upon the great successes of her administration . . . and doing her best to keep her visitors' attention diverted from the Klingon disruptor she was very slowly sliding out of the holster on her hip.

When she felt the muzzle of an unfamiliar weapon at her neck, she knew her efforts at discretion had been in vain. "Drop the pistol," Kira whispered in her ear.

Opaka merely smiled.

"I said, drop the pistol," Kira hissed, pressing the weapon against her skin.

"I think not," Opaka whispered back. "Take a good look around you."

She felt the younger woman's head turning, first left and then right, and slowly the weapon at Opaka's neck eased off. The entire camp had fallen silent. Following Winn's silent orders, both the "workers" and the "overseers"—nearly three hundred strong—had drawn disruptors of their own, each and every weapon targeted at the visitors.

"All right, look," Captain Kira Nerys said as the alternate Winn Adami moved in to confiscate their phasers. "We're not who you think we are."

Opaka laughed. "Oh, I'm quite certain of who you are, young woman. I knew it the moment I saw *him*." She pointed a finger at Vaughn. "What I demand to know is why you've come here, and why you're posing as the Intendant."

Kira grinned involuntarily, a nervous rictus catalyzed by the sheer absurdity of seeing Opaka Sulan as the gun-slinging master of a labor camp, and Winn Adami as her lieutenant.

Vaughn, for his part, seemed preoccupied studying the faces around him. What he expected to learn from doing so, Kira had no clue. They'd spoken little during the two hours it had taken them to walk here from Akorem's Rock—after Nog had successfully beamed them across the dimensional gulf from Deep Space 9—pausing in their journey only to snatch some indigenous clothing from a vacant farmhouse in order to conceal their uniforms as they continued toward Vekobet.

"I came here because of Iliana Ghemor," Kira told their captor.

Opaka stuck her disruptor under Kira's jaw. "Where is she? If she's dead, if you've killed her—"

"She's all right," Kira said calmly. "Only two of us could make the journey, but she's safe, I promise you. It was she who told us where to find the religious enclave from which she received her . . . information about her counterpart."

"Then why the subterfuge?" Opaka asked.

"Frankly, I wasn't sure who among you I should trust. Ghemor didn't have time to tell us what we should expect, or who we should speak to. When I saw that Vekobet is a labor camp, I thought posing as the Intendant was my best option until I could make contact with members of the enclave." She looked around ruefully at the small army arrayed around them. "I never imagined that the entire camp was in on it."

Opaka seemed to be studying Kira very carefully. Suddenly she reached out and grasped Kira's bare left ear between thumb and forefinger. Kira gasped slightly but stood her ground. The older woman closed her eyes, and after a few silent moments, the disruptor slowly withdrew, and Opaka released Kira's ear.

"They mean us no harm," Opaka told Winn. "Have our people stand down, and give our visitors back their sidearms."

Winn frowned. "Are you sure about—?"

"Do it," the other woman said, "and bring them to the refectory. We'll continue our conversation there." Opaka turned and went on ahead, speaking quietly into a comm device that she retrieved from the pockets of her long coat.

Winn was eyeing them with suspicion as she handed back their phasers. "Move," she told them, ordering Vaughn and Kira to walk in front of her as the three of them followed in Opaka's wake toward one of the camp's larger buildings.

Kira noted that Vaughn was still searching the faces of the alien "laborers," all of whom had already returned to their mining. Mostly they were humans, but Kira had also noticed some Tellarites among them, as well as a few Bolians and representatives of several other familiar species.

"What is it?" she whispered.

Vaughn hesitated before answering. "I'm looking for someone who can help us."

"Let's hope we've already found them," Kira said, though she was glad Vaughn was continuing to attempt to assess their options.

They were led to an elaborate wooden building, built entirely of nyawood. Massive timbers that may have been decades or centuries old lent the structure the solidity of stone—something that could endure the test of time. Inside it was revealed as a large, rustic dining hall, empty but for a dozen or so long tables and benches, which were arranged in orderly rows, and the presently unoccupied serving stations that ran along one wall. Large oval windows on the eastern and western walls allowed daylight to fill the refectory, and the smell of cooking permeated the place.

Opaka was already waiting for them at the head of one of the tables; Kira and Vaughn were made to sit opposite one another on the long sides. Shortly after they were seated, a male Bajoran emerged from a door that presumably led to the kitchen, bringing a tray of bread and fruit along with several mugs containing something that smelled like freshly brewed *deka* tea. The server nearly stumbled when he saw Kira, but after receiving a stern look from Opaka he set down his tray and quickly retreated into the kitchen.

Winn remained standing near the door through which they'd entered, her weapon still conspicuously drawn but pointed at the floor.

"Please eat," Opaka said. "The third member of Vekobet's leadership triad will join us soon. In the meantime, you're welcome to enjoy our hospitality, such as it is."

"We appreciate your generosity," Kira said. "Though we're grateful simply for the opportunity to speak with you."

Opaka chuckled. "You're not like your counterpart at all, are you? That imperious air you put on earlier—it doesn't come naturally to you."

"Was I that obvious?" Kira asked as she reached toward the tray for a ripe *moba*.

"Not terribly," Opaka said. "But I see qualities in you that she couldn't even begin to emulate, and I say that as someone who has made a study of Intendant Kira for many years, albeit from a safe distance."

"Lady Opaka," Vaughn said. "Is it true that the Bajoran religious enclaves are aligned with the Terran Rebellion?"

Opaka's expression as she turned toward Vaughn seemed to border on amusement. "Yes," she answered. "In fact, you could almost say that Vekobet represents the marriage of the two groups. Years ago, I was one of the first to rally to Benjamin Sisko's banner, after he took up the cause of freedom for the Alliance's underclass. I fought at his side until we both came to realize that a violent uprising of former slaves would not be enough."

"What did you think you'd have to do next?" Vaughn asked.

"There wasn't much more we could do, at least not without widening the conflict," Opaka said. "For the rebellion to succeed over the long term, it needed sympathizers within the Alliance itself—willing accomplices who could support the rebels secretly, with resources and intelligence. I left the front lines of the struggle and returned to Bajor to see what I could accomplish behind the scenes on the rebellion's behalf, for I knew I was not alone in my dissidence; others on Bajor felt as I did— men and women who yearned for the dissolution of our unholy pact with the Klingons and the Cardassians, for a return to the kind of world that Bajor *used* to be. But it wasn't until I came to Vekobet that I learned what it would truly entail to recapture that lost identity.

"Here I found kindred spirits among the enclave's leaders," Opaka went on, nodding toward Winn. "And working together we have tried to unify the Bajoran dissident movement with the Terran Rebellion. As you've undoubtedly gathered by now, Vekobet is far more than a labor camp. It is both a religious sanctuary and a secret training facility for freedom fighters. The workers here are not really slaves; they are soldiers awaiting their moment. They continue to do the work of mining ore in order to maintain our cover . . . and because our mines yield far more uridium than even the Bajoran Parliament knows. This makes it possible for us to smuggle out a sizable quantity of unprocessed ore through third parties to rebel bases beyond the B'hava'el system."

"And the other enclaves?" Vaughn asked.

"Not all of them are like this one, but each does what it can to advance the dual causes of Bajoran renewal and freedom from the Alliance."

"That must be a huge risk for all of you," Kira said.

"The risk to our *pagh* would be far greater if we did nothing, child," Winn said.

"Well spoken, Adami," said a new voice. Vaughn and Kira turned to see a tall man with close-cropped white hair entering the refectory through a back door. He strode toward the table, his tan-and-blue medical smock flattering his broad-shouldered frame. "Please forgive my tardiness. I was with a patient, but I came as soon as I could."

The words had been softly spoken, but had an edge like steel. Kira recognized him at once—as the man who, in her universe, had once attempted to seize power on Bajor by leading a military-backed political coup. She rose automatically.

"Jaro."

"Doctor Jaro Essa," the man clarified. "I'm the camp physician, and the third leader of the Vekobet enclave. I'm quite pleased to make your acquaintance, Ms. Kira."

"It's Captain Kira, actually," she said. "This is my first officer, Commander—"

"Elias," Jaro breathed, a glint of surprised recognition suddenly evident in his dark brown eyes.

"You know my counterpart," Vaughn said, evidently making the same deduction that Kira had.

Jaro merely nodded, studying the human commander in apparent fascination.

"Since we're all here now, let's get to the heart of it, shall we?" Opaka said as Jaro pulled up a chair to the foot of the table and Kira reseated herself. The older woman addressed Kira directly. "You're from that other universe. Iliana Ghemor went there to stop her counterpart weeks ago, and we haven't heard from her since. But within the last hour we've received word that Terok Nor is under attack by Alliance forces, and now here you are. I take this to mean that the situation is grave."

Kira nodded, then launched into the story of everything having to do with the two Ilianas that had recently transpired in her continuum, including the fact that the real Intendant Kira was now presumed to be dead, replaced by the Iliana Ghemor of Kira's home universe. Kira's hosts listened attentively, usually with equanimity, but at other times with profound surprise. They asked many questions, all of which Kira and Vaughn tried to answer as fully as they could. Finally Kira told them of her attempt to warn the rebels, and of the energy field that was now constricting and disrupting dimensional transport in and around Terok Nor and Bajor—possibly a defense engineered by the false Intendant to prevent further interference from the other universe.

"Once we were cut off from your station, I was faced with having to decide quickly how the two of us might do the most good by beaming to your Bajor," Kira explained. "Your Ghemor told me where to find your enclave, and we decided to come here in order to warn you. My hope was that you—or somebody like you—might have the resources and the will to take action against the impostor."

"A laudable effort, Captain, but a fool's errand," Opaka told her. "If what you say is true, and Iliana's counterpart is carrying out the military assault on Terok Nor, there may be nothing we can do but await the outcome of the battle."

"We could expose her," Kira argued. "Alert your government and the Alliance that the woman leading the attack is a fraud."

"It would take far more than either your word or ours to convince anyone on Bajor—much less in the Alliance leadership—that she isn't the rightful Intendant."

"You don't need our word," Vaughn said. "Despite her outward appearance, this Intendant's physiology is Cardassian. That can be proven medically. In addition, her quantum resonance signature is the same as ours, and it's possible to show that this signature is different from everyone else native to your universe. Surely that evidence—"

"No one will listen," Winn insisted from her place near the door. "Certainly not while she's leading a campaign directly over the surface of Bajor."

"Then what about the rebels?" Kira asked. "The ones on those interstellar bases you mentioned? If you're exchanging matériel with them, then you must have a way to make contact with them. Maybe they can be persuaded to come here and help to repel the Alliance fleet."

Opaka shook her head. "What you're proposing is quite impossible. As I said before, we reach the rebels in other star systems only through third parties, and that method of communication will take too long to do us any good, at least before *this* crisis resolves itself."

"And the people you're training here?" Kira asked, feeling her desperation level steadily rising. "You said they're awaiting their moment. Well, I'd say their moment is *here*!"

"If we had access to armed spacecraft capable of going into battle against the Alliance fleet, then the men and women here would gladly take them and go," Winn said. "But such is not the case. Vekobet trains soldiers for the rebellion, yes. But it has no means of staging offworld attacks."

"But there has to be *something* we can do!" Kira said. "For whatever reason, my continuum's Iliana has decided to go after Terok Nor before she begins her search for the wormhole. That gives us a huge opportunity. We can't simply squander it!"

"We must put our faith in the Prophets," Opaka said. "And we must trust the rebels of Terok Nor to prevail against the Intendant."

"And if they don't?" asked Vaughn. "Are you willing to just wait around and hope for the best without a contingency plan?"

"What would you suggest?" Jaro asked.

Vaughn leaned forward. "If the Intendant takes back Terok Nor, then the station will once again fall under Bajoran oversight, yes?"

"Of course," Jaro said.

"Then I imagine your politicians will wish to make a show of the Alliance victory over the rebels," Vaughn went on. "Some will want to go there as soon as possible once the station has been secured."

"Your Ghemor told us that there are highly placed dissidents in Bajor's secular leadership," Kira chimed in. "If you have any influence with them, we need to be ready to get someone up to the station as quickly as possible. You can send me."

Jaro was nodding thoughtfully. "Perhaps."

"Consider this carefully, Essa," Winn cautioned.

"I am, Adami, rest assured. And I believe Commander Vaughn's point is well taken: we must be prepared to take swift action should the station fall."

"You do have influential people you can count on, then?" Kira asked.

Jaro smiled. "While my position here is ostensibly that of a humble physician, Captain, there are indeed favors I can call in from certain dissident politicians, several of whom possess the authority to arrange a 'fact-finding visit' to Terok Nor, if it does fall under Bajor's dominion once again—and they would do it gladly if it meant exposing the Intendant as a fraud."

"But would this false Intendant even allow such a visit?" Winn asked. "Given what we know of her, I'm not convinced she would feel obligated to honor our protocols."

"Ever the pragmatist, Adami," Jaro said. "I'm fairly certain it's why I married you."

Winn harrumphed but otherwise let the comment pass.

"You're quite right, of course. There are no guarantees," Jaro continued. "However, I must remind you and Sulan both that we do not follow a path of guarantees, but rather one of choices. The Prophets gave us free will so that we might light our *own* way in the darkness."

Kira blinked.

"You must forgive him," Opaka said, noticing Kira's expression. "He can be quite florid when he puts his mind to it." She shot Jaro a warning look. "It begins to grate after a while."

"No, it's all right," Kira said. "It's just—you speak so much like the vedeks of my world, Doctor Jaro. The other Bajorans I've met from your universe seemed completely ignorant of—"

"Most of my people have forgotten the Prophets," Jaro said, interrupting. "But as you already know, we three belong to a movement that labors toward a renewal of the faith. Years ago I belonged to one of the first enclaves dedicated to preserving our ancient teachings. Eventually some of our group's followers ventured out to become founders of their own enclaves. It wasn't until my wife and I came to Vekobet, when we rediscovered the Shards of Dava, that we came to understand what was truly at stake for our people—that the time foretold by Trakor is finally upon us—and together we set about preparing for the coming of the Emissary."

"The Shards of Dava?" Kira asked. "Dava Nikende? He was a kai on my world centuries ago, the leader of our faith—"

"On ours as well," Winn said. "It was he who foresaw the destruction of the Tears."

Kira's shock was absolute. "The Orbs of the Prophets were destroyed? How could that happen?"

"The Terran Empire," Jaro said. "Our conquerors disapproved of our religion. They forbade its practice, and systematically wiped out its priests, its scriptures, and its icons."

Kira felt as if she'd been punched in the gut. Even the Cardassians of her universe hadn't gone so far during the occupation of Bajor. They had been curious enough about the Tears to confiscate them, but they had never taken the Bajoran religion seriously enough to attempt to eradicate it.

And maybe that alone explains why the Terran Empire went that extra kellipate, Kira thought. The Bajoran faith had been the thing that held Kira's people together during the Occupation, giving them the will to continue resisting. Perhaps that was something the Terrans had already understood when they came to Bajor—and why they had feared its power enough to want to wipe it out.

No wonder this world fell in with the Alliance, and why it breeds people like the Intendant.

"It was during this purge that the first enclave came together, dedicated to preserving what prophecies remained," Opaka went on. "But centuries before, Kai Dava foresaw the darkening of the Tears, and he took what steps he could to preserve their light. With great reluctance, he took from each of the Nine a fragment, set them in bands of metal, and hid them to await the day when Bajor would need them again."

"Orb fragments," Kira whispered, and she and Vaughn exchanged a look of understanding.

"Yes," Opaka confirmed. "And I believe I can guess what you wish to ask us next, Captain. Let me save you the trouble: the Shard discovered on your world came from ours."

Kira shook her head in amazement. "How?"

"Those of Dava's writings that survived from this period reflect the torment his visions caused him, as well as his anguish over the actions he felt compelled to take," Opaka said. "One of the more oblique scrolls seems to suggest that before he hid the Shards, the Orb of Souls called to him. He describes meeting his reflection when he opened the ark, and entrusting the Shard of Souls to this second Dava."

"*My* world's Dava," Kira realized. "But it was all for nothing. The Shard has fallen into the hands of a madwoman bent on fulfilling Trakor's prophecy. It doesn't make sense."

"Perhaps not in hindsight," Opaka conceded. "But consider it from our Dava's perspective. His visions of apocalypse had affected him so profoundly that he willingly defaced the Tears in order to save them. Perhaps he also foresaw some tragedy involving the Shard of Souls that he wished to avert, and only by removing it from this world did he believe it would be safe. Prophecy is often vague, Captain. That's why we must test it."

The familiar words brought a smile to Kira's lips, but she wasn't completely reassured. On the one hand, it seemed as if the Dava of this universe was indirectly responsible for giving Iliana Ghemor a weapon of incalculable power. On the other hand . . .

Is it possible that this is exactly what the Prophets intended should happen? But why would They—?

"Sulan," someone said.

Kira looked up at the sound of the voice. Vaughn did not. Instead, he closed his eyes. Behind him, running toward their table from the door through which Jaro had entered earlier, was Elias's daughter. But not *his* daughter.

Her cheeks were streaked with tears.

"Prynn, you shouldn't be here," Opaka said, rising from her chair as the young woman threw her arms around her. "What's wrong, child? Has something happened?"

"Ashalla," she whispered.

Kira braced herself.

"What about Ashalla?" Winn asked, leaving her place at the door and approaching the table for the first time.

"It's gone. Ashalla's gone," Prynn wept. "The city's been destroyed."

PART ONE

HARKOUM
2376

1

Far below the cracked ochre wasteland of Harkoum's surface, Iliana Ghemor turned away from the reading screen, her anguish and rage competing for dominance as she wedged the knuckles of her left fist between her teeth. She savored the sensation of her skin breaking against the pressure, the metallic taste of her blood mingling with the salty tears that flowed freely down the cheeks of Kira Nerys.

Her cheeks.

Dead, she thought as her eyes traveled tremulously back to the shatterframe monitor atop her desk. *They're all dead. And they've been dead for years.* Her mother, her father, Entek, the Obsidian Order itself . . . And now, if this newest intel from her spies was to be believed, even Gul Dukat was gone—consumed in Bajor's Fire Caves during an arcane confrontation with the Emissary, a battle that had evidently claimed them both.

In truth, she'd half expected this. From the moment she'd learned the full scope of the Dominion War and the attempted genocide on Cardassia that had marked its end, Iliana had accepted the very real possibility that all the people she'd known in her old life were among the nearly one billion slain. But instead, after scouring the files of Dukat's personal database—copied from his secret safe house beneath the lunar prison on Letau—she learned that they'd met far different fates.

Her mother had been first. Less than a year after Iliana had departed Cardassia for her covert mission to Bajor, Kaleen Ghemor had fallen into a despair from which she had never recovered. She resigned from the judiciary, withdrew from the world, and eventually became gravely ill following a prolonged struggle with a crippling depression. She finally expired in a hospital room seven years after she'd last seen Iliana.

Corbin Entek met his end three years later, after he'd become one of the highest-ranking strategists of the Obsidian Order, and during a predictably convoluted plot to expose her father's covert involvement with a growing dissident movement on Cardassia. That the eroding certainty of her father's political beliefs had eventually led him to become one of the movement's leaders was a revelation, but it was as nothing compared to the shock of learning that Entek's scheme had involved manipulating Tekeny Ghemor with the promise of restoring his long-lost daughter to him, using a surgically altered Kira Nerys—the *other* Kira Nerys—to convince him that she had finally returned from her assignment on Bajor.

That her old mentor—and the architect of her metamorphosis—had chosen to defile her memory in order to achieve his ends came as little surprise. Entek had done a poor job of concealing his true interest in Iliana during her tutelage, and the things she had heard Dukat say to him at Elemspur on the day of her memory transference left little doubt that Entek had manipulated her from the start, and that his frustrated obsession with her was directly responsible for the course her life had subsequently taken. Fittingly, the farce he had perpetrated against her father had been Corbin's final undoing, though it had thrust Tekeny into exile and had allowed the other Kira to survive unscathed.

The final insult, however, had come two years later, at the time of her father's death of Yarim Fel syndrome aboard Deep Space 9. The bond that Entek's plan had created between Tekeny and Kira had endured right up until Tekeny Ghemor drew his last breath. He had sought to spend his last days in Kira's company, even sharing with her the final, supremely intimate rite of *shri'tal*! Had he known that Kira shared responsibility for killing the love of Iliana's life? Was it really possible that he had given up any hope of ever finding his real daughter, and had turned to the creature Iliana had been sent to replace in some pathetic need for a surrogate, just so that he wouldn't have to die alone?

They gave up on me. All of them.

It had been no less devastating to learn about the deaths of her Bajoran loved ones. Thanks to the memories of Kira Nerys, Iliana recalled the mortal wound Cardassian soldiers had inflicted upon Kira's father, Taban. But Kira's mother, Meru, had apparently lived for years as Dukat's concubine, long after her daughter had thought she'd died of malnutrition in the refugee camps of Singha. Dead too were Kira's brothers, Pohl and Reon.

Most of Kira's resistance cell—the Shakaar—were gone as well. Some had fallen during the Occupation, like Dakahna Vaas, whose loss had been so painful to Kira that it drove her into a self-destructive spiral from which she had only barely escaped; others had been murdered in recent years by a vengeful Cardassian who'd survived Kira's bombing of Gul Pirak's compound on Bajor—the same bombing that had killed Iliana's beloved Ataan Rhukal. Ataan's death had driven Iliana to the Obsidian Order in her need to exact justice—and there she had drawn first blood by killing one of the Order's captured terrorists, Dakahna Vaas.

Ataan and Vaas. She remembered loving them both. She remembered *killing* them both. And the terrible symmetry of those memories often seemed too intolerable to contemplate.

And now to learn that Dukat, too, was dead . . .

She would have been the first to admit the source of the new information was dubious—*if* she had lacked Kira's appreciation of Bajoran metaphysics.

The report, filed by members of the Vedek Assembly and now glowing out from her desktop screen, told of an account given by the wife of the Emissary. This Kasidy Yates claimed to have experienced her husband in the aftermath of his final encounter with Dukat, and that he had told her that the gul was lost forever to the very entities he had tried to unleash—the Pah-wraiths. From a Cardassian perspective, it was utter nonsense.

But from the perspective of a devout Bajoran, it was an entirely logical and fitting end to the life of the planet's most universally hated enemy. Adding to that the information she'd gleaned from Dukat's own files on Bajoran mysticism and the many inexplicable events of the last eight years, and Iliana could well believe that the inscrutable alien beings who resided within the Bajoran wormhole had spun a complex web that had ensnared many lives, including that of Skrain Dukat.

And perhaps even her own.

That's it, isn't it? she thought. Cardassia and Bajor, her life and Kira's, Tekeny and Taban, Kaleen and Meru, Shakaar and Corbin, Vaas and Ataan—they were all somehow intertwined; entangled by invisible strands that formed the pattern of whatever obscure and intricate tapestry the Prophets were weaving behind their impenetrable curtain of timelessness.

And the thread of my life? Where does it lead now? How do I make myself whole again? Cardassia lies in ruins. Bajor has no place for me. Vengeance against Dukat is denied me. Entek is long dead. My mother succumbed to her own broken heart. And my father . . . My father's love was stolen from me forever.

By Kira—

"Nerys?"

Iliana started, but didn't turn toward the voice, hastily moving instead to close the file on her reader and wipe the tears from her face.

"What is it?" she asked sharply.

She sensed Shing-kur's hesitation. Ever since they'd broken out of Letau, together with several other inmates, the Kressari had been her devoted right hand, and she'd had the clearest understanding of everything that Iliana had endured these last two decades.

Shing-kur alone knew that Iliana was not the Bajoran she appeared to be. But she seemed to appreciate none-theless Iliana's all-consuming need, after fifteen years of physical and psychological torture in Dukat's private dungeon, to cling to the identity of the Bajoran woman that she should have replaced—the woman whose iden-tity was the only one that had any meaning to her now. Consequently, during the months since their escape to Harkoum, Shing-kur had become acutely sensitive to Iliana's moods, and it had to be obvious to her now that she had intruded upon Iliana at a moment of acute vulnerability.

"Well?" Iliana demanded. "Out with it!"

The Kressari seemed to take the hint, though she gave no further sign that she thought anything was amiss. "There's been news out of Bajor."

Her interest piqued, Iliana turned her head halfway toward Shing-kur, so that the Kressari would see her profile. "What sort of news?"

Shing-kur's voice carried an air of possibility. "There's a Jem'Hadar soldier aboard Deep Space 9."

Harkoum proved to be everything Iliana could have hoped for, and more: Dukat's secret Dominion trans-porter on Letau had deposited her band of fugitives deep within the abysmal Grennokar Detention Center. This was one of many underground secret prison installations that the Obsidian Order had quietly maintained over the last century, until Cardassia finally abandoned the remote planet for good. Rumor had it that mummified corpses still resided in many of those forsaken facilities, and that the so-called enemies of the state who had been incarcerated here at the end of the Order's reign—many of them having served as test subjects for the Order's medical research initiatives—had simply been left to die in their locked subterranean cells. Iliana had tried to imagine what it must have been like for those poor souls, caged and starving, their ever-weakening screams for help and rescue going unheard until they had at last faded into eternal silence.

But if those rumors were true, then Grennokar was a notable exception to current Cardassian policy. The initial search that she and her cohorts had made of the facility showed considerable evidence of *recent* use, which appeared to have ended both suddenly and disastrously. Between the detention center's still-intact records, which had included copies of Dukat's personal files, it hadn't taken long to piece together what had happened here, or why Dukat had taken such an interest in this place that he had used the Dominion subspace transporter in his secret Grennokar safe house exclusively for travel to and from Harkoum.

Dukat had first learned about Grennokar's existence during the time of his great disgrace several years ago, during the period when he had been relegated to captaining a military freighter that serviced some of the Cardassian Union's most remote holdings. But it wasn't until he'd begun his negotiations with the Dominion to drive out Cardassia's then-occupiers, the Klingons, that he had started formulating new plans.

Plans that were to make considerable use of the Grennokar facility.

To bring those schemes to fruition, Dukat had successfully tracked down two of the Order's former medical researchers, Doctors Omek and Vekeer, and recruited them for a very bold and risky project. Once he'd returned to power as the new Dominion-backed ruler of the Union, Dukat had quietly set the two men up at Grennokar. He then began discreetly redirecting useful bits of Dominion technology, thereby slowly rebuilding and improving upon the experimentation facilities that already existed on the detention center's bottommost level.

These covert machinations were all directed toward a single purpose: to secretly undermine the intricate genetic programming that governed the Jem'Hadar's loyalty to the Founders—part of a long-term plan to challenge the shape-shifters' mastery of Cardassia *and* the Dominion by transferring their soldiers' genetically mandated loyalty to *him*.

Research subjects were initially the corpses of Jem'Hadar soldiers recovered from battle. Later, sedated live specimens were pulled off massive offensives against the Federation and the Klingons, abattoirs of battle from which a few fallen cannon-fodder troops would never be missed; these eventually found their way to Grennokar, providing Vekeer and Omek with as much raw material as their work required.

In hindsight, it came as no surprise to Iliana that not a single individual, neither Cardassian nor Jem'Hadar, was left alive in Grennokar by the time the war had ended. Iliana recalled Shing-kur's incredulous reaction upon studying the project data, likening the doctors' experiments on live Jem'Hadar to studying lightning from the top of an iron tower.

Nevertheless, the research had continued for two years—until quite recently, it seemed. According to the records, at the time of Dukat's last visit to Harkoum to check on their progress—shortly after he'd had himself surgically altered so that he could pass for a Bajoran— Omek and Vekeer were convinced that they were on the verge of a significant breakthrough. Dukat led them to believe that he intended to return in order to put the fruits of their long labors to work, once his latest task on Bajor was completed.

But he never did. And less than a month after that final visit, both the scientists and every member of their support staff died horribly—moments after their "breakthrough" Jem'Hadar test subject broke through quite literally, overcoming his restraints. The creature's berserker rage wasn't spent until everyone in the lab lay dead, including the Jem'Hadar itself, which apparently had fallen victim to a massive and fatal cerebral hemorrhage.

It was the grisly aftermath of the doctors' arrogance that greeted Iliana and her gang when they had first beamed in from Letau, some weeks after the disaster had taken place. Still, these gruesome findings had done nothing to discourage her from recognizing Grennokar's enormous potential utility. The secrecy of the facility and the remoteness of Harkoum—to which Grennokar was linked via Dukat's subspace transporter—offered Iliana and her band of fellow travelers a long-term haven. The fugitives spent many of their early days at Grennokar simply taking inventory of their new home, assessing its resources, and debating the possible uses to which they might be put—computers, medical technology, weapons, a communications system linked to the Cardassian subspace relay network. The place even had a number of small, nondescript spacecraft that were clearly intended not to attract any unnecessary attention.

While each of her fellow escapees started to imagine how they would resume the various individual pursuits, legal or otherwise, that had landed them in Letau's prison levels in the first place, Iliana began to formulate how she would fold their ambitions into her own. The more she learned about the strange new galaxy into which she'd emerged, the more the scope of her desire for revenge expanded outward, becoming a need that couldn't be satisfied simply by eliminating her double aboard Deep Space 9.

She craved far more than that: she wanted—needed—to *hurt* Kira Nerys profoundly before finally killing her. The exact shape of that vengeance was something she still had to determine. But Iliana had become convinced that whatever form her revenge would take, it would best be achieved with an organization at her back.

Fortunately, convincing her fellow former prisoners to continue following her lead proved to be far simpler than she had hoped. Shing-kur's devotion to her since

Letau was pure, and could be called upon to serve as an example to the others; the Kressari seemed satisfied to make Iliana's needs her own, and supported her every decision. She was, in fact, Iliana's sole confidant.

The others were fairly simple creatures at their cores, motivated by little beyond a thirst for profit and a contempt for the respective societies that had either rejected them, hounded them, or betrayed them. To build upon the tentative loyalty Iliana had earned from them during their escape, she needed to provide all of them with what they desired most.

With Shing-kur's support, Iliana painted a picture of an organized group of criminal operatives working out of Grennokar, with themselves at the top of the organizational hierarchy. She told them that this emerging brave new age of protectorates, in which the Allied powers were carving up the battered Union into swaths of loosely policed space—ostensibly to assist in preventing a descent into complete anarchy while Cardassia licked its Dominion War–inflicted wounds—would not last forever. But it *would* give them a definite window of opportunity they could not afford to squander. She argued passionately that the ships and worlds of this region would never be more vulnerable than they were at the present moment. This vicinity of space was now ripe for the picking, and the five of them were uniquely positioned to bring in that harvest.

The young gunrunner, Fellen Ni-Yaleii, bought into her vision at once; Iliana felt certain she could fan the Efrosian woman's interest into passionate enthusiasm before very long. Mazagalanthi, the Lissepian smuggler of illicit technologies, had been somewhat more reserved, but finally gave his full support to the proposal. Telal, ever the skeptic, had taken some convincing, but in the end even the Romulan freelance assassin had allowed himself to be ensnared by the very real possibilities and opportunities that Iliana had laid out for the group.

The group spent the weeks that followed bringing the most useful sections of Grennokar back online, as well as recruiting mercenaries from those few old industrial communities on Harkoum that still clung to life as havens for every type of outlaw from dozens of worlds. And as the structure and aims of Iliana's emerging criminal enclave gradually emerged, the group began undertaking seemingly random acts of piracy in several of the adjoining sectors, slowly escalating to more ambitious targets: outposts, colonies, even elaborate confidence games.

And as the rewards began pouring in, Iliana gradually exploited her inner circle's growing euphoria, reaching out to them as trusted friends. Eventually she confided in them the tale she wanted them to believe about her imprisonment on Letau—that she was the victim of an imposture being carried out to this very day, by a fraud who had claimed Iliana's real identity aboard the Federation's starbase in the B'hava'el system.

Iliana's subtle manipulations had their desired effect: Bit by bit she was transforming their already solidified loyalty into something much larger, much more heartfelt, and far more difficult to quantify: zeal.

These pirates and former prisoners were no longer merely Iliana's accomplices, or even her friends.

They were now her followers.

"Nerys, did you hear what I said? There's a Jem'Hadar aboard Deep Space 9!"

Iliana sighed and turned all the way around to face Shing-kur, who was standing just inside the threshold of the modest quarters Iliana had claimed as her own shortly after their arrival at Grennokar. Her Obsidian Order training had given her valuable insights into the detention center's design, and she had immediately recognized the unremarkable-looking room for what it really was by its very inconspicuousness.

True to her suspicions, she had discovered that the room's rather ordinary workstation allowed—with some painstaking navigation of its labyrinthine security system—exclusive access to some of the detention center's more interesting amenities, such as a personal armory, a secure subspace communications booth, a self-destruct system, and a vault containing a shocking amount of latinum. If the dust present was any indicator, Dukat and his scientists hadn't known about any of it. Whoever had been in charge of this place when it was first built certainly had a flare for the dramatic. But then, she reflected, that was true for most Cardassians.

Kressari, by contrast, possessed notions of drama that were not immediately recognizable outside their species. Their rough, hard-edged faces, lacking the flexibility of either Cardassian or Bajoran skin, did not emote in the manner of most humanoids. It wasn't until Iliana looked into Shing-kur's eyes that she saw the excitement there, evidenced by the deep black that filled her irises. Iliana had become quite fluent in the chromatic language of Kressari emotions, including even the subtle variations in Shing-kur's ocular palette. She had learned to decode instances such as when one color encircled another, and the meaning conveyed by the expansion and contraction of those colors. It was a fascinating vocabulary of visual signals, in many ways as complex as the kinesics of any of the various species Iliana had studied during her Obsidian Order training. Interpreting the meaning behind those cues was usually easy, Iliana found, though she had to *see* Shing-kur's eyes to fully grasp the emotional context of her words.

Even so, there were still times when it could be a challenge to "read" the Kressari accurately. News of a Jem'Hadar visitor to the other Kira's station was odd, to be sure, but Iliana failed to understand why this was a source of excitement for her confidant. It certainly offered Iliana no solace from the bitterness she was finding increasingly difficult to tamp down.

"A Jem'Hadar on Deep Space 9. What is that to me, Shing?"

The Kressari stepped farther into the room and, as if suddenly concerned about being overheard, lowered her voice to a whisper. "According to what I've been able to find out, he could be there awhile," she said. "His name is Taran'atar. Supposedly he was sent by the colonel's changeling lover as some kind of cultural observer, and the assignment is open-ended. This may be the opportunity we've been waiting for."

Iliana thought she understood where Shing was going with this, and she shook her head irritably. "If you're thinking of doing to the colonel's new pet what Dukat's fools did with the Jem'Hadar on Harkoum, so that he'll go into a berserker rage and kill her, I won't have it. She's mine to destroy, Shing."

Flecks of blue grew inside the Kressari's eyes, conveying mild disappointment. "I'm not suggesting anything of the kind. I'm proposing that we put the Jem'Hadar under *your* control. Directly."

Iliana stared. "What in the world are you talking about? You were the one who couldn't believe Omek and Vekeer were arrogant enough to tamper with creatures that dangerous! Now you want to follow in their footsteps? Are you insane?"

"Hear me out," said Shing-kur, spreading her hands placatingly. "I've been studying the research that was done here, and I think I've figured out where Dukat's men went wrong. If I'm right, there may be a non-invasive way to override the Jem'Hadar's behavioral programming and transfer his obedience imperative to you. And the best part is this: We won't need to strap him down to a table and pray that he doesn't kill us before his brain explodes. We can do it remotely, from the safety of Harkoum."

Iliana was beginning to think she might have to re-evaluate her estimation of the Kressari flair for the dramatic. She folded her arms before her.

"How?"

"The short version? A subliminal waveform embedded in a subspace communications signal."

Iliana almost laughed. "That's it?"

"It's actually considerably more complicated than that. But as I said, that's the short version."

"And you're telling me that once he's exposed to this . . . waveform, he'll obey my every command?"

"*Every* command," Shing-kur assured her. "And if it works the way I intend, he won't even be aware of what we've done to him . . . especially since his new master will appear identical to his current one."

A sleeper. How deliciously ironic. Iliana turned and started pacing the office.

"Nerys, are you listening to me?"

"I'm listening, Shing. I'm just trying to consider all the implications." She stopped in front of the Obsidian Order's spectral Galor-emblem that still decorated one wall of her quarters and focused on it while she spoke. "How soon can you put your plan into effect?"

"I'll need several weeks at minimum to configure the pulse correctly," Shing-kur said. "One of our people will need to hack into Deep Space 9's medical database and download a copy of any scans the station's doctors have made of the creature."

Iliana nodded, knowing that several of their hirelings were sufficiently proficient with Cardassian computer systems to pull off the job. After learning that Bajor was spearheading relief efforts to Cardassia Prime from all over the quadrant, and that those efforts were being coordinated from Deep Space 9, Iliana knew it afforded her the perfect means by which to keep tabs on what was going on aboard the station, as well as on the two worlds Iliana had lost.

At her instruction, several of the smugglers in her employ began hiring themselves out legitimately as freelance cargo carriers, making regular runs as part of the relief effort. The required stopovers at Deep Space 9 allowed them some freedom of movement aboard the station for brief periods at a time, and they reported what they observed or overheard during those visits back to Shing-kur. Visits to the station's Infirmary were not uncommon.

"All right," she said. "Put someone you trust on it, and get started on developing the pulse as quickly as you can. And Shing . . ."

"Yes?"

"Thank you."

Shing-kur's black irises became ringed with vermilion—the pattern Iliana saw most often when she looked into her confidant's eyes. "You never need to thank me, Nerys," she said softly before turning and leaving Iliana's quarters.

Iliana watched her go. She had known for some time that Shing was in love with her. Not in any way that could be consummated, of course; the profound differences between their respective species made such a thing impossible, even if Iliana's ordeal of the past fifteen years had not purged her of any interest in physical intimacy. And for her part, Shing-kur made no such overtures. Her love for Iliana clearly wasn't about that. Rather, it was the adoration of one individual for the essence of another—a tender and unconditional affection for the intangible part of another person's being.

Had Iliana believed herself capable of reciprocating those feelings, Shing-kur certainly would have been more than deserving.

But she understood all too well that her own emotional spectrum had been bled of such vivid colors a long time ago.

The next several weeks went by swiftly. A seemingly galaxywide crisis erupted during that time, involving the spontaneous opening of innumerable transspatial gateways. The brief period of instability that had grown out of the event came and went before Iliana could decide how she might take advantage of it—much to the relief of her lieutenants, who had considered the situation too dangerous and unpredictable for their liking.

Still, the transient emergency had made Iliana imagine how she might employ such power had she been in a position to gain control over it.

As Bajor's movement toward Federation membership accelerated in the aftermath of the gateway crisis, Shing-kur reported that her subliminal waveform was ready at last. They were delayed from putting it to work, however, when Deep Space 9 became engulfed in a conspiracy by a species of hostile sentient parasites bent on dominating the Bajoran civilization; the discovery of that threat had forced a lockdown of the B'hava'el system.

The deceptively small creatures had already usurped the body and the identity of Bajor's political leader, the man Iliana remembered as her friend and commander in the Bajoran resistance, Shakaar Edon. Iliana's emotions at learning of his death were decidedly mixed. On the one hand, she had found the fact of Edon's demise and the circumstances surrounding it both horrific and heartbreaking. On the other hand, the fact that it had all happened right before Kira's eyes seemed to make it all worthwhile.

It was during the days that followed the successful ending of the parasite menace—a resolution that had brought with it both Bajor's admission to the Federation and the inexplicable return of Benjamin Sisko, the supposed Emissary—that a relative calm settled over Deep Space 9.

That was when Shing-kur told Iliana that she thought she was ready to attempt the subversion of Kira's Jem'Hadar, because there was finally a reasonably high chance of success.

Bypassing the station's comm system so that their signal wouldn't alert station personnel to the incoming transmission—and then following that system to the correct companel—took a bit of finessing. But when the shatterframe screen in Iliana's secure comm booth suddenly came to life with the Jem'Hadar's grim visage, Iliana smiled at him from across the many light-years that separated Harkoum from Deep Space 9 and uttered the words she'd been waiting months to say.

"Hello, Taran'atar."

2

THREE MONTHS AGO

Shing-kur's waveform performed exactly as she had predicted; Taran'atar's altered thralldom made him the perfect mole, enabling him to collect all manner of interesting intelligence that was stored aboard the station, transmit it to Iliana, cover his actions from detection, and retain no memory of what he did—except perhaps in the way one might remember a fading fragment of a dream.

"I'm surprised you're using him purely as a spy," Shing-kur volunteered one day, finding Iliana as she often did these days: sitting alone in the old prison administrator's office, reading from a padd.

"For now," Iliana answered, her eyes never leaving the device. She had developed a particular interest of late in the Celestial Temple and the Orbs, both of which had been absent from Kira's life until after the Occupation. Taran'atar had obligingly performed exhaustive searches on Iliana's behalf for any data relating to them. "Let me guess: you thought that if we were successful with Taran'atar, I would immediately begin preparations to infiltrate the Gamma quadrant so we might put your waveform to more widespread use, bending the armies of the Dominion to my will."

"Something like that," the Kressari admitted.

"Patience, Shing. Leading untold billions of Jem'Hadar soldiers back through the wormhole and onto Captain Kira's very doorstep just before I place her head on a pike is a tempting idea, but it lacks a certain . . ."

Iliana trailed off, suddenly frozen by the content of the file she was reading.

"Nerys?" said Shing-kur. "What's the matter?"

When Iliana found her voice, she could manage only a strangled whisper. "Another Kira."

"What?"

"Another Kira," Iliana rasped. "Another *universe*."

"What are you talking about?"

"Look!" Iliana shouted, holding the padd out to Shing-kur. "A parallel universe with another Kira Nerys!"

Shing-kur took the padd and read through the file while Iliana paced the room, scarcely able to breathe, clutching fistfuls of her hair in both hands, feeling as if she might come apart at any moment.

"All right," the Kressari said finally. "But why is this upsetting you? This woman had nothing to do with—"

Iliana stopped in front of Shing-kur and backhanded her across the face. The impact against the Kressari's hard skin was more painful for Iliana than it was for Shing-kur, but her confidant shrank from her anyway, letting the padd drop to the floor, her eyes turning lavender with sadness as Iliana's rage poured out and broke across her like a wave striking a rocky shore.

"How can you know me as well as you do and still not understand what this means to me? *Another Kira* is out there, Shing, claiming my identity, keeping from me what's rightfully mine!"

Shing-kur said nothing. Iliana grabbed her by the front of her tunic and shoved her against the wall.

"And doesn't that imply that there's a potential infinitude of alternate Kiras," Iliana screamed, "in innumerable alternate universes, *each of them carrying a piece of* me?"

Iliana recalled very little of what happened after that, but when she became aware of herself again, she was on the floor, surrounded by the wreckage of the office, weeping uncontrollably. And Shing-kur, bloodied and bruised, was cradling Iliana's head in her arms, rocking gently back and forth, whispering softly in her ear.

"We'll get them somehow," she promised Iliana. "We'll get all of them."

In time Iliana returned to herself, but she was not the same afterward. She could feel it. Something deep inside of her had changed somehow. She became consumed with the belief that she would only feel whole again once all the other Kiras had been eradicated. Once she had punished each and every one of them for the torment she felt, for the love they'd taken from her, for the life she'd been cruelly denied.

She spent days sequestered in her quarters. Shing-kur ran interference for her with the rest of her followers, taking responsibility for the outburst that had led to the Kressari's injuries and the destruction of the office. Iliana thought she could imagine what the others thought of Shing-kur's excuses and evasions, but she was beyond caring. Nothing they were doing seemed to matter anymore. None of it would fill the void in her soul.

She should have known that Shing-kur would never give up trying.

"Nerys," Iliana heard as she sat alone in the soul-salving darkness of her quarters. A trapezoid of light stretched across her floor, ascending the wall that faced her chair; illumination from the outer corridor, let in by the open door. The light framed Shing-kur's shadow. "Nerys, there's something I want to show you. I think you'll like it."

Iliana said nothing. Shing-kur's shadow grew larger. Iliana became vaguely aware of a padd being placed in her lap.

"Take your time with it," the Kressari said, and then she was gone again.

How many hours passed before Iliana finally summoned the volition to read what Shing-kur had brought her, she couldn't say. She knew only what she felt afterward, that her friend had left her with a precious gift.

A ray of hope.

It was a grouping of several files, selections from the data Taran'atar had sent her about the Orbs, the wormhole, and the alternate universe. Some of it Iliana had already read, but all of it was cross-referenced with a file that was entirely new to her, an obscure paper by a Bajoran philosopher named Ke Hovath, from a backwater village in Hedrikspool Province:

SPECULATIONS ON THE ARCHITECTURE
OF THE CELESTIAL TEMPLE

Highlighted parts of the selected files stressed the popular belief that the Bajoran Orbs were structured vortices of the energy within the wormhole, and the fact that the wormhole itself was transspatial in nature, as evidenced by the passage it once facilitated to and from the alternate universe.

The connection Shing-kur seemed to be making immediately became clear enough: perhaps the Orbs themselves offered a way to access other realities. Ke Hovath's whimsical thesis seemed to imply something of the sort, though it didn't go quite so far in its speculations. Still, Iliana could see that it represented a promising beginning . . . especially after she finished reading several attached log transcripts describing the Deep Space 9 crew's single interaction with Ke and his village, years ago, and the curious object that was in Ke's care.

An Orb fragment. An artifact that hardly anyone knows about, and which wouldn't be missed until far too late, provided we take the proper precautions. This thing could be the key to unlocking all *the doors of the wormhole.*

An infinitude of doors, beyond which existed an infinitude of Kiras.

In the pale glow of possibility that Shing-kur had given her, Iliana delved back into the mountains of data that Taran'atar had sent her, acquainting herself intimately with every last detail she could find concerning the wormhole, the Orbs, the prophecies of the Emissary, the so-called Intendant of the alternate universe, and the state of that continuum.

And Iliana began to plan anew. . . .

From the safety of her cloaked shuttlepod, Iliana watched the live images beamed from the Besinian freighter in grim amusement. The sight of Captain Kira and her crew scouring the ship for answers to the puzzling questions raised by the events of the last twenty-six hours was enormously entertaining. But it was apparently not a sentiment shared by Iliana's current captive.

"You're not her," Ke Hovath snarled. "You're not Kira Nerys. Who *are* you?"

Iliana shot him a bemused look over her shoulder. Safely contained behind a force field in the pod's aft section, Ke seemed to have recovered somewhat from the manifold traumas she had inflicted upon him over the course of the day. It was an admirable feat; the immolation of almost everyone in his beloved village of Sidau still had to be fresh in his mind, right alongside the threats Iliana had made against his young wife, Ke Iniri.

Perhaps the young scholar was made of somewhat sterner stuff than appearances had led her to believe.

Or it might just be his shock at seeing the image of Captain Kira's face on Iliana's monitors, a sight that contradicted the man's earlier belief that the Kira he knew was the one responsible for the recent horrors he'd been made to endure. This revelation seemed to have restored some of Ke's shattered world, if only slightly. But apparently it had been enough to embolden him.

Iliana would need to deal with that.

She continued to watch as events unfolded on her screens. Kira was studying the bodies her people had found in the freighter's engineering section. The captain was clearly taking great pains to reconstruct what had happened aboard the Besinian ship, but she evidently had yet to notice the active-scan cameras that were catching her every move, every nuance of every facial expression.

The destruction of Sidau had been regrettable but necessary—a precaution Iliana had taken to delay the inevitable pursuit she expected to come from Deep Space 9—by ensuring that no witnesses survived to tell the authorities what had happened, or what had been taken from them.

Kira and her medical officer were moving toward the airlock now, following the trail of life signs that had led them to poor, hapless Iniri. Iliana was careful to restrict that feed to a monitor that was out of the restrained Ke's present line of sight, and routed the accompanying audio to her own personal earpiece. There was no value in allowing him to jump to the comforting conclusion that his beloved wife was being rescued. She was, after all, the most effective lever Iliana had over him.

"Oh, my God."

The voice that issued from Iliana's monitor came out as a whisper, from Kira's medical officer, a young man the captain had addressed as Doctor Tarses. A young man who seemed overwhelmed by the killing ground he had found aboard the freighter. To his credit, the doctor appeared to recover from his revulsion quickly enough; Iliana watched impassively as he beamed out with a hysterical and traumatized Iniri.

Then Iliana kept her camera's eye focused tightly upon Kira as the captain moved on to the corpse-strewn bridge, where a heavily disruptor-burned female Arkenite and a charred, hulking Nausicaan lay unmoving in the bloodbath's grisly epicenter.

The Besinian freighter and its variegated and anarchic crew had been among the more troublesome of Iliana's assets. It had lately become *so* troublesome, in fact, that Iliana had come to consider it more liability than asset. The cargo vessel's crew members were widely known within her organization for thinking themselves deserving of greater rewards for their contributions and for encouraging other mercenaries to voice similar sentiments.

Using them for Iliana's mission to Bajor—without informing them it was intended to be a one-way trip— had given her the opportunity to rid herself of a growing nuisance, and also served to demonstrate the price of dissent to any like-minded mercs that might have remained in her employ.

When *Defiant* had finally caught up with the freighter, Iliana had immediately stowed the bound and gagged Ke in the vessel's shuttlepod, then made quick work of the Besinian crew before rejoining her sole live captive, with whom she quietly slipped away from the scene of carnage that she had wrought. Then she had activated the little auxiliary vessel's cloaking device to cover her departure from the freighter's modest, single-craft-sized shuttlebay.

And from this remote and rapidly retreating place of

relative safety she continued to monitor in detail everything that transpired on the doomed cargo ship.

Iliana watched as Kira received a report on the freighter's bridge monitor. *"Captain, I've managed to get the warp drive operational,"* the young engineer said, *"and have already initiated a restart sequence, which should take no more than fifteen minutes."*

As the engineer continued to furnish additional details, Iliana beamed inwardly. Her pursuers now had less than a minute before the sabotaged antimatter injector would do its lethal work. She leaned forward in her seat aboard the shuttlepod, watching the captain's face intently, waiting to see if Kira would put it all together in time. It would be very disappointing if she didn't.

"Thank you, Lieutenant," the captain told her engineer. *"Stand by for further instructions."*

Kira stood on the bridge, a thoughtful expression on her face. Iliana leaned forward anxiously in her seat.

A grin escaped onto Iliana's face, then began to falter. Was killing her nemesis really going to prove to be this easy?

On the viewer, Kira's expression suddenly changed.

"We've got to get out of here," the captain told her subordinates.

There you go, Iliana thought as her doppelganger ordered her boarding parties to prepare to return to *Defiant* on her command. She felt perversely gratified by her opposite's quick thinking and prudent suspicion; she had obviously begun to suspect that the fifteen-minute engine restart sequence her engineer had begun had also set into motion a far briefer autodestruct program.

Iliana glanced down at the chronometer on her wrist. *But have your suspicions awakened in time to do you any good, Nerys?*

Tapping the Starfleet combadge on her chest, Kira said, *"Kira to Nog."*

"Nog here, Captain." came the response from the freighter's engine room.

"Shut down the restart sequence, Lieutenant."

"Sir?"

"Shut it down, Nog," the captain said curtly. *"That's an order."*

"Aye, sir," replied the engineer. *"Initiating core shut-down . . . . Uh-oh."*

"What is it?" Kira wanted to know, her face abruptly going pale.

"The antimatter injector isn't responding. It's continuing to cycle up to release, and the rate is accelerating. Sir, this thing is going to rupture any second."

As *Defiant* extracted Kira and her people in a light-ning-fast emergency beam-out, it occurred to Iliana that Inari could no longer serve as a tool to ensure Ke Hovath's cooperation. As she settled back into her chair and executed the pod's preset course for Harkoum, she decided there was no longer any point in allowing him to learn that she had been rescued.

Just as there was no longer any point in sparing the poor wretch's feelings. The universe, after all, could be a terribly cruel and arbitrary place.

"Say good-bye to Iniri, Hovath," she said softly as she allowed the Bajoran to see everything that was now appearing on her own monitor.

A few heartbeats later the freighter's engine core exploded, and all the monitors aboard the shuttlepod went blank with static. Iliana lifted her hand and considered her prize, the green jewel of the *Paghvaram* glittering seductively in her palm.

Behind her, Ke Hovath screamed as if he would never stop.

3

EIGHT WEEKS AGO

Something was wrong.

Despite the near flawlessness of the manner in which Iliana had gained possession of the so-called "Soul Key," the artifact obstinately refused to work for her. Her first attempts to access its power purely by force of will had been a dismal failure. When she'd questioned Ke about it, the Bajoran had merely tried yet again to convince her that he knew of no use for the *Paghvaram* other than the one to which it had been put for generations: the annual ritual of the Dal'Rok—an elaborate morality play contrived to pacify the historically volatile villagers of Sidau.

Iliana then did what she considered the only logical thing: she demanded a demonstration. The Dal'Rok had always been a construct, after all—the collective fears of the Sidau villagers given form. If that was truly all Ke was capable of conjuring from the *Paghvaram*, then it was a beginning. Iliana wanted to see it, to know how Ke made it work.

She released him from his underground cell and took

him to Harkoum's surface, where Fellen and Telal had already rounded up a dozen or so of the most wretched transients from Iljar, the abject starport community on the edge of the broiling wasteland known on Harkoum as Tarluk V'Hel. Made up of undesirables from at least five different species, the miserable-looking group became wide-eyed with terror when they saw Iliana arriving with Ke.

Ke's face registered disgust. "These people are afraid of you."

"With good reason," Iliana said.

"What did you do to them?"

She turned to look him in the eye. "I made sure their fear would be at your disposal." She slipped off the *Paghvaram* and held it out to Ke. "Now show me."

The Bajoran reached for the artifact, but Iliana yanked it back. "Know this first, Ke. Do as I ask, and I'm willing to let these people return to their lives, such as they were. But if you try any tricks, they die."

Ke glared back at Iliana, his face a mask of pure hatred as he took the *Paghvaram*. She could see the flicker of indecision on his face before he roughly forced his palm through the gap in the bracelet into which the artifact was set. She could see that she had been right to threaten the captives; despite everything, Ke simply did not seem capable of enduring the idea of more innocents dying because of him.

He turned and stretched out his hand to the cloudless sky, palm out.

Once again, nothing happened.

Ke's brow furrowed. He thrust his hand out again,

squeezing his eyes shut in intense concentration. Beads of sweat formed on his brow in response to his mental exertions.

Still nothing changed.

"Why isn't it working, Ke?" Iliana asked.

Ke opened his eyes. He lowered his hand and stared at his palm, shaking his head in disbelief.

"I don't know."

Iliana could see that he meant it. He was genuinely mystified by his failure. He truly expected the *Paghvaram* to work. A troubled expression enveloped his face, and after a moment he offered her a possible explanation.

"I'm no longer worthy."

"Then you're useless," Iliana said, disgusted.

She drew her disruptor and shot Ke point-blank in the head. His body thudded heavily onto the dry earth, which greedily drank the blood that seeped from the imperfectly cauterized blast wound.

Telal sighed and stepped toward her. "Are we done here?"

The Romulan's brusque tone irritated Iliana. None of her inner circle, save Shing-kur, seemed to appreciate the interest she had taken in the Bajoran artifact. And this latest failure to show them the reason Iliana had gone to so much trouble to acquire it could not help but raise doubts in their minds about her judgment.

But that's a problem for another day, she thought.

"Yes, we're done," Iliana answered, still staring at Ke's body.

Telal cocked his head toward their captives. "What do you want us to do with *them*?"

Iliana stooped to take back the *Paghvaram*. "Dump them back in Iljar."

"Are you sure? They know what you look like."

She restored the bracelet to her hand and started back toward Grennokar.

"I didn't say they had to be alive," she said over her shoulder.

Iliana wasn't ready to give up. If anything, her obsession with the *Paghvaram* was only intensifying. Now the thing's ineffable mysteries seemed to taunt her, making her more determined than ever to unlock the secret of its use.

At Shing-kur's suggestion, Iliana turned the artifact over to her for scientific analysis while Iliana pored over file after file of Bajoran prophecy and theological scholarship, looking for insights that went beyond the empirical. For the part of her that was Kira Nerys, becoming reacquainted with her culture's sacred scripture and spiritual philosophy felt a lot like coming home.

Even so, it was difficult to find anything that brought her closer to understanding the *Paghvaram*, in part because there was no reference to it in any of the texts that Taran'atar had sent her. It seemed to occupy no place in the history of the Bajoran religion, or in the indistinct visions of the future that paved the Paths walked by the faithful.

Needing a break from what increasingly felt like a pointless exercise, Iliana set aside her reading to look in on Shing-kur, who had spent most of the last several days in the workshop that she had transformed into her personal laboratory.

"Any progress?" Iliana demanded as she entered the lab. The Kressari was making adjustments to a ceiling-mounted sensor array whose scanning nodes were presently triangulated on the illuminated table directly below them, upon which rested the enigmatic bracelet.

"That depends on your point of view," Shing-kur told her.

"Explain," said Iliana.

"The scans I've taken are consistent with the Orb studies done aboard Deep Space 9. This stone *is* an Orb fragment," Shing-kur confirmed. "But like its larger cousins, it defies any more meaningful analysis by conventional scanning equipment. I can't tell you what it's made of, or how it works, or *why* it works."

Iliana found it difficult to keep the frustration out of her voice. "So what you're saying is, you can't determine anything beyond what Starfleet has already been able to learn about the Orbs."

"Not quite," Shing-kur said. "There is one important difference. I can tell you with absolute certainty that this object is not from this universe."

"We already know that! It came from the wormhole—"

"That isn't what I'm talking about."

"What, then? How can you know it came from another universe if the scans can't even tell you . . ." Iliana stopped herself and looked at the artifact, realization slowly settling in. "The bracelet?"

Shing-kur nodded as blackness swelled in her eyes. "The bracelet."

Although Iliana was willing to concede that the

bracelet that held the Orb fragment was beautiful, it was otherwise unremarkable. "What's so special about the bracelet?"

"Nothing, in and of itself. The metal is simply a solid band of gold composite, consistent with pre-modern Bajoran craftsmanship . . . but its quantum resonance signature places its origin in the Intendant's universe."

The Intendant's . . . ? Iliana thought, her mind racing. *But according to the files, the alternate Bajor doesn't have any Orbs. They haven't even discovered the wormhole that the Orbs came from yet!*

Then suddenly, she had the answer.

"Of course," Shing-kur continued, "I'm not quite sure yet how this information can help us, but it is a curious . . . Are you all right, Nerys?"

Iliana had started pacing the room, feeling a smile begin to spread across her face that Shing-kur was already sharing with her.

"It's fate," Iliana whispered.

Shing-kur's eyes adopted the aquamarine-and-pink hues of mild confusion. "I'm . . . not sure I understand."

Iliana could scarcely contain her mounting excitement. She went to the Kressari and grabbed her shoulders.

"We've been thinking about this all wrong, Shing," she said. "This thing is an Orb fragment. It's a construct of the Prophets. The Prophets exist outside of time. A Bajoran would say it works when it's *fated* to work."

"Meaning what?" asked Shing-kur. "We have to wait for this thing to decide when the time is right before we can get any use out of it?"

"No. Yes. No—" Iliana gestured with her hands, groping for the words that would explain her sudden flash of insight. Finally she said, "It can't be a coincidence that my need for justice has led me to this, to the *Paghvaram*, so soon after I learned about the Intendant! Don't you see? I'm not meant to use this thing here. I'm meant to return it to where it belongs—to the place where it's needed—where there's a Bajor that's still waiting for the one who is destined to open the Gates of the Celestial Temple."

Shing-kur's eyes shifted to pale blue—the color of her profound uncertainty—as she tried to process what she was hearing. Iliana couldn't help but feel pity for her. Shing-kur couldn't *see*. She wasn't Bajoran, and she couldn't possibly understand the immense vista of possibility that had just opened up before Iliana, now that she finally understood which Path she needed to walk.

The Path of the Emissary.

"But what about Captain Kira?" Shing-kur asked.

Iliana grinned. "Captain Kira can wait. First we deal with the Intendant."

The plan that Iliana ultimately approved was Shing-kur's, and it was shocking in its audacity.

Iliana's immediate goal was to eliminate the Intendant and take her place. The solution seemed obvious enough: Taran'atar had already confirmed that scans of the dimensional transport module—the handheld device that could bridge the two known universes, invented by the same clever human who was now leading a doomed rebellion against the Klingon-Cardassian

Alliance—were stored in Deep Space 9's computer system. It seemed reasonable to think Iliana could use those files to fabricate her own DTM and beam across the dimensional gulf to the alternate Harkoum. From there. . .

From there, everything got a lot more complicated. For one thing, their knowledge of the alternate universe was limited to the information collected by the crew of Deep Space 9, and it was appallingly superficial—there was no way to be sure about what might await them on the other side of the dimensional gulf. For another, while Iliana might be physically identical to Intendant Kira, she lacked sufficient knowledge of her target to pull off an effective long-term impersonation.

It was Shing-kur who suggested a less direct, though perhaps more audacious, approach. The key, she argued, was not to risk crossing over to the alternate universe too quickly, but rather to trick the Intendant into believing she had an interest in bringing Iliana to *her*. The Kressari hypothesized that the DTM could be used as a basis for communication with the other side, and that if they could make contact with the Intendant, then it would simply be a matter of making the alternate Kira an offer she would be incapable of refusing.

Once Taran'atar had provided them with the specs for the DTM, it took Shing-kur surprisingly little time to reverse-engineer the mechanism. More problematic would be using it to locate the Intendant. She could be anywhere, after all. But Shing-kur reasoned that the government of the alternate Bajor must, of a necessity, have the means to contact at need a Bajoran as politically powerful as the Intendant, no matter where she was.

That information would doubtless be classified, but computer records of it had to exist.

Accordingly, it became the first test of the Kressari's device to establish an uplink with the alternate Bajor's government comnet. It then fell to Iliana herself, calling on all the technical skills she'd mastered during her time in the Obsidian Order, to circumvent the maze of virtual safeguards that protected the system's most secure files . . . and find the candle in the Fire Caves, as the old proverb went.

For many hours, Iliana labored nonstop from her secure comm booth, expertly sidestepping virtual tripwires and working constantly to stay one step ahead of the system's more elaborate security measures, until . . .

There.

First Minister Li's most recent intelligence briefing, a long and tedious litany of issues great and small to eat up the workday of this world's supreme political leader, plus a contact list of important offworld Bajorans. Kira Nerys was at the top of the list, followed by her current location aboard the Klingon vessel *Negh'Var* and a secret protocol for reaching her.

Armed with that information, Shing-kur could begin the next phase of Iliana's plan.

It was a thing of beauty to watch. The Kressari had a surprising gift for manipulation, one that she deftly employed to ensnare the Intendant with the promise of what she coveted most: power. Shing-kur offered the alternate Kira access to a different quadrant of the galaxy, and the means to rally the most formidable army she might ever encounter—the Jem'Hadar of the alternate universe—

with which the Intendant would be able to conquer the Klingon-Cardassian Alliance. Shing-kur sweetened the deal further, claiming that the rewards of their partnership were not limited to the universe of the Alliance, but that Kira would have access, without restriction, to the considerable resources of Deep Space 9's continuum . . . and, if she wished, to other realities as well.

Best of all, Kira was made to believe that she had been talking to Taran'atar himself the entire time. It had required only one of the many Jem'Hadar corpses still in stasis on Grennokar, some controlled lighting and carefully managed static, and a voice distorter to convince the Intendant—being the vain and venal creature she was—that she had been contacted by a disillusioned soldier in search of a leader more worthy of what he had to offer.

Now everything had come down to waiting while the Intendant completed the preparations that "Taran'atar" had told her would be necessary to begin their enterprise—preparations that would actually pave the way to her own downfall.

Iliana's inner circle was growing impatient. She had been keeping them at arm's length for too long, telling them only what she wanted them to know about her plans, which they still believed extended no further than expanding their criminal organization and eventually using her pet Jem'Hadar to inflict some cruel retribution against the commander of Deep Space 9. But it was obvious to them that Iliana was holding back, and her increasing detachment from their operations was encouraging doubt to flower where once there had been only faith.

Iliana tried to ease those doubts, to offer Mazagalanthi and Fellen and Telal the reassurance they so clearly craved, even though their partnership was nearing the end of its usefulness to her. The bonds they had forged during their escape from Letau and since were not irrelevant, but they were becoming as far removed from Iliana's sense of her own destiny as her artistic pursuits had become after she had learned that Ataan would never be returning from Bajor.

Her inner circle would never understand those changes, she knew. And with Shing-kur's willing help, Iliana made sure that none of them would ever survive an attempt to turn against her. A brief search of the arsenal of clandestine equipment in Grennokar's old storage compartments yielded enough essential components to enable Iliana and Shing-kur to fabricate neurotoxin-filled implants, tiny subcutaneous poison-delivery devices capable of releasing their lethal payloads upon receipt of a specific and individualized remote command. Once the devices were completed, filled, and sealed, Shing-kur used a silent hypospray to inject the devices into the bodies of each of the others, one by one, while they slept.

Afterward, while standing before Iliana, Shing-kur made the ultimate gesture of supreme fealty, willingly giving herself a shot as well.

It was as if her friend already knew that even she would not be able to follow Iliana down the Path that her personal destiny demanded. Moved once again by Shing-kur's selfless devotion, Iliana insisted that they each take a remote subcutaneous kill-switch, to use against any one of her inner circle at will should any of them ever be compromised, or become disloyal.

It was the nearest thing she would ever know to exchanging vows with another.

"The more I learn about her, the more amazed I am that Intendant Kira has survived as long as she has," Shing-kur said between bites of a plant that looked a little like a Bajoran desert cactus. "You'd think her superiors in the Alliance would have put down a megalomaniac like her long ago." She paused, her rising concern coloring her eyes a bright orange-red. "Aren't you going to eat your dinner?"

Iliana spared a glance at her cooling slab of roast *porli* before shaking her head. The refrigeration unit full of Bajoran delicacies had been a pleasant surprise when it was found among the cargo taken in one of her organization's recent pirate raids, but she found herself unable to think much about food at the moment. She felt strangely ill at ease, almost as if she'd forgotten something important, and the feeling had already utterly sabotaged her appetite.

Seated across the table from her in the otherwise empty Grennokar mess hall, Shing-kur made another attempt to engage Iliana in conversation. "I'll say this for her, though: When the Intendant embarks on a new scheme, she doesn't fool around."

"Then she and I *do* have something in common after all," Iliana said, absently rubbing the hand that held the *Paghvaram*. The bracelet felt cool against her skin.

"Well, she definitely lacks your imagination, but she *is* resourceful," Shing-kur acknowledged. "She actually seems to be manipulating her patron, the Klingon regent, in much the same way we're manipulating her."

"A fitting symmetry then," said Iliana, now acutely aware that something was wrong. Her hand and wrist were growing colder, as if the bracelet were made of ice. She raised the artifact to her eyes, catching what seemed like a flicker of movement in the tiny bead of green it carried. Iliana gazed deeply into the *Paghvaram* at that moment.

Then the Orb fragment gazed as deeply back into her. And all at once, Grennokar was gone.

She was enclosed instead in whiteness, surrounded by a void in which only the cadence of her heart seemed to exist. She became aware of its echo, a sympathetic rhythm that did not fade, but seemed to gain strength . . . and she understood that it was not an echo at all.

Somewhere in the perfect emptiness, another heart was beating in tandem with hers.

She turned and saw herself . . . yet not herself: Iliana Ghemor as she might look today, had she never been altered to replace Kira Nerys—the ghost of a life she'd never lived, her black hair and her gray, ridged skin achingly familiar, like a lost reflection.

The specter was watching her intently, and Iliana suddenly saw the truth behind the other's deep brown eyes—the essence of who she was, and all she had ever been, revealed in shards of memory that seemed to explode from her like broken glass, fragments of a life that assailed Iliana, assaulted her.

Mocked her.

No.

The Cardassian's expression had changed. Where once there had been confusion and curiosity, now there was alarm. There was no mistaking the abhorrence Iliana saw in the familiar eyes, the utter loathing, the undisguised contempt.

And there was something else in those eyes now: resolve.

Iliana recoiled as the other woman took a determined step toward her.

Stay . . . away . . . from . . . me!

"Nerys!"

Iliana gasped as the white nothingness all around her abruptly vanished, along with her nemesis. She was once again back in Grennokar, the accusing stare of her distorted reflection replaced by Shing-kur's vermilion worry. The Kressari's hands held her own tightly, covering the *Paghvaram.*

"Nerys, are you okay?"

"What—what just happened to me? Where did I go?"

"You didn't go anywhere," Shing-kur told her. "You just . . . froze where you were sitting for a few minutes. You didn't blink. I'm not sure if you were even breathing."

Iliana jerked her hands away from Shing-kur and stumbled away from the table. She forced herself to look again at the artifact on her wrist, but the Orb fragment now seemed as inert as any ordinary piece of jewelry.

"She's coming for me," Iliana whispered.

"Who?"

Iliana felt her panic slowly giving way to anger. "This place . . . this place needs to go on high alert, effective immediately," she said.

The vermilion in Shing-kur's eyes intensified. "What?"

"Tell our people! There's a dangerous Cardassian woman on her way to Harkoum, an assassin. Put a bounty on her head, promise them anything—just make sure everyone knows she has to be stopped before she gets anywhere near Grennokar!"

Iliana paused, glancing at her palm again. "I have to make my move," she told the Kressari. "You have to put pressure on the Intendant, Shing. Tell her she's running out of time, that it has to be soon."

Shing-kur's eyes had yet to change to a calmer hue, but she didn't question her orders—even though she must have known they meant that she and Iliana would necessarily be parting ways sooner than planned.

"I'll take care of it," the Kressari promised. "But then I want you to tell me exactly who is coming after you, and how you know about it. Will you do that for me?"

Iliana nodded. It didn't even occur to her to refuse. It was first time Shing-kur had asked her for anything. And it would likely be the last.

"What about Taran'atar?" asked Shing-kur.

Iliana smiled. "It's time we brought him home."

PART TWO

DEEP SPACE 9

4

Ghemor ran through the Habitat Ring, on the hunt.

It was clear to her that her target was taking steps not to be found. Maybe he knew she was on him, maybe he didn't, but his movements through the station during the last fifteen minutes were decidedly evasive. Back on Terok Nor, this wouldn't have been a problem. But the very limited access she'd been permitted to the labyrinthine recesses of Deep Space 9—however familiar this station seemed—meant that she needed to find her target before he found refuge in some part of the station that had been denied to her.

Instead, he found her.

"Is there something you want from me, Ms. Ghemor?"

Iliana shook her head and turned, momentarily unable to believe that he had out-hounded her. It wasn't the sort of skill she'd expected from a human.

"How did you do that?"

Benjamin Sisko arched a nearly nonexistent eyebrow at her from the jutting bulkhead against which he'd concealed himself. "I picked up a few tricks over the years from a Cardassian who used to live here. He was good."

"He'd have to be," Ghemor said.

Sisko stepped out into the corridor. "Now do you mind telling me why you've been following me around the station?"

"I wanted to talk to you."

"That much I'd gathered. What about?"

"When we were in ops earlier, Captain Kira was ready to take me back to my universe, to help my people against my counterpart. Commander Vaughn changed her mind, convinced her to take him instead. I want to know why."

Sisko shrugged. "You'll have to ask Commander Vaughn."

As if that were an option now! "I'm asking *you*, sir."

"I'm afraid I can't help you, Ms. Ghemor," Sisko said as he started to walk away.

"You mean you *won't* help me," Ghemor countered.

Sisko stopped and looked at her.

"I saw the look Vaughn gave you before he beamed out," she continued. "I'm well trained at reading people's faces. He was acting at your behest. So I'll ask you again: Why?"

"Let me ask *you* something, Ms. Ghemor. Why this sudden preoccupation with returning to your universe? Considering all the trouble you went to to get here, you seem strangely eager to return."

Ghemor felt her anger rising. "I only came to your mixed-up continuum to stop my counterpart before she stole the mantle of Emissary in my universe. I would have thought you of all people would appreciate the enormity of that."

Sisko's tone remained even. "I'm surprised to hear you say that, given that we both know you had the perfect way to stop your counterpart while you were still on the other side. And you didn't use it."

Damn him. "So you sent Vaughn?"

"Someone had to step up," Sisko said. "Because up to now, too many people have been dropping the ball." He moved on down the curving corridor.

"You're playing a dangerous game, Captain," she called after him.

"That's the difference between us, Ms. Ghemor," he answered over his shoulder. "This isn't a game to me."

"But it is to Them, isn't it?" Ghemor asked.

Sisko stopped. *That got to him,* she thought, gratified that her words had finally struck a sensitive spot.

"They treat our lives like *kotra* pieces," she pressed. "Tell me, Captain, how do you go along with it—putting your own people's lives on the line for some abstract concept of fate, abandoning any sense of free will, any sense of choice—"

Sisko turned to meet her accusing stare one last time. "Everyone has a choice, Ms. Ghemor," he told her. *"Everyone."*

He left her alone in the corridor, and never looked back.

It was with a profound sense of irony that Ro Laren had become an expert on Bajoran prophecy, studying for endless hours in her quarters.

She'd never been the religious sort—not since the death of her father, anyway. If growing up during the Occupation had made her doubtful of the Prophets, Ro Gale's cruel and senseless murder before her seven-year-old eyes had solidified her complete rejection of the Bajoran faith. She didn't deny the existence of the wormhole or the sentients within it, of course. But that wasn't the same thing as believing they were gods. As far as Ro was concerned, any mysticism attached to them wasn't merely unnecessary; it served only to muddle the truth, effectively widening the gulf between the darkness and the light that her people's religion was ostensibly supposed to narrow.

And yet, quite inexplicably, it was Ro's very skepticism that fueled her absorption of Bajor's wealth of religious writings. Because of the accepted transtemporal nature of the wormhole entities, no one disputed that the prophecies were essentially imperfect attempts to understand genuine flashes of precognitive insight—courtesy of contact with beings who existed outside of linear time—going back thousands of years. Where people differed, of course, was in their interpretation of those quasimystical ancient insights. Deciphering those florid descriptions had long been the passion of scholars and theologians all over the planet, as well as a serious area of inquiry—ever since the rediscovery of the long-lost Book of Ohalu—of one agnostic security officer on Deep Space 9.

Admittedly, Ro's attempts to understand the frame of mind of Iliana Ghemor were leading her into turbulent philosophical waters. If Iliana's intention was indeed to fulfill the prophecy of the Emissary in the alternate universe, Ro needed to understand what she expected to achieve by doing so.

The obvious first stop was to review the prophecies that foretold the coming of that religious icon. Those texts, at least, tended to agree on the specific circumstances that would define the Prophets' fated intermediary with the Bajoran people: the Emissary was the one to whom the Prophets would call, the one who would open the Gates of the Celestial Temple, and the one to whom the Prophets would give back life. For Iliana, Ro knew, the key variable in that formula would be the second one. It was the condition that, in Benjamin Sisko's case, had been fulfilled literally when he discovered the wormhole. The other two criteria were much more open to interpretation, and thus easier to rationalize.

Was that enough to make her Emissary, though? Ro had studied the incident with Akorem Laan, the time-lost Bajoran poet who had, in the opinion of many at the time, fulfilled the prophecy more perfectly than Sisko had. And yet, in the end, it was Sisko—alien, nonbeliever, and wounded spirit—whose connection to the wormhole beings had been reaffirmed.

Sisko . . .

Ro rubbed her eyes. She needed a break. And thanks to the bargain she'd struck with her physical therapist, Etana Kol, she was sworn to leave her quarters and take her meals on the Promenade; this was to force her to practice using the powered exoframe that allowed her to exercise her legs while her spine continued to heal following Taran'atar's back-breaking assault.

She reached for her cane and struggled to get out of her chair. How quickly things seemed to change. Had it really been less than a year since she had begun a semblance of friendship with a Jem'Hadar soldier? Ro had always been slow to warm up to people, and those she counted among her friends were few. One of that small number, DS9's former science officer, Shar, had recently gone back to visit his homeworld of Andor and had never returned. And now Taran'atar—

Theirs was an unlikely friendship to be sure, if one could even call it that. They'd first bonded during a harrowing mission to Sindorin, each one learning unexpected things about the other. Later he had helped Ro expose and capture the assassin of Bajoran First Minister Shakaar Edon. It still made her laugh when she recalled the tense moment when Taran'atar had admitted to being unable to provide Shakaar with reliable intel, and he suggested that she, Ro Laren, make a leap of faith.

People think he has no sense of humor, she thought. *I know him better than that.*

She looked down at the jointed metal struts that covered her uniform from the waist down.

Or at least I thought *I did.*

She pressed her cane down upon the deck, and with slow, difficult steps, she made her way toward the door and out into the corridor.

5

Prynn Tenmei flung her padd onto the table and grabbed two handfuls of her spiky black hair, groaning in frustration at the insurmountability of the puzzle she'd been tasked with solving.

"I'm guessing that sound doesn't signify a breakthrough," Julian Bashir said gently.

Tenmei glared at the doctor from across the table, noting as she did that a number of the staff and patrons at the bar had turned their heads to see what was the matter. Embarrassed and thoroughly demoralized, she buried her face in her hands.

She wondered if Quark had a holosuite program that featured a deep hole she could drop into, with a very large rock to roll in on top of her.

"Steady, Ensign," Bashir said. "You aren't the first person to feel defeated by a mystery involving the wormhole aliens. I can recall more than one occasion when Lieutenant Dax's immediate predecessor wanted to smash the Orb of Prophecy and Change for defying her attempts to analyze it. Consider yourself in good company."

"That's all very well and good, Doctor, but respectfully, it doesn't actually help me solve my problem."

Bashir smiled and set down the tricorder with which he'd been running diagnostics on a modified combadge. The doctor had been collaborating with the station's engineering staff to upgrade the neuropulse device he and Lieutenant Nog had developed to reverse Taran'atar's brainwashing. From what Prynn could tell, they had made excellent progress so far.

That makes one of us, she thought glumly.

Bashir placed his elbows on the table and leaned toward her. "You really need to relax, Prynn. You're never going to figure out how the *Rio Grande* wound up in the alternate universe in your present state of mind. That means the first thing you need to do is seek out a little perspective—get comfortable with the fact that the answer you're looking for won't be found by conventional Starfleet methods of investigation. You need to think outside the box."

Tenmei threw her head back and stared at Quark's ceiling. "Outside the box. Terrific."

Ezri Dax's upside-down face suddenly entered her field of vision. "How's your work progressing, Ensign?"

Tenmei nearly jumped out of her chair as she quickly straightened her posture. "Sorry, Lieutenant. I'm afraid that every simulation I run gives me the same results: there's just no reason why an improperly collapsing warp field or a leaky plasma injector should open up a passage into the alternate universe."

"Prynn, listen to me," Dax said as she pulled a chair

up to the table. "I know how hard you've been working on this. I knew it wasn't going to be an easy assignment, but I also knew that if anybody was going to explain what happened to the *Rio Grande*, it was going to be you. I still believe that. But Doctor Bashir is right: the waters of conventional wisdom tend to get muddy in and around the wormhole. Get used to it."

Tenmei nodded, but she was spared having to make what she felt certain would have been a half-hearted verbal reply when Quark arrived with their food.

"Well, good afternoon, Lieutenant," Quark said, addressing Dax as he set down Bashir's mug of Tarkalean tea and Tenmei's bowl of Andorian *vithi* bulbs. "Any more funeral processions you'd like to recruit me for? Just say the word; I'm sure I can find an opening in my schedule—"

"All right, Quark, enough already," Dax said. "Let's move on, shall we?"

"Move on, you say?" Quark held up a finger and reached for an empty chair, evidently having decided to join their table. "You know, that reminds me," he continued in a quiet voice. "There's a nasty rumor going around that *you're* thinking of moving on—as in, *transferring off the station*. There wouldn't be any truth to that ugly bit of gossip, would there?"

Instead of making a face, as Dax was wont to do when confronted by something she thought was preposterous, the lieutenant merely blinked in surprise, which Tenmei immediately took as a bad sign. And she apparently wasn't the only one to think so.

"Ezri," Bashir said slowly. "Is that true?"

Dax sighed. "I haven't put in for a transfer, all right?"

Bashir's eyes narrowed. "But you *are* thinking about it."

Dax threw both hands into the air. "Yes, all right, I've been thinking about it. From time to time. As in, *not very often.* Can we change the subject, please?"

"Change the subject?" Quark asked. "What's wrong with the subject? Doctor, do you have a problem with the subject?"

Bashir folded his arms as he regarded Dax. "No, actually I'm quite interested in the subject."

"Ensign?"

"Please don't get me involved in this, Doctor. She outranks me."

"There, you see?" Quark said to Dax. "A clear table majority has no objection to the subject. Democracy in action, which I know you Federation types *love* to see."

Dax bowed her head. "Why are you doing this to me?"

Bashir fumbled over his next comment. "It just seems rather . . ."

"Sudden," Quark put in.

"Yes," Bashir agreed. "Sudden. It seems rather sudden."

"Oh, please," Dax said. "Neither of you has the slightest idea how long I've been thinking about this—and I want to stress again, I'm only *thinking* about it—so don't try to draw me into some sick passive-aggressive wordplay. Remember who you're talking to."

"You know, Ezri," Quark said, lacing his fingers in front of him as he leaned into the table. "It's widely accepted on Ferenginar that there are certain places in the universe that function as the nexuses of interesting activity—focal points, you might say, for commerce, love, adventure, discovery, you name it." He tapped his finger on the table. "This happens to be one of them."

"The table?" Ezri asked.

"The station," Quark snapped. "Why do you think I've stayed here as long as I have?"

"Lack of better prospects?" Bashir asked.

"Your bill just went up." To Dax, Quark said, "Remember Rule of Acquisition Number One-Ninety-Nine: Location, location, location."

Tenmei blinked.

"I think we're done," Dax said, starting to rise.

"Location," Tenmei repeated. "That's it. That's the answer."

"*What's* the answer?" asked Bashir.

Tenmei pointed at Quark. "Nexuses of interesting activity." She pointed at Bashir. "Outside the box." She pointed at Dax. "Change the subject."

Quark stared at her and spoke to Bashir out of the corner of his mouth. "Does anybody have any idea what she's going on about?"

Dax settled back into her seat. "Prynn, what are you getting at? Does this have something to do with the *Rio Grande*?"

Tenmei laughed. "That's just it, Lieutenant . . . . I don't think it was *ever* about the *Rio Grande*. It was about the wormhole. Don't you get it? It was about the wormhole all along!"

"Explain it to me," Dax said.

Tenmei sighed and held up her useless padd. "I've been running simulations trying to recreate the *Rio Grande*'s voyage into the alternate universe, but none of them have worked. Why? Not because there's anything wrong with my data on the workings of the ship, but because I can't duplicate the exact conditions inside the wormhole."

"Why not?" Dax asked.

"Because those conditions aren't restricted to the ones we can measure. It's as much a mindspace for the aliens living inside it as it is a subspace tunnel for ships to travel through. And when you take that into account, then maybe the *Rio Grande* didn't cross over into the alternate universe because its malfunction made it possible after all. Maybe it crossed over because its malfunction was the *precondition* for the wormhole aliens to permit its passage."

"It sounds as if you're saying the Prophets *sent* the *Rio Grande* to the alternate universe," Bashir said.

"That," Prynn said, "is *exactly* what I'm saying!"

"So all we need to do," Dax mused, "is duplicate the original malfunction while we're inside the wormhole, and we should be able to reach the Alliance's continuum?"

Tenmei laughed. She couldn't help it; hearing someone actually say it out loud was the last straw. "Beats me. It still doesn't make any sense, not really . . . until you factor in the will of the wormhole aliens, that is. They're the ones calling the shots in there. But if the conditions they set are constant and not variable, then there's every reason to think we can do it again."

Dax smiled. "I like it."

"You intend to put Ensign Tenmei's hypothesis to the test?" Bashir asked.

"You bet I do. Nog hasn't been able to make a dent in the scattering field—or whatever it is—that's blocking our ability to transport over there. This may be the only way to assist Captain Kira and Commander Vaughn. How's your modified combadge coming along?"

"I was just running the final diagnostics before authorizing Ensign Leishman to upload the specs into the replicator database."

"Good," Dax said. "I want us to be ready to depart first thing tomorrow morning." She rose from her chair. "I'm going to tell our interdimensional visitor the good news. Care to join me?"

Bashir nodded and downed the last of his tea before he gathered up his things. Dax gave Prynn an approving nod as they left the table. "Well done, Prynn."

After they left, Quark said, "So let me get this straight. You solved this unsolvable problem after I recited the One-Hundred and Ninety-Ninth Rule of Acquisition. Is that about right?"

"Well," Prynn began, not quite sure how to answer. "I suppose that's one way of—"

A burst of applause rang out through Quark's, throwing Tenmei off. She turned around and immediately saw the reason for the enthusiasm: Lieutenant Ro was slowly making her way into the bar, helped along by a cane and the bracelike exoframe fastened around her legs. She scowled at the applauders, but Tenmei could see her smiling behind it as she worked her way toward a table to join Nurses Etana and Richter.

Quark was suddenly grinning from ear to enormous ear. He straightened his topcoat, breathed into his palm, and stood. "If you'll excuse me, Ensign, duty calls," he said, and headed straight for Ro's table.

Tenmei popped a *vithi* bulb into her mouth, thinking that perhaps the day had just taken a turn for the better, for everybody.

6

"You have the look of someone lost," Shing-kur told her visitor.

Ghemor stood with her arms folded outside the holding cell, staring at the Kressari, acutely aware of the nearby Bajoran guards who were watching them both. Major Cenn had been gracious enough to let her see Shing-kur, but he was wise enough not to leave Ghemor alone with her, even separated by a force field.

"You must have me mistaken for someone else," Ghemor said.

Shing-kur's eyes, conveying pleasure, resembled orbs of obsidian glass. She sat in repose on the bench against the back wall of her cell. "Oh, I think I read you well enough, Iliana. Is it all right if I call you that? She never let me use her old name."

"I don't give a damn what you do."

"No? Then why are you here?"

Good question. "I'm trying to understand why someone with your obvious intellect could be so self-destructively devoted to someone like her. What exactly is the hold she has on you?"

"No hold, Iliana," Shing-kur said.

"What, then?"

"She needed someone, and I was there for her."

"That's it?"

Shing-kur regarded her for a moment. "Haven't you ever been needed?"

Ghemor took a half step toward the force field. "Help me stop her."

"Why would I do that?"

"Don't you care about the all the harm she's done? The harm she still plans to do?"

"Ah, yes, all the harm *she's* done." Shing-kur's eyes turned white. "You're like everyone else. You spare no thought for the harm that's been inflicted on *her*. For the betrayals *she's* endured."

"Help me to understand, then."

Shing-kur sat up. "I was right about you. You truly do feel lost right now, don't you? Something's changed since we last spoke. It's in your face."

"Nothing's changed," Ghemor said through her teeth. "She's still out there, and you're still in a cage."

"Then I daresay that makes two of us," Shing-kur said, her eyes shifting back to deepest black.

"Ghemor?"

She turned. Dax and the doctor were standing near the exit. The Trill tilted her head toward the door.

"A moment of your time, please."

Ghemor cast a final glance at the Kressari and followed the officers out. Dax led them into the interrogation room. Whatever she had to say, she obviously wanted to do it in private.

The petite lieutenant folded her arms before her. "What were you doing in there?"

Ghemor shrugged. "Taking care of some unfinished business."

Dax seemed to be considering whether or not to insist that Ghemor elaborate, then apparently decided to let the matter pass.

"If I may say, Ms. Ghemor, you look at bit drawn," Bashir said. "How are you feeling?"

"Honest answer? Pretty useless. But thank you for asking."

"When was the last time you slept?" the doctor pressed.

"Probably too long ago."

"Then I advise you to get some rest," Dax said. "That's why we came to see you. We have a new theory about the wormhole. We're launching *Defiant* tomorrow so we can put it to the test. If we're right, we could have you back in your universe before lunchtime . . . and maybe give your counterpart a little surprise as well."

Ghemor merely nodded, suddenly too drained to say anything out loud. She caught her reflection in the interrogation room's two-way mirror. The doctor was right—she was a mess.

The look of someone lost.

She didn't recognize herself anymore. Iliana thought she knew what she was doing, but ever since her conversation with Sisko, she'd felt adrift. Every choice she'd made up to now had been a disaster. She could only hope she still had enough time to set things right before the other Iliana became the new face of the Prophets.

There's a thought. A new face.

With a burst of renewed energy, Ghemor turned to face her hosts. "I think I have an idea. . . ."

PART THREE

THE ALTERNATE UNIVERSE

7

FIVE DAYS AGO

"My patience is wearing thin, L'Haan," Iliana said as she considered the view beyond the panoramic window of her suite aboard the *Negh'Var*, watching the elongated starlight stream past—an illusion of the warship's superluminal velocity. She'd long since grown weary of the view. Her rendezvous with the Alliance battle fleet at Regulon was now only minutes away, and still the Vulcan handmaiden had not kept up her end of the bargain they had struck prior to Iliana's arrival in this twisted universe. "You assured me you understood the mechanism's function."

In the reflective transparency of the window, Iliana saw L'Haan bowing deeply, the scanty silken veils that passed for servants' attire in this place once again billowing around her slender frame as she moved. Iliana's predecessor had clearly been a creature of vulgar sensibilities.

"With respect, Intendant," L'Haan said, "the fault is not with my understanding, but with the mechanism itself."

Intendant.

The title brought a faint smile to Iliana's lips, which she admired in her reflection. She was a perfect match for the Kira Nerys of this universe, from the gaudy silver headpiece that crowned her red hair to the toes of the narrow boots that completed her clinging black bodysuit. Three days after the she'd claimed her new identity, the euphoria of slitting that other Kira's throat lingered like the heady effect of an exquisite wine.

But she knew that she owed some measure of her success thus far to L'Haan. Reaching out surreptitiously to Intendant Kira's handmaiden had been a tricky but essential maneuver. As a personal slave, and a Vulcan, L'Haan was uniquely positioned to take note of Kira's most closely guarded secrets, and to advise Iliana on how to carry off her masquerade. She needed only to be convinced to stay out of the way until the switch could be made during the *Negh'Var*'s detour to Harkoum. And despite her lowly station in the hierarchy of the Alliance, she was already proving that she was not without useful skills of her own.

Iliana turned away from her reflection to look at the Vulcan. "Exactly what are you telling me?"

L'Haan kept her eyes fixed on the floor. "I am saying that Professor Ke's dimensional transporter does not function as it was intended."

Iliana glanced toward the elaborate array of equipment surrounding the blank wall at the far end of her spacious quarters. "That's impossible," she spat. "We made the journey over, Taran'atar and I, using that very device. How can you stand there and tell me—"

"That involved the use of the transporter in a manner that is already proven to work," L'Haan explained. "To bridge the two known parallel universes. But Professor Ke warned your predecessor that the system he created to broaden the dimensional reach of the transporter was unstable. I suspect he was trying to prepare her for the possibility of failure, and that he would require more time to perfect it. Unfortunately, she killed him before its ability to reach other alternate realities was substantiated."

Iliana wanted to scream. How supremely stupid could this continuum's Kira have been to kill the machine's creator before it could be tested? Wasn't it enough that Shing-kur had fed the Intendant the idea of creating a metadimensional transporter in the first place? The Kressari's technical genius had served Iliana well over the last year, but even she admitted to being woefully unqualified to devise a transporter capable of bridging multiple realities. Far better to leave that task for Intendant Kira and the considerable resources someone of her power and influence could doubtless call upon—or so Shing-kur had believed. The DTM had been invented here, after all, and used repeatedly by people who seemed to be obsessed with the other universe. But had Iliana known the Intendant would botch it so completely, she certainly would not have placed nearly so much reliance on that hedonistic narcissist!

But perhaps it was better this way. The metadimensional transporter had always felt like overkill to Iliana, the fruit of Shing-kur's unvoiced skepticism toward her epiphany. Now the device's failure seemed almost to be a sign affirming Iliana's instinct about the pivotal role she was fated to play in this universe.

It would have been so sweet—beaming across the dimensions at my leisure to slay one Kira after another. But all things in their proper time. Iliana gazed down at the golden bracelet that encircled her hand. *And there's so much else we need to do first, isn't there?*

The stars beyond her enormous viewport condensed from streaks into pinpoints, and the *Negh'Var* was suddenly surrounded by a combined fleet of Cardassian and Klingon warships, magnificently arrayed in formation.

"Here we go," Iliana whispered aloud. She turned to consider the tall figure that stood vigilantly some distance away on her right. "How do you feel?"

"Obedience brings victory," Taran'atar said. He watched her constantly, ever ready to follow her slightest command without question.

Iliana offered him a thin smile. "That's not an answer, but no matter. General Kurn is growing impatient about the true nature of the 'package' his Intendant received while the *Negh'Var* was orbiting Harkoum. Soon it'll be time to make your existence known, and to sell our story. I trust you remember what to say?"

Taran'atar answered without hesitation. "I will tell anyone you designate that I am a Jem'Hadar soldier, from a world far beyond the Alliance's borders. I was captured by a Bajoran scientist in your service, Professor Ke Hovath, who studied my neurochemistry and learned that I could be made to serve the Alliance. Professor Ke contacted you and presented me as a gift on Harkoum. As a test of my servitude, and in order to preserve the secrecy of my existence, your first command was that I kill Professor Ke."

Iliana nodded. "Good. I'll persuade them that with your help I'll be able to find the rest of your kind and sway them into serving the Alliance as well. By the time anyone realizes I have no such intentions, the wormhole will already be mine. And then—"

The dull tone of the Klingon comm system heralded a call from the bridge. *"Kurn to Kira."*

Iliana sighed at the interruption. "If you're going to tell me we've arrived at Regulon, General, I can see that for myself."

"No, Intendant. But we received a Code Black transmission as soon as we dropped out of warp."

Iliana cursed silently. Code Black was an alert from the Obsidian Order.

"Gul Macet is standing by to beam an Alliance official over to us from the Trager," Kurn continued. *"The official is demanding an audience with you."*

"Is he now?" Iliana mused. "Well, we mustn't keep him waiting. By all means, welcome this dignitary to your ship, General, and escort him to your office. "

"My office, Intendant?"

"Do you have a problem with that, General?"

After a slight pause, Kurn answered, *"Of course not, Intendant."*

"Good," Iliana said. "Keep him occupied until I arrive. Kira out." Iliana returned her attention to L'Haan, and pointed to Professor Ke's device. "Have that equipment dismantled and destroyed. Download the specifications to a datarod, but remove all trace of it from the computer system. Is that understood?"

Again, L'Haan's eyes went to the deck. "Yes, Intendant."

"Why would an official from the Obsidian Order wish to see the Intendant *now*?"

L'Haan shook her head. "I cannot say. My previous mistress had little use for the Order. I gathered she held them in some contempt."

Iliana laughed at that, and turned to adjust her hair in the reflection of the viewport. "Just when I thought she and I couldn't be more dissimilar . . ."

As with most Klingon ships, the *Negh'Var* reeked of the excesses of its builders. Not the builders per se; individual Klingons exuded a strong and distinct odor that in itself was not wholly unpleasant. But when that scent was magnified by their preference for overcrowded living conditions and mingled with the pervasive stench of the rich, meaty foods they favored, the air quality of a spaceship's interior, even one as atypically spacious as the *Negh'Var*, was almost unbearable. Outside the Intendant's quarters, Iliana felt as if she were suffocating in the vessel's warm, acrid atmosphere—even in the executive turbolift she took to the command deck and Kurn's office, a private elevator reserved for the ship's seniormost officers.

Iliana steeled herself and soldiered on through the

Negh'Var's narrow warren of corridors toward Kurn's office.

She would need to dispense with the Order's messenger as quickly as possible. There was much she needed to do, and such delays were intolerable. Still, she knew she had to tread carefully; though she was confident of her ability to play the role in which she'd cast herself, she understood that her impatience to reach her endgame could easily prove to be her undoing.

The guards stationed outside the office door carefully avoided eye contact as she approached. The show of deference was amusing in its way; whatever else she might think about the Kira of this universe, the woman had clearly made a masterful ascent within the political structure of the Alliance, and in doing so, had cultivated the fear as well as the respect of the aliens around her. It made Iliana tingle to imagine how she would use that power in the days ahead.

But when the thick door to Kurn's sanctum opened, her excitement quickly evaporated into the pungent air. The general was facing her as she entered. He was speaking to a tall Cardassian who had his back to the door, a man dressed in neat brown civilian attire. She couldn't yet see the Cardassian's face, but there was no mistaking either his silhouette or his posture. He turned toward her as she entered the room, and though the face was sixteen years older than the one she remembered, it gave her pause nevertheless.

The Cardassian's large, probing eyes met hers, one eyeridge rising appraisingly.

"Intendant Kira, I presume?"

Iliana said nothing in response, and into the silence that followed Kurn finally said, "Intendant, I give you Senior Operative Corbin Entek of the Obsidian Order."

Iliana took her time summoning forth an arrogant smile. "Thank you, General. You may return to your duties. I'll speak to the operative. Alone."

Kurn's eyes blazed with unconcealed resentment. She was still learning the nuances of their relationship, but clearly he wasn't accustomed to receiving such dismissive treatment from Intendant Kira. Iliana knew she would have to rectify that, but now was not the time. For the moment she merely held his stare as if daring him to defy her.

"I'll be on the bridge," Kurn said through his teeth, then marched out without sparing another word for either of them.

Ignoring Kurn's emotional display, Iliana kept her own manner businesslike as she gestured Entek toward the office's single guest chair, which was made of the same hard, unforgiving metal that comprised the *Negh'Var*'s decks.

"Are you unwell, Intendant?"

"Is there a reason I should be?" Iliana asked imperiously as she retreated behind Kurn's cluttered desk.

"Not yet," Entek answered. "But perhaps you're unaware that operatives of the Obsidian Order are trained in kinesics. It seemed to me that you appeared unsettled for a moment."

"I'm well aware of the skills that the Order prizes, Mister Entek. It just troubles me to think that all its agents may be as poorly trained and impertinent as *you* appear to be."

"Then I'll be sure to make your concerns known to Director Lang when next I speak with her," he promised. "I understand that she's developed a keen interest in your thoughts of late. As have others."

Iliana leaned back in Kurn's massive, too-hard chair and manufactured a scornful gaze. "Kindly dispense with your veiled insinuations and come to the point, Mister Entek. If you know anything about me at all, then you know I'm not one to be trifled with. And if I find that you are wasting my time, Director Lang will also develop a keen interest in the whereabouts of your body."

Entek smiled, clearly not intimidated. Without taking his eyes off her he produced a padd, carefully set it down on the desk between them, and pushed it gently toward her. "You've been summoned before the regent," he said in matter-of-fact tones. "You're to present yourself to him at Raknal Station within three standard days."

Iliana refused to look at the padd. She concentrated instead on keeping her outrage contained, however imperfectly. "That's quite impossible, Mister Entek. I'm on a vital mission on behalf of the Alliance, on the regent's own authority—"

"Which he is free to rescind at any time," Entek reminded her. He seemed to be enjoying her discomfiture. "And your 'mission,' as you call it, is precisely *why* you've been summoned. It appears that some . . . concerns have been raised about some of your recent activities. Particularly as they pertain to this military force you've amassed here at Regulon."

Iliana finally looked down at the padd. She saw the official command displayed on the device's tiny screen, and wondered what this turn of events might mean. L'Haan had assured her that Intendant Kira had successfully negotiated the use of Regent Martok's personal fleet. Something had changed, apparently. But what?

"You may, of course, decline the summons," Entek continued. "But I daresay the regent might find such a decision on your part . . . irritating." From the Cardassian's tone, she strongly suspected he would love to see her try.

Iliana paused to consider the somewhat narrow palette of choices available to her. As infuriating as this diversion was, her success depended in large part upon not making enemies of these people too soon. Simply defying Martok's summons wasn't an option, as Entek knew perfectly well. In a fleet rife with power-hungry opportunists, her flagrant disobedience of the regent would invite a quick assassination from those wishing to curry Martok's favor—and she strongly suspected that Kurn would be at the head of the line.

Still, while she might have little choice except to adapt on the fly to these suddenly altered circumstances, that wouldn't necessarily prevent her from taking steps to affect how events would unfold.

Iliana touched the companel on Kurn's desk. "Kira to bridge."

"This is Kurn," came the terse reply.

"Send out the word, General," she said pleasantly. "We are to make best speed for Raknal Station at once. I want the entire fleet ready to get under way within the hour."

"As you command, Intendant. Bridge out."

"A wise choice," Entek said.

"Choice has nothing to do with it," Iliana said. "As the regent's loyal servant, I'm bound to obey him, as are we all."

"Well spoken," said Entek. "Tread as carefully before Martok, and you may yet come out of this with your whole skin intact after all, Intendant."

Iliana leaned forward with her elbow on the desk, propping her chin up on a languidly posed hand. "Oh, please . . . call me Nerys," she pouted. "And you seem to think I'm guilty of something, Mister Entek. That hurts my feelings."

"I doubt that sincerely," Entek said. "And if the Order has taught me anything, it's that everyone is guilty of something."

"Too true," Iliana said. "So what are *you* guilty of, Entek?"

"Quite a great deal less, I suspect, than you are."

"Indeed." She dropped her arm and leaned in to whisper conspiratorially. "Would you like to see just what I'm guilty of?"

Entek laughed. "Are you serious?"

"Completely," Iliana said, placing her hand on her heart. Dropping her coquettish façade, she spoke her next words loudly and sharply. "Taran'atar . . . show yourself."

Instantly, the air next to Entek shimmered, and her Jem'Hadar pawn solidified, tall and imposing as he stared down at the Cardassian. She had ordered him to stick close to her since their arrival three days ago, but not to reveal himself until she was ready to make his existence known.

Now seemed to be a particularly useful time to unveil him.

Entek stood up quickly and stumbled backward, startled. "What—what is that?" he demanded to know.

"The future," Iliana told him, allowing an almost flirtatious purr to return to her voice. "Now, Corbin—may I call you Corbin? it feels natural somehow—now, Corbin . . . you're going to tell me what this is all *really* about. Or else I'm going to tell my friend here to take his time with you."

"You cannot threaten me, Intendant."

"Don't be too sure of that," Iliana said. "Oh, I know all about that little wire in your brain that's supposed to make you resistant to torture. But wired or not, I'm willing to bet you can't produce nearly enough endorphins to do you much good while you're watching yourself being dismembered, once small piece at a time."

Entek licked his lips—apparently a nervous tick that Iliana had never observed the spymaster's counterpart to exhibit—as he watched the Jem'Hadar warily.

She sighed. "I'm still waiting, Corbin. Now why are you here, really?"

Apparently finally recognizing the better part of valor, Entek said, "Twenty hours ago, you transmitted an inquiry to the Central Records Office on Cardassia Prime, for information on one Ataan Rhukal."

Iliana swiveled around in her chair, hiding her face from Entek. "What of it?"

"It raised a flag on the Obsidian Order's surveillance

grid," he said, "since all information pertaining to Rhukal is classified."

"Why is it classified?" she purred.

Entek's equanimity appeared to have returned, at least somewhat. "I can't disclose—"

Speaking in the same commanding tone she had used to conjure the Jem'Hadar, Iliana said, "Taran'atar, remove his left thumb."

"Wait, I'll tell you!" Entek shouted, once again on the ragged edge of panic as the monster took its first determined step toward him.

"Stop," Iliana said calmly, and the Jem'Hadar immediately halted his advance. Addressing Entek in ingratiating tones, she said, "You were saying, Corbin?"

Still clearly flustered, Entek said, "Rhukal was one of ours—an operative of the Order. But he has been positively identified as the assassin of the organization's previous director, Tekeny Ghemor."

Iliana's hand curled into a fist. "And Martok . . . Martok believes that my interest in Ataan stems from complicity with—with Ghemor's murder?"

"They all believe it," Entek said. "The regent, Director Lang, the supreme legate. Everyone."

"Everyone," Iliana echoed, her voice mild. But the sudden realization of her own profound carelessness ignited a sudden firestorm of anger and frustration deep within her soul.

Ever since the *Paghvaram* had shown Iliana her counterpart, she'd found it mercifully difficult to recall the broken kaleidoscope of memories to which she'd been subjected once the other's life had been opened to her.

But there was one thing she'd retained—or thought she had retained, because it had invaded her sleep so many times during the intervening weeks: the face that still, after all these years, caused her nothing but sorrow.

Ataan's face.

On her first night aboard the *Negh'Var*, Iliana had in a moment of weakness arisen from her troubled sleep and filed an inquiry on the Cardassian information net, requesting any information on Ataan's counterpart, just to know who he was in this continuum. She had found nothing. Ataan Rhukal had seemed not to exist in this universe, and Iliana became convinced that she had simply imagined having seen him in the *Paghvaram*'s whirlwind glimpse of her counterpart's life.

Now she knew the truth. The Order had made Ataan disappear.

She considered how her Obsidian Order training, aggregated with every tragedy and betrayal she had experienced since those days, had eroded away most of her emotional core. *How ironic*, she thought. *After all I've gone through, and everything I've had to do to get myself to this point along my Path . . . to be undone by my own sentimentality. . . .*

How her mentor must be laughing at her now.

She took another moment to gather her wits before she stood up from behind Kurn's desk.

When she turned to face Entek again, she wore one of the Intendant's brightest, most personable smiles. Using the pleasant tones of a magnanimous host, she told Taran'atar, "Bring him."

"Wait," Entek cried as the Jem'Hadar grabbed him roughly by his jacket and dragged him after Iliana as she strode to the office door. "Intendant, please! I see now that this is all an unfortunate misunderstanding. You obviously didn't know about any of this. I'll make that case to the regent for you. I swear it!"

Iliana was still smiling as she led them out of the office. "I know you will, Corbin. You've always been *such* a help to me."

8

THREE DAYS AGO

Tethered by gravity to the planet for which it was named, Raknal Station hung like an immense spider within the iridescent haze of the Betreka Nebula.

Its design reflected the sensibilities of its Cardassian builders, the dozen duranium "legs" of its docking pylons arching outward from its saucerlike central mass. Easily five times the size of Terok Nor and possessing ten times its firepower, Raknal was undeniably the most heavily fortified base in its region of the galaxy. Virtually every major joint operation of the Klingon-Cardassian Alliance was staged from here, at what was—symbolically if not quite literally—the midway point along the axis between Cardassia Prime and Qo'noS. In every way, Raknal Station represented the collective might of two great galactic powers, as well as the tenuous bond that held them together.

Nearly fifty years ago, a Cardassian survey of Raknal V had uncovered the hulk of a crashed Klingon vessel, a discovery that had nearly unraveled the still-young Alliance in the ensuing dispute over which side had the truer claim to the system. As in the past, it was Bajor that had brokered the accord the two empires finally reached; Raknal V became the symbol of a stronger and more unified Alliance, and Raknal Station was built to affirm that partnership.

In retrospect, Iliana now knew she should have realized that a command to appear before the regent of the Klingon Empire at Raknal Station would also mean appearing before the supreme legate of the Cardassian Union.

After crossing the airlock from the *Negh'Var* and clearing interminable security checkpoints throughout the station, Iliana reached the audience chamber and pushed open its enormous doors with an impatient shove; Intendant Kira's reputation for brazen arrogance had to be maintained, after all. The ostentatious room stretched away before her, its long metal walls and high ceilings overlaid with thick decorative slabs of volcanic rock. She started confidently down the main aisle toward the raised black marble dais with its two occupied thrones at the other end of the room, pointedly ignoring the Klingon and Cardassian guards who had drawn their weapons as she made her entrance.

But when she saw Dukat seated upon one of the thrones, she slowed almost to a complete stop.

"Well?" the legate snapped. "What are you waiting for? A procession of slaves to cast flower petals at your feet?"

Knowing that this wasn't the same Dukat she had known in her own universe now seemed to be an utter irrelevancy. The fact remained that it was *his* voice that she heard in her nightmares.

His face that she longed, even now, to flay from its skull.

Suppressing her sudden desire for violence, Iliana marched forward, keeping her eyes fixed upon Martok, who made a far more imposing figure than did the legate. But the attempted self-diversion did her little good. Dukat was a beacon in her peripheral vision, impossible to ignore, and she knew that pretending he wasn't there would avail her nothing. And still another presence made itself known as well, lurking quietly in her peripheral vision.

As she approached the thrones, she reminded herself that encounters like this one, and the earlier one with Entek, were to be expected; meeting the counterparts of people she'd known, friend and foe alike, seemed inevitable—and in a way, almost comforting. The subtle if inexplicable forces that caused many of the same sets of lives to intersect in both universes might also prevail in other realities as well, and therefore were likely to make her ultimate goals easier to achieve.

She fixed on that idea, clinging to it like a lifeline. And at the foot of the dais, just beyond the edge of a centrally placed, floor-mounted viewscreen that was angled toward the thrones, she prostrated herself before the rulers of the Alliance, just as L'Haan had coached her.

"My lords," she said humbly.

The crowned heads of the Alliance took their time giving her their leave to rise. Iliana understood that they were merely making a point about who was in charge here, thereby setting the tone for the audience.

It wasn't until Martok released her to stand that she

got a good look at the small, low table that stood between the two men. Upon the table's polished surface was arranged the square marble board and bone-carved pieces of what appeared to be a half-finished game of Terran chess. There was even a tradition, as old as Raknal Station itself, among the leaders of both sides: once a year, no matter which of the two powers was in ascendancy, they would meet at Raknal to play chess—not *kotra* or *klin zha*, the favored pastimes native to their respective empires, but rather the seminal strategy game of their long-vanquished Terran adversaries; more symbolism, intended by the rulers of the Klingon Empire and the Cardassian Union to remind themselves, and each other, of all that they had accomplished by working together, despite their longstanding mutual competitiveness.

"Tell us, *Intendant*," Dukat began with his familiar drawl, his voice practically dripping with disdain as he used her title. "Where are your loyalties?"

"With the Alliance, of course, Legate," Iliana said automatically, laboring to keep her smile genial. "As always."

"And yet," Martok said, his regent's cloak gathered around him like the webbed wings of the giant avians that roosted among the peaks of Bajor's mountains, "you answer my summons with my own Ninth Fleet at your back, accompanied by a host of Legate Dukat's ships as well."

"A fleet that you yourself released to me, Regent," Iliana said smoothly, "so that I could bring you the results I vowed to achieve: the destruction of the rebels. Already their infestation has been purged from the Badlands.

Terok Nor is to be next—a mission I would be on at this very moment, but for your summons."

"Do not presume to remind me of what I already know," Martok rumbled, his eyes burning with scorn. "I'm well aware of your successes in driving the Terran rabble from their hiding places among the plasma storms . . . but I also know that that isn't *all* you've been up to."

Iliana spread her hands in a gesture of openness. "I have no secrets from you, Lord Regent."

"Then explain your interest in Ataan Rhukal," came a shout from across the room. The command had been flung like an accusation, intended to rattle her. But Iliana had expected it, having already noted the presence of the dark-clad speaker, who had been skulking restlessly in the audience chamber's shadows when Iliana had entered.

Martok seemed incensed by the interruption. "Legate, if you cannot control your people—"

"Natima!" Dukat scolded, his embarrassment plain. "I specifically instructed you to remain silent while we questioned her!"

"My lords, I beg your forgiveness," said Director Lang of the Obsidian Order, the heels of her black boots clacking loudly as she marched toward the dais. "But since I have been charged with the responsibility for the security of our Alliance, I cannot hold my tongue while this Bajoran traitor pretends her innocence!"

"You *will* hold your tongue," Martok said, the gravel-strewn timbre of rebuke in his voice. "Or I will cut it out myself."

Properly chastened, Lang moved off to one side, taking a position off the dais to the left of Dukat's throne. Iliana quickly took stock of the Cardassian woman: she was older than Iliana, but still athletic and attractive, her shimmering brown hair styled in a manner that was undoubtedly calculated to seduce. Likewise, the dark fabric of Lang's smart civilian suit was cut in all the right ways, both to flatter her shape and to make her appear as formidable as possible. Iliana noted that it also afforded her just the right amount of room to conceal all manner of useful technology beyond the standard comcuff and padd that were already in evidence. She guessed that Lang was carrying at least six small weapons, a homing device to allow her movements to be tracked, a minitricorder, and a full-spectrum imaging device to record the proceedings.

Clearly she was not long out of the field; she had not yet acquired sufficient confidence to "travel light" in her recently attained position of authority.

Lang caught Iliana staring at her. Iliana covered by sending her a kiss, hoping it was a sufficiently Intendant-like taunt. She added a flirtatiously lifted eyebrow just to be sure, and was rewarded with Lang's angry but ultimately ineffectual glare.

"Director Lang speaks out of turn," Dukat said, turning his scowl upon Kira. "But she does speak to the very question that has brought you before us today. What *is* your interest in Ataan Rhukal, Kira Nerys?"

"Only the interest of a loyal subject of the Alliance, Lord Legate," Iliana answered smoothly.

"Do you think this is a game?" Dukat asked, rising

angrily from his chair. "I warn you, *Intendant*, your plati-
tudes serve only to enlarge the cloud of suspicion that
already hangs over your head."

Iliana's eyes narrowed. She considered the Cardassian
leader's expression, his body language, the timbre of his
voice. This wasn't just professional, she realized. This
was personal.

Of course it is. For years the Klingons had been the
dominant partner in the Alliance, helped in no small part
by Bajor's support, which had been strongly influenced
by Iliana's predecessor. But during Intendant Kira's temporary disgrace over a year ago, Dukat had successfully
installed his own Bajoran concubine, Ro Laren, as the
new Intendant, and for that brief time Bajor's political
axis had swung toward Cardassia.

Kira's return to grace had meant Ro's downfall, accompanied by a quick shift back toward more Klingon-
friendly votes in the Alliance Council. *Evidently the legate
is still nursing a bit of a grudge*, Iliana thought.

Dukat's wounded pride might also serve to explain
the constant emphasis he was placing on her title today:
he was mocking her with it, in effect telling her that he
didn't feel she deserved it.

Or rather, that he didn't feel that the Kira of this
universe deserved it. *But that Intendant's reign is over now*,
she told herself silently. *And very soon it'll be time to give
these fools a glimpse of who and what they're really dealing with
now.*

"Cloud of suspicion, Legate?" she shouted back.
"Suspicion of what? If you have charges to bring against
me, level them now!"

She sensed the chamber's guards advancing behind her. Martok sent them back to their places with but a look.

"Have a care, Kira," the regent cautioned her. "Yours may still be a valued and powerful voice in our Alliance— for now—but I remind you that you've fallen from our favor before. You would do well to tread carefully now. *Very* carefully."

Iliana bowed her head, hoping that Martok would see the gesture as an adequately contrite one.

The legate returned to his throne and nodded to Lang. The Obsidian Order director came forward and placed the padd she'd been holding into Dukat's outstretched hand, which he in turn held out to Iliana. Taking it, she saw that it showed the face of a Bajoran female.

It was Lupaza, from Kira's old resistance cell—Lupaza as she would have looked, had she lived to the present day.

Lupaza . . .

"I take it from your expression that you recognize the woman," Dukat said.

Iliana saw little point in denying it. "She looks like someone I remember from my youth."

"Then you deny any current association with her?"

For a fraction of a second, Iliana hesitated. She had been anything but idle during the voyage to Raknal; L'Haan had compiled dossiers of all of Intendant Kira's known associates over the last ten years, even the most casual ones, and Iliana had spent hours reviewing the files, committing their details to her eidetic memory. Lupaza had not been among those associates, but her absence from the files far from ruled out the possibility of recent contact between the two women. Still, if the Order had taught her anything, it was to stay as close to the truth as possible.

"I *do* deny it," she told Dukat.

"Then you lie," Lang said. She leaned toward Dukat. "My lord, end this now. She recognized the Bajoran woman. The Bajoran woman was tied to Rhukal. Rhukal confessed to Ghemor's murder, and Kira has sought information about Rhukal. What more do we need? The truth is plain: Rhukal was obviously in Kira's employ. The dissident movement on Bajor and Ghemor's assassination are clearly linked." She pointed at Iliana. "Through *her*!"

Iliana frowned. "*What* dissident movement?"

"You deny *that* as well?" Dukat asked. "Then let me speak plainly. We know that treason is stirring on Bajor."

"And you suspect my involvement?" Iliana said.

"I note that you do not seem surprised by the accusation. And yet, why *should* you be? As my Klingon brother rightly points out," the legate said, nodding toward Martok, "you've fallen before. And while your resourcefulness in clawing your way back to your old rank and office was exceptional, not everyone believes you can still be trusted, *Intendant*."

Dukat turned to Lang, who took that as her signal to address Iliana directly. "The Bajoran national you see on the device was recently apprehended on Cardassia Prime as she was attempting to make contact with Ataan Rhukal, at a time when he was under suspicion of Ghemor's assassination, but not yet under arrest. Before she died during her interrogation, she had confirmed Rhukal's guilt and admitted to being a member of an underground movement on Bajor—a movement of which we weren't previously aware, one fueled by the ancient religion that once held your people back."

"Strange, isn't it?" Dukat asked. "Your reports from Bajor have never even mentioned such a group."

Iliana scoffed and tossed the padd with Lupaza's face back to Lang, who fumbled to catch it. "I wouldn't waste my time or yours with updates about a pitiful little cult of religious fanatics, my lord—even if I'd known they existed."

"You maintain that you had no prior knowledge of this group?" Lang asked.

"None," Iliana said honestly. "Which leads me to conclude they're unworthy of my notice."

"And yet this movement appears to be enjoying something of a resurgence of late," Dukat said. "Driven by the expectation that a deliverer they call the Emissary will soon rise to lead Bajor into a new era . . . against the Alliance."

Iliana chuckled, hoping it would not seem forced. "And you *believe* this nonsense? A deliverer! The very notion is laughable!"

"I tend to agree," Martok said gravely. "And yet . . . even laughable ideas may be dangerous. Some prophecies have a way of becoming self-fulfilling. They can stir up a populace, invite discontent, even inspire open revolt without so much as a particle of truth behind them."

The regent leaned forward in his chair, a growing menace in his gaze. "Bajor is too important to the continued prosperity of the Alliance for us to risk ignoring any such danger. So I ask you plainly, Kira: Is there rebellion in the hearts of your people?"

Iliana faced him squarely, offering him a predatory smile. "If there is, my regent, then I vow here and now to root it out. Just as I am already rooting out the Terran Rebellion."

"And as you have recently attempted to 'root out' Ataan Rhukal?" Dukat scoffed, evidently not expecting a serious answer. "Let me put another question to you, then, *Intendant*—and I would advise you to consider your words most carefully before you answer. What do you know about the death of Tekeny Ghemor?"

"Everything," Iliana said without hesitation.

Martok cursed under his breath and shook his head, his great black mane obscuring his face.

"A confession?" Dukat asked with a sudden grin. "Then you admit your guilt—"

"I admit nothing, except to possessing certain knowledge, Lord Legate. But nothing about Bajoran treason."

"Do not tempt our patience, *Intendant*," Dukat said. "We know these matters are connected."

Iliana shrugged. "Perhaps they are, Lord Legate. But I am not their common denominator."

"Then explain yourself!" Martok said. "What is your knowledge of Ghemor's death, and why did you seek out his assassin, Rhukal?"

"My knowledge is that Ataan Rhukal is *not* the assassin of Tekeny Ghemor, Lord Regent," Iliana said calmly.

Lang laughed. "We have his confession, as well as the corroborating testimony of the Bajoran dissident,

Lupaza. We have the record of your request for information about Ataan Rhukal—"

"You have all those things, yes," Iliana agreed, then resumed addressing the Alliance rulers. "But ask yourselves, my lords . . . if Rhukal truly is as guilty as the Obsidian Order would have us all believe, then why would I have sought information about him so openly, when surely that act would have drawn the Order's suspicion to me?"

"Your attempts to confuse the issue will not succeed, Intendant," Lang said, her satisfied smile suggesting she had Iliana exactly where she wanted her. "The fact is, our investigation into Ghemor's assassination has been a closely guarded secret, including Rhukal's arrest. You didn't know we already had him, or that we had already obtained his confession and linked him to your fellow traitors on Bajor. Your own arrogance has finally betrayed you—as it had to eventually."

"Or," Iliana said, reflecting Lang's smile back at her, "the Order's vaunted secrecy isn't as absolute as you believe, Director Lang. And if it's not, then it's entirely possible that a loyal servant of the Alliance who was deeply troubled by the untimely demise of Tekeny Ghemor might suspect that matters were not at all as they seemed. Such a loyal servant might well calculate that a sudden inquiry into the status of Ataan Rhukal would flush out the *real* assassin . . . which is precisely what it did."

Iliana produced an isolinear data rod from inside one of the sleeves of her gleaming black bodysuit, and held the translucent object up before the supreme legate and regent. "The real traitor's confession is recorded here, my lords—testimony from the same man who rather conveniently arrested the woman, Lupaza; the man who coerced the statements from her that led to the arrest of Ataan Rhukal; the man who, in turn, tortured Rhukal into confessing to a crime he had nothing whatsoever to do with."

Iliana stepped forward and held the rod out to Martok. "The same man who raised suspicions about my loyalties after I submitted my very open inquiry about Rhukal to the Central Office of Records on Cardassia, and who personally came to relay your summons to me aboard the *Negh'Var*: Senior Operative Corbin Entek of the Obsidian Order."

"This is absurd!" Lang spat. "My lords, do not let this farce continue! This woman is—"

"Silence!" Martok shouted, cutting off Lang and whatever Dukat might have added to her rant. He took the rod from Kira's hand and inserted it into the dataport on the arm on his chair. "I will know what this contains."

At Iliana's feet, the Klingon-style screen that was tilted toward the thrones came to life. She didn't bother to watch the recording herself, already being thoroughly familiar with its contents; she much preferred to watch the expressions of Martok and the two Cardassians as Entek's face filled the screen and he began speaking. His expression remained stoic throughout the recording; Iliana had cautioned him against trying to slip out code-phrases, tonal clues, or facial movements intended to signal that his statements were being made under duress.

Naturally, Entek had resisted at first. But Iliana

had made good on her vow to bring her wrath down upon him in ways that even the state-of-the-art pain-suppression technology the Order had wired into his brain would do little to ease. She had not even needed Taran'atar for that part; her own interrogation skills, though rusty, had been more than effective, requiring only that L'Haan be on hand to provide medical assistance sufficient to prolong Entek's suffering without killing him. After that, he had offered his "confession" with almost pitiful eagerness.

"My name is Corbin Entek," he began. *"I'm making this recording of my own free will in order to reveal the truth about what I've done. I was the real assassin of Tekeny Ghemor. Ataan Rhukal is innocent. I forced him to confess to a crime he did not commit. I did these things at the command of my supervisor, Natima Lang, who coveted Ghemor's position as head of the Obsidian—"*

Lang's outrage drowned out the rest of Entek's statement. There was an almost comical quality to the widening of her eyes. "You traitorous, deceitful witch! Where *is* he? *What have you done with my operative?"*

Iliana gave the answer to Lang's question to Martok. "Corbin Entek committed suicide several hours after this recording was made, a fact that General Kurn and his men will corroborate. I believe his remorse finally became too much for him to bear. He simply couldn't live with the guilt of carrying out Director Lang's orders and betraying the Alliance."

"I'll kill you!" Lang screamed as she advanced on Iliana. *"I'll kill y—"*

There was a sharp *thunk* and Lang stumbled back a

half step, her eyes falling to the Klingon dagger that was suddenly buried to the hilt in the center of her chest.

She looked up at her killer is disbelief. Martok was standing now before his throne, his regent's cloak flung back, the short scabbard on his belt now conspicuously empty.

"You fool," Lang said to Martok just before she tumbled to the floor, lifeless.

Martok turned toward one of the Klingon guards. "Retrieve my *d'k tahg*," he ordered with a grunt. "And clean up that mess."

For his part, Dukat appeared stunned. "Regent," he began. "Surely you must realize that Entek's confession had to have been coerced. You can't possibly believe—"

"What I cannot believe, Legate, is that you are suggesting that a senior operative of the Obsidian Order can be coerced into doing *anything*," Martok said, peering at Dukat through slitted eyes. "And yet, given the plague of disloyalty and utter incompetence within the organization of late—defections by prominent agents, conspiracies and assassinations—it's hard to know *what* to believe at the moment. Except that better care will need to be taken in choosing the Order's *next* director."

The regent recovered the isolinear rod from the armrest of his throne and tucked it into his gauntlet. "I'm quite satisfied that we have found the source of the treachery in this sordid affair . . . as I'm quite sure the Alliance Council will be."

"But there's still the matter of the Bajoran dissident movement!"

"*What* dissident movement?" Martok asked. "The

only evidence of that is the word of a dead Bajoran who was interrogated by a confessed traitor."

Still seated, Dukat was clearly fighting to hang on to his composure. "It was you who said that even laughable ideas can be dangerous."

"So I did," the regent said, turning to Iliana. "And in view of what we've just learned, I can think of no one better qualified to get to the truth of this matter than Bajor's Intendant, who has already vowed to root out whatever traitors to the Alliance may exist on her planet."

Dukat was now speechless, and the regent pressed on, nodding toward the chess set on the table between them. "This game has been most diverting, my Cardassian brother, but I grow weary of it. It is time we all returned to our respective domains, don't you think?" With a sweep of his cloak, Martok turned away before Dukat could reply, leaving the audience chamber through a guarded private door in the corner nearest to his throne. Dukat stood before his throne, fists clenched in frustration.

With Martok's leave granted implicitly, Iliana likewise gave Dukat her back as she started back down the room's main aisle.

"This is far from over, *Intendant*," he called after her.

Iliana turned and offered him a mocking bow. "On that we can certainly agree, Legate. I'll look forward to meeting your next appointment to head the Obsidian Order."

She turned and left the audience chamber, enjoying the sound of Dukat kicking over the chess table before the great double doors closed behind her.

Iliana found it difficult to keep the spring out of her step as she made her way back through the station, and was surprised to find Martok waiting for her when she finally reached the airlock port that led back to the *Negh'Var*. The regent was alone, unaccompanied by guards or retainers.

"My lord," she began. "I trust you're pleased with how—"

With unexpected speed, Martok grabbed her by the throat and shoved her back against a wall, his chipped and filthy fingernails digging into her neck.

"Don't imagine for a moment that I don't know what you just did in there, Intendant," he said. "You and the Cardassians may share a taste for these little maneuvers and manipulations, but I have no stomach for them. Your interest in Ataan Rhukal, whatever it truly is, created an embarrassment for me that could have allowed Dukat to eclipse my influence over the Alliance Council."

She tried to reply, but a single hard squeeze of his powerful hand convinced her not to try to speak again until she was certain he had finished.

"As it is," the regent continued, "the only reason you are still alive is because your scheme had the appearance of vindicating my patronage of you—and because it gave me a convenient excuse to rid myself of that Cardassian cow's shrill braying. I therefore congratulate you on slithering your way out of yet another calamitous indiscretion. But you would do well not to test my capacity for forgiveness further. Do we understand each other, Intendant?"

Iliana nodded as best she could in the Klingon's viselike hold, and Martok released her with an attitude of disgust. "Now tell me of this creature General Kurn has advised me about—this monstrous pet you acquired during your unscheduled visit to Harkoum. Is he the new ally you promised me? The Jem'Hadar?"

Iliana rubbed her neck. "He is."

"And the rest of his kind? Where are they?"

"They aren't yet within my reach, Lord Regent. But they soon will be."

Martok growled deep within his throat. "I allowed you the use of my Ninth Fleet because you promised to deliver unto me an army to rival the forces of Qo'noS and Cardassian combined."

"And so I will," Iliana said, her voice regaining some of its strength. "Taran'atar is a soldier like none you've ever seen before, Regent, separated from his people by a cruel fate. But with him at my side, I'll find the rest of his kind and provide you with soldiers who will make the Alliance invincible."

"You make weighty boasts, Intendant," the regent said. "See that you live up to them . . . or you will assuredly die under them."

"Once I've finished crushing the rebels on Terok Nor, I vow to open the way to the rest of the Jem'Hadar."

"Indeed you will," Martok said. "But you will attain both objectives without your armada."

"*What?*" Iliana exclaimed. "Terok Nor holds Bajor hostage from orbit and you wish me to—"

"A dozen ships," Martok said. "The *Negh'Var* and your choice of support vessels. If you cannot retake Terok Nor while protecting Bajor with a force of that size—and in the process uproot whatever obscene cult is flourishing on your planet—then perhaps my trust in you has been misplaced after all."

Iliana fumed, the subtext of the regent's words crystal clear to her. The truth was, Martok really didn't trust her at all. Whatever the truth might be about a religious resurgence on Bajor, Lang and Entek had blundered onto a sizable portion of Iliana's true agenda, suspecting that she might be positioning herself to lead a Bajoran revolution. And on that suspicion alone, Martok was setting her up either to fail, or to betray herself.

Either way, achieving her real objectives was going to be far more difficult now.

Or would it? If she destroyed the station outright, it would be at most a temporary setback for the Alliance. Martok, Dukat, and the Alliance Council would be furious at the loss of such an important strategic asset, to be sure, but probably not enough to eclipse the glory of her decisive victory over the rebels who'd been using Terok Nor to stalemate the Alliance for the past four years. She would regain the Alliance's trust, whatever the station's fate, and by the time Martok and Dukat realized that their first instinct about her had been the right one, it would be too late for them to do anything about it.

But no, Iliana thought, shedding her newly germinated plans like springtime *nerak* petals. *There's the balance to consider—the symmetry that needs to be maintained as I go to claim my destiny. That means first becoming Terok Nor's master,*

not its destroyer. And maybe . . . maybe there's a way to achieve
that and still pacify this grotesque fool, even with a smaller strike
force. . . .

"Very well," Iliana said. "I'll take what you offer . . .
and I'll return to you victorious."

"See to it that you do, Intendant," Martok warned.
"For if you fail, it will better for you if you do not return
at all."

9

Taran'atar dreamed.

He floated naked and weaponless beneath the surface of a golden ocean and knew that he was adrift in the divine substance of the Founders. It surrounded him and moved through him, buoyed him and pushed him outward until his eyes broke the surface of the Great Link and saw the black sky into which he'd been born to obey, and fight, and die.

But the Founders had not released him. Coated in their slick residue, they clung to him with viscous tendrils that stretched up from the surface of the Link. They entangled his body and his brain, infiltrating every muscle and every thought, restricting his movements, impeding his ascent.

Taran'atar looked out across the endless sea of his creators and remembered how the Founders he had known had denied their divinity, how they had led him to question what it meant to be a Jem'Hadar without gods. As the memories stirred, he felt the Link's hold on him ebbing, and he knew that he was close to understanding something important.

As quickly as the tendrils began to recede, they suddenly ceased their withdrawal, holding fast to his body; they darkened and transformed, as did the entire ocean below. No longer golden and fluid, the tendrils became dry ropes of streaming copper, fine strands that constricted his arms and legs, choked his windpipe, dragged him down into the flowing chaotic mass that had somehow usurped the Great Link, tainted it, smothered the answers he seemed so close to grasping. Their hold on him was indissoluble; he was paralyzed, an impotent shell of flesh and bone, powerless to act—powerless even to conceive of acting.

My mind to your mind . . .

It was only a whisper, but he heard it as if it came from very far away.

. . . Your thoughts to my thoughts . . .

Closer now. A presence that seemed to be approaching from everywhere and nowhere, even as more strands of copper lashed out from the hideous mass below and pulled him down.

Fight what you see. Fight what you feel. Follow my voice. Listen to me. . . .

The voice was feminine, familiar. *Who are you?*

I am L'Haan, came the answer, as if she were there beside him. *I believe that I can help you. But I need you to help me in return.*

You can help me how?

Close your eyes.

He strove to remember how to do that, but the knowledge eluded him. *I cannot,* he told her somehow, speaking without speaking.

You can, L'Haan insisted. *You fail because your altered mind will not permit you to follow the commands of anyone but her. But I do not seek to command you, Taran'atar. I merely offer an idea, and I invite you to make the choice to close your eyes.*

Not a command. An idea. A choice.

Somehow, Taran'atar closed his eyes.

Well done, said L'Haan. *When you're ready to open them again, things will seem different.*

Taran'atar opened his eyes. He was no longer ensnared. The black sky and endless red ocean were gone. He was simply standing in the midst of nothingness.

Facing him was the stoic figure of L'Haan.

"Where are we?" he asked.

"You are still asleep in the Intendant's quarters aboard the *Negh'Var.* I've risked reaching out to you with a mind-meld, helped you from your dreamstate into one closer to wakefulness, in order to make a proposal."

"You betrayed your last master. Now you wish to betray your new one."

"I have no master," L'Haan claimed. "My servitude is pretense. I am in reality a member of a secret movement that seeks a fundamental reordering of this part of the galaxy."

Images invaded Taran'atar's mind, memories: He saw a corrupt and decadent stellar empire, stagnating and doomed to inevitable ruin; he saw the rise of a bearded Vulcan, his vision of a better world, and the complex plan of historical inevitability—ebb and flow, action and reaction, choice and consequence—that he had set in motion in order to achieve it. Taran'atar saw it all, spooled through his consciousness at lightning speed, delivered in a single blinding instant of revelation.

"And you hope to recruit me into your cause?" Taran'atar asked.

"No," L'Haan said. "I wish only to ask your help in correcting the mistake I made by helping to bring you and the false Intendant into my universe."

Taran'atar watched as the Vulcan's impassive face became uncharacteristically creased with regret as she paused before continuing. "I thought that by bringing her here I would be accelerating the political and social change toward which my group works. My plan was to replace my Intendant with one who would be sympathetic to our cause."

"You misjudged her," Taran'atar said.

L'Haan nodded. "This new Kira is as malign, if not more so, than the one she murdered. I understand now that her agenda against the Alliance is a self-serving one. In my arrogance and impatience, I fear that rather than advancing my people's plan, I may have put it at risk." She paused again, her dark eyes both probing and pleading. "Now, to repair the damage I have done, I look to you."

"What exactly do you wish me to do?" Taran'atar said.

"What I cannot do without risking the exposure of my movement: kill her."

"She is my god."

"Is she? Are you sure of that?" L'Haan asked. "Is her

claim to your obedience truly any greater that that of your previous gods, these 'Founders' I saw in your mind, the creatures who denied their own divinity to you? The beings who banished you into the unknown so that you might learn to redefine your entire state of being?"

Banishment, Taran'atar thought. Was that truly what his gods had done to him? And how could anything other than continued obedience to his gods bring him succor?

Speaking in patient tones, L'Haan pressed on. "I perceive the conflict within you, Taran'atar . . . the thing that was done to make you forsake your true gods for another . . . to abandon your purpose in order to serve her will."

"My life is hers," Taran'atar said. "That is the new order of things."

"If the old order can change, then so, too, can the new," L'Haan said insistently as she closed the already narrow distance between them. "That is an axiom we have in common, I think. And I believe that I can offer you an alternative to the order of things."

"What alternative?"

"Consider how I empowered you to escape your dream. I believe my telepathic skills can help you to do much more than that. I can break the hold she has on you. Your choices will forever afterward be your own. No one will have a claim on your loyalty, your obedience, or your enmity ever again, unless you choose to give it to them. Do you understand what I'm telling you, Taran'atar? You'll be free."

Free.

Every time he heard the word, it sounded more profane than it had before. Within the Dominion, freedom was synonymous with chaos. It was anathema. Yet he also knew that many, particularly among the humans of the Alpha Quadrant, prized their freedom more highly than they did life itself. Odo had told Taran'atar that he wished him to understand that perspective, to somehow apply that insight to himself so that he might provide a template for the future of the Jem'Hadar species as the Dominion learned to live in peace with its galactic neighbors.

But such a fundamental change was contrary to the design, the very concept underlying the Jem'Hadar's creation. They had been engineered to be the perfect soldiers, their purpose pure, their loyalty unassailable. What sort of future, then, had Odo imagined was really possible for them?

Perhaps it didn't matter. For if the Founders were not gods, then the perfection of the Jem'Hadar was a lie. If the Founders were not gods, then Taran'atar's mission to Deep Space 9 had been a farce from the beginning. If the Founders were not gods, then perhaps Odo was wrong, and the Jem'Hadar really *had* no future, only an unending gray present.

A future that was defined solely by the function for which they were created.

To obey. To fight. To die.

And with that acceptance, Taran'atar paradoxically made a choice. He closed his eyes again, exerted his will, and bore down on L'Haan, driving her from his mind and forcing himself into a state of full and complete wakefulness.

He opened his eyes in the near darkness of the Intendant's quarters, where he still leaned against the bulkhead in the spot where he'd fallen into sleep. He stood at the edge of the panoramic viewport, past which the stars still streaked as they had ever since the *Negh'Var* had departed from Raknal Station. L'Haan stood before him, her fingers still touching the sides of his face. Her eyes suddenly widened with the understanding of what he had done, but too late.

In a blur of motion, Taran'atar slapped her hands away from his face. He spun her around and pulled her close, clamping one hand over the Vulcan's mouth, and the other against the back of her head.

"I was never meant to be free," he whispered into her ear, just before he snapped her neck.

Then he flung the body away from him and went back to his nightmares.

10

TWO DAYS AGO

"That thing should be put to death."

"Now, Kurn, be reasonable," Iliana purred from the guest chair in the general's office.

"I want that creature off my ship," Kurn demanded. "It introduces an element of . . . uncertainty that I will not tolerate."

"I'm afraid you'll have to learn to tolerate it, General. Taran'atar isn't going anywhere."

The Klingon bared his teeth. "You brought it aboard without my knowledge or consent! Now it has killed your own handmaiden!"

"You heard what he told us," Iliana said. "L'Haan planned to betray me. Taran'atar may have responded to that threat impulsively, but it was the *correct* response. As long as you and your men remain loyal to me, you have nothing to fear from him."

"Do not insult my honor, Intendant," the general warned her. "My men and I fear nothing, and our loyalty—"

"Your loyalty was negotiated, General," Iliana reminded him. "So let us forgo the posturing, shall we? This is about your having come to appreciate just how dangerous Taran'atar can be when it becomes necessary. That's good, because now you know you can believe what I've told you about what we have to gain by finding his people."

"I now also know what we have to risk," Kurn said. "I've looked into the creature's eyes, Intendant. That thing is soulless. And when it chooses not to obey you anymore, it will not differentiate friend from foe."

"He can't make that choice, Kurn. He's bent to my will. I control him, and when we find the others of his kind, I'll control them just as completely. Imagine it . . . an army of creatures like Taran'atar, led by you as you go into battle against Martok and Dukat, to claim the glory that has wrongfully been withheld from you. And when the dust settles, there'll be no more Alliance—just a single, all-encompassing, invincible imperium . . . led by us."

Kurn's eyes glittered with the possibilities, though they were still tinged with doubt. "I will not lie to you, Intendant. I crave what you offer. But there is much I still do not understand about our undertaking. You tell me that we seek a stable wormhole within the Bajoran system that will take us to the region of the galaxy where the creature comes from. Why then, should we even bother with the rebels on Terok Nor?"

"Because there is far more to be achieved here than just the conquest of the Alliance. The wormhole will open the way not just to the other side of the galaxy, but also, when we're ready, to the other universe. Retaking Terok Nor is merely the first step toward those ends. That's why the dimensional static field your engineers are working on is so important, General, and why it has to be finished before we enter the B'hava'el system. I won't risk interference by those meddlesome alternates before we've achieved our goals here."

"Then you'll be pleased to know that the tests on the static field have already been completed," Kurn said. "It will be ready to deploy by the time we reach Bajor. But why do you fear invasion by the alternates now? They shrink from confrontation."

"No, Kurn. They don't. They're coming. Or they'll try to, at least."

Kurn eyed her suspiciously. "How do you know this?"

"That doesn't really matter, does it?" Iliana asked as she rose from the chair and stretched lasciviously. "What *does* matter, though, is that you've given me your trust up to now, and that it would only hurt you if I were to lose that trust when we have both gotten so close to achieving everything we want."

Kurn strode toward her and stood very close, breathing in her scent. "You *could* reassure me," he said with a suggestive leer.

"I could," Iliana said, forcing a grin as she slinked away, just out of his reach. "But you ordered our fleet to maintain combat readiness from the moment we departed Raknal, and with good reason. Remember, our enemies could attack at any moment. What sort of message would it send to the crew of the *Negh'Var* if its

commander were to lead them into battle without his
pants on?"

"I'll risk it," Kurn said as moved toward her.

"Bridge to General Kurn."

Kurn growled, halting as he answered the comm.
"What do you want?"

*"We've reached the rendezvous coordinates, sir. The Union
vessel* Aldara *is ready to transfer its prisoner to us. Your presence
is requested on the bridge."*

"On my way," Kurn snapped, and Iliana breathed a
discreet sigh of relief. Taran'atar was in her quarters, and
she feared she might be forced to kill Kurn herself if his
lust got the better of him.

The frustrated look on his face told her how narrowly
he had avoided forcing the matter with her. "There are
times, Intendant, when I believe you are a demon sent
to madden me," he said. "Where do you want me to put
our . . . guest?"

"Visitor accommodations on deck six should be ad-
equate," Iliana said, making an effort to sound casual.

"The same level as your own suite," Kurn observed.
"Should I be jealous?"

She suddenly dropped all pretense of enjoying their
banter and offered him an icy glare. "What you should
do is remember your place, General."

Kurn's eyes narrowed slightly at the rebuke. "Then
I trust you will not object if I post guards outside his
quarters. Whatever you hope to learn from him, he is
not to be trusted."

Iliana waved her assent as if it was of no consequence,
and the general left for the bridge. She watched him go,

thinking that perhaps eliminating Kurn at some point—perhaps sooner rather than later—would be in her best interests, after all.

Ignoring the two scowling Klingon soldiers who flanked the doorway to the guest quarters on deck 6, Iliana barked her access code into the bulkhead-mounted panel. It wasn't at all difficult to forget about the hulking armored sentinels that stood on either side of her; the moment she glimpsed the man on the other side of the sliding hatch, she instantly forgot about everything else.

He was sitting on the protruding hard shelf that passed for a bed aboard every Klingon warship she had ever seen, his elbows resting on his knees as he stared at the deck in apparent contemplation. He looked up at her as the door opened, his face leaner and harder than the one she remembered, but in a pleasing way. His shapeless orange prison fatigues failed to hide his lean and powerful physique, which clearly did not need to be accentuated by the flattering shape of Cardassian military armor.

Ataan appeared to have aged very well indeed.

"May I come in?" she asked quietly.

He frowned and nodded, clearly puzzled by the courtesy, as well as more than a little suspicious of it. As Iliana stepped inside, he rose to his feet in a show of either respect or defiance, or perhaps both.

Iliana let the door slide closed behind her before she spoke again. "Please sit down," she told him.

He did as she asked, and she took the single chair with which the small cabin had been outfitted. The bareness of the room reminded Iliana of the stark cell she'd been assigned when she had first joined the Obsidian Order.

They sat in silence for a few moments. Iliana thought she knew what she would say when she went to see him, but now that the moment was finally upon her, she was finding it hard to recall how she wanted to begin.

Fortunately, Ataan spared her the trouble. "I understand I have you to thank for my release," he said.

"That's right," Iliana said. Her throat was dry, and her words came out as a sandpaper whisper. She swallowed and tried again. "That's right," she repeated, more clearly this time. "The charges against you—conspiracy, murder, treason, all of them—have been summarily dropped."

Frowning, he folded his arms across his chest. "May I ask why?"

"Does that really matter?"

Ataan's eyes panned quickly across his surroundings before his gaze settled again on Iliana. "If I'm to understand my unusual new circumstances—being brought aboard this ship at the summons of Bajor's Intendant— then yes," he said, smiling crookedly. "It really *does* matter."

"I see your point," Iliana said. "Regent Martok has tasked me with investigating rumors of sedition on Bajor—"

"I don't know anything about that," Ataan said firmly.

"—and I was able to persuade the regent that you could be quite helpful in that regard," she continued, speaking over his denial. "Any assistance you could provide would certainly help in my vindicating you."

"I thought you said I had been exonerated."

"I said that the *charges* had been dropped," Iliana reminded him. "I never said that anyone really believes you're *innocent*."

"I see. But if that's the case . . . then it seems likely that if I *were* able to offer you assistance, Intendant, it would simply confirm the suspicions surrounding me."

"I can promise you it won't. In fact, if you agree to help me, I give you my word that your status and reputation will be completely restored, and your record expunged."

"I'm not sure I can believe that."

"You underestimate me."

Ataan studied her face. "Maybe I do. Certainly Corbin Entek did, not to mention Director Lang and the Supreme Legate of Cardassia."

Iliana tipped her head in a gesture of mock modesty. "Word travels fast."

"Of course. Intendant Kira of Bajor has a far-reaching reputation."

Iliana chuckled. "Well, I hope I can convince you that not all of it is deserved."

"Why?"

"Excuse me?"

"Why would you hope to convince me of anything? And why *me*, Intendant?"

"As I've tried to explain . . . I believe we can help each other. I want you to trust me."

That seemed to catch Ataan off guard. "I'm beginning

to believe what you said about your reputation. You're not at all what I expected, Intendant."

"Then I'd say we've already made a good beginning," Iliana said. She rose to leave, realizing that she needed to avoid putting too much pressure on Ataan or moving too quickly.

Pausing near the door, she said, "I'll leave you to think about my offer. In the meantime, I'll arrange to have some decent food and more suitable clothing brought to you. We'll be arriving in the B'hava'el system in two days' time, but I hope we'll be able to continue our conversation sooner than that."

"I'll consider it," he told her, his expression guarded.

Iliana nodded and smiled at him. "Then, pleasant rest, Ataan."

11

"**B**ajor directly ahead," the helm officer announced. "Preparing for reduction to sublight speed."

Iliana was leaning over the back of Kurn's command chair as the general settled into it and said, "Sound battle alert throughout the fleet."

"All ships acknowledging," reported his first officer.

"General," said the officer manning tactical. "We're detecting an unusual transmission being received by Terok Nor."

"What type of transmission?" Kurn asked.

"It appears to be a communication, but . . . I cannot isolate the source."

Iliana straightened her posture. "Can you put it on speakers?"

"I believe so. One moment . . ."

A squeal of white noise rose and crescendoed before a feminine voice pierced it, carrying across the bridge of the *Negh'Var*: "*. . . also have a stake in seeing this woman stopped. She's proved herself a threat on our side as well as yours. My people and I stand ready to assist you.*"

Kurn had swiveled in his chair to face Iliana, a puzzled scowl twisting his snaggletoothed visage. "That sounded like *you*."

Iliana's mind was racing. *Kira. Somehow she's found a way to bridge the two universes, the way Shing-kur did.*

The helm officer called out, "Dropping out of warp in three . . . two . . . one . . ."

Iliana thrust a commanding finger toward tactical. "Jam that transmission!"

"Status of the fleet?" Kurn asked his first officer.

"All ships reporting in. The fleet is continuing toward Bajor at full impulse."

"Status of targets?"

"Terok Nor has raised shields and is powering up weapons. No sign of *Defiant*."

"They could be cloaked," Iliana pointed out.

"Instruct all ships to begin sensor sweeps of the B'hava'el system," the general said, giving his orders in a clipped, martial cadence. "If that cursed vessel is anywhere nearby, I want it *found*!"

Iliana turned again to the man at tactical. "Are we blocking that signal?"

"We are, Intendant. Do you wish to deploy the scattering field?"

Iliana hesitated. "Not yet. Can you patch into the transmission?"

"Yes, Intendant."

"Do it," Iliana said. "Put it on the main viewer."

"What are you doing?" Kurn asked.

Iliana smiled as she stepped around to stand alongside

his chair, facing the screen. "I'm enjoying myself, General."

The viewscreen took a few moments to resolve the image, but the end result proved to be well worth the wait. For the first time, Iliana and Kira faced one another in real time, the Starfleet captain's brow already knotted with worry when the *Negh'Var* cut into the transmission, her expression now turning to shock as Iliana's smile greeted her.

"Well, hello . . . Captain," Iliana purred. "What an unexpected surprise. And how clever of you to have devised a way to communicate with Terok Nor. You've no idea how pleased I am to see you alive."

"I sincerely doubt that," Kira answered, her now-angry glare almost making Iliana laugh.

"Oh, believe me, I wasn't at all happy to learn what Taran'atar had done to you. That was a task I'd reserved for myself. It's actually reassuring to know that I get to come back for you . . . once I'm done here, of course."

"You won't succeed."

"Of course I will," Iliana said. "Haven't you heard? I walk with the Prophets." She held up her hand and showed Kira the *Paghvaram* wrapped around it, wiggling her fingers in a little wave before signaling the *Negh'Var*'s communications officer to cut the connection.

"Are you finished?" Kurn asked.

Iliana ignored the general. "Deploy the scattering field," she told the weapons officer.

"Done," he said. "It's expanding as we speak. It has already blanketed Terok Nor and should completely envelop the planet in the next few minutes."

"Good," Iliana said. "Begin scanning Bajor for anomalous quantum resonance signatures, and continue until further notice."

"What is it you expect to find?" the general asked, raising a single thick eyebrow.

"If the scattering field operates the way you claim it does, nothing. But I've learned not to underestimate my counterpart. And not to put too much faith in experimental technology."

Kurn's voice took on a suspicious tone. "You told your counterpart you weren't happy to learn what Taran'atar had done to her. What did you mean by that?"

Kosst! How could I have been so careless as to openly make the connection between Taran'atar and the other side, she thought. *Especially after I led Kurn and his superiors to believe that I had found the Jem'Hadar in* this *universe!*

"That's a tale for another day, General," Iliana said, tamping down her frustration at her own overeagerness. "But I trust you understand now why I expected interference from the other universe."

That seemed to redirect Kurn's line of thought. "It's abundantly clear that the alternates are conspiring with the enemies of the Alliance," he conceded as the blue-green crescent of Bajor slowly expanded on the viewscreen before him. "We will need to deal with that threat more directly before long."

"And we will," Iliana said. "But first things first."

"Agreed," said Kurn, who then turned to face his first officer. "Enemy status?"

"The space station's shields are at full strength and its

weapons are now hot. The fleet reports no other hostile contact."

"It appears the rebels' vaunted warship is missing in action after all," Kurn mused. "A pity. But no matter. This may yet turn out to be a battle worthy of song."

"Sing all you want, General," Iliana said as Terok Nor became visible off Bajor's eastern limb. "Just don't forget that I want that station captured, not destroyed."

"You heard my executive," Kurn said as he gestured toward the screen. "The rebels are prepared to fight. You may need to abandon your hopes of taking Terok Nor intact."

Iliana leaned down so that only the general would hear what she was going to say next. Humiliating Kurn in front of his bridge crew was the surest way to get him mad enough to attack her, and while she felt confident of the outcome, she just didn't have the time right now.

"Let me remind you that while I may get what I'm after whether Terok Nor is captured or not . . . you most assuredly won't get what *you* want, my dear general. Now, please carry out my orders."

Kurn's eyes seethed with the desire for violence, but he held it in check. Stalking away from Iliana, he began snapping orders to the various members of his bridge crew. "Helmsman, continue to approach until we get within transporter range of Terok Nor, then hold position there. Weapons, you will withhold fire until the Intendant gives the order. First officer, relay these instructions to the rest of the fleet."

Moments later, the first officer said, "All ships acknowledge, General."

"Transport distance achieved," the helmsman reported.

"All stop," said Kurn.

"Acknowledged, all stop."

The *Negh'Var*'s commander glared at Iliana. "It's your move now, Intendant."

Iliana went to the tactical console and shoved the weapons officer aside. "Raise the rebels," she ordered as she manipulated the targeting sensors.

"Channel open," said the comm officer.

"Attention, occupants of Terok Nor," she began. "This is Intendant Kira Nerys of Bajor. Your unlawful seizure of this space station is now at an end. By the authority granted me by the Alliance, I hereby place you all under arrest for assorted acts of terrorism and murder. You have one minute to stand down and surrender."

She was answered by several seconds of silence before the face of the rebel leader filled the screen, his expression defiant and hate-filled.

"*I don't need a minute to tell you and your Klingon lapdogs to go to hell, Intendant,*" O'Brien said. "*We aren't surrendering to you or anyone else. I have a torpedo lock on Bajor's capital.*"

"Yes, that gambit has worked quite well for you up to now, hasn't it, *Smiley*?" Iliana taunted. "Holding an entire planet hostage, threatening billions of lives—it seems so *ruthless*. But a bit *too* ruthless for the likes of you, I think."

"Don't make the mistake of being overconfident, Kira," the rebel leader shot back. *"You make one move against this station, and I promise you Bajor will pay the price. Now back off."*

"No," Iliana said calmly.

O'Brien was seething. *"You think I'm joking, Intendant?"* he shouted. *"I said back off!"*

Iliana made sure to watch his face as her hand fell on the firing button. The ship's hull answered with the vibrations of multiple torpedo launches at the same time that they registered on O'Brien's instruments.

His eyes went wide. *"My God—what the bloody hell have you done?"*

Iliana stepped around the tactical console and strode toward the viewscreen, savoring the horror she read on the human's face. "I've called your bluff."

"General," the first officer said. "Sensors are showing . . . massive detonations on the surface of Bajor. In the capital city!"

"What?" Kurn was on his feet, whirling to face Iliana as she walked past him and stopped directly in front of the screen. Tears were forming in O'Brien's eyes. The man seemed to be on verge of total collapse.

"I've taken away your hostage, Smiley," Iliana said. "And before your grief turns to rage, and you begin pouring out the station's firepower at my fleet in some misguided need to avenge those poor people down there, let me point out that I've destroyed only a single city. If you don't surrender Terok Nor to me immediately, I'll open fire on another, and then another, and then another . . ."

O'Brien clenched his eyes and pounded the console before him. His breathing became ragged, erupting into uncontrollable sobs.

Iliana took that as her answer.

"General Kurn," she said. "Have your troops prepare to board Terok Nor as soon as its shields come down."

12

Kurn's soldiers were efficient, if not entirely in control of themselves. Of the nearly seven hundred rebels aboard the station, twenty-nine had been killed by overzealous troops who'd found it too easy to forget that their orders had been to confine the Terrans and their cohorts, at least until arrangements could be made for their public executions on Bajor. After all, Iliana had made a point of assuring the surviving ministers—all those who had not been in the capital when the city's end had come, of course—that the mad and murderous Terrans who were responsible for the atrocity of Ashalla's destruction would be remanded to Bajoran custody in the days to come. After Iliana had gotten from them what she wanted.

O'Brien was a broken man, unable to refuse her commands for fear of what she might do if he did. Obedience kept his friends alive, kept more Bajorans from suffering the same fate as Ashalla—at least for now. But there was no need to burden Smiley with too much information, after all. She needed him to focus on the new task she had set out for him.

Moving the station to the mouth of the wormhole.

At first, he insisted that what she was asking of him was impossible, until she presented him with the exact specifications for getting the job done, per the documents she'd had Taran'atar steal from Deep Space 9's computers. O'Brien's counterpart had made it work once, eight years ago, using a low-level subspace field to reduce the station's inertial mass just enough so that six of the station's maneuvering thrusters had been able, if only just barely, to push Deep Space 9 to the edge of the Denorios Belt in less than a day's time.

While O'Brien and his people labored under the watchful glare of Kurn's men, Kira made herself at home in the station commander's office, trying to enjoy the view of Bajor outside the huge window behind her desk. The only thing spoiling it was the dark, fuzzy patch that hovered over the spot where Ashalla had been. She took heart in the fact that she wouldn't have to look at it much longer.

"It was a bold move," Kurn acknowledged next to her, as he reached across the desk to pour himself another celebratory bloodwine. "But a bit too lateral as stratagems go. Klingons prefer more direct confrontations." He took an appreciative sip from his metal stein and nodded. "Still, it was a bold move. Are you certain you won't join me?"

Iliana swiveled in her chair and looked up at him, watching as the general capped off his drink. "You don't approve of my decision," she said.

Kurn shrugged. "It is not for me to approve or disapprove of your choices, Intendant, as you have correctly reminded me on more than one occasion since this mission began. Noncombatants are always among the inevitable casualties in any war. Yet seldom are they the *only* casualties. And it is . . . unseemly to deny responsibility for such an act. It will be interesting to know the regent's reaction to all this, once word of it reaches him."

"The regent," Iliana said, "made very clear to me that he believed treason was brewing on Bajor. With one stroke, I've snuffed out whatever spirit its agents may have had, while crushing the rebellion in this system and proving that my loyalty to him comes before anything else."

"And you believe Martok will be less inclined to look suspiciously at your activities from now on," Kurn said. "Freeing you to pursue the overthrow of his rule."

"Well stated. As for the Bajorans . . . by the time they learn the truth, their image of me will be considerably different, believe me. This will pass."

Kurn was silent for a moment as he paused to study her intently. "You're not the woman I once knew, Intendant."

Iliana blinked. "I beg your pardon?"

"You've changed. Ever since you acquired your Jem'Hadar pet, you've been . . . different in ways I've found difficult to properly quantify."

"Perhaps you should keep those opinions to y—"

The office doors parted and admitted the station's only Cardassian.

Kurn set his stein down forcefully on her desk. "What is *he* doing here?"

"Rhukal is here on my authority, General," Iliana said, injecting a tone of warning to her words. "So please remind your men that he is to be extended every courtesy." She stood up and gestured toward the double doors. "Now if you'll excuse us, General, I'd like to talk with our guest in private."

Kurn let out a low growl and stormed out of the office and back into ops.

"Sorry about that," Kira said to Ataan. She was pleased to see that he was wearing the dark green suit she'd gotten him after she'd learned that the *Negh'Var*'s replicator database had a limited wardrobe selection meant to accommodate visiting Cardassian VIPs. "Kurn gets grumpy between meals. Low blood sugar."

Ataan said nothing. He kept his eyes fixed on her desktop.

"Come and sit down," Iliana said, gesturing toward the soft chairs in the sitting area. They were stained and frayed—clearly cosmetic maintenance had been a low priority for the ragtag rebels.

Ataan did as she bade him, but still he didn't speak. His silence concerned her. They'd had several pleasant conversations over the last two days, and he'd been unfailingly cordial to her on each of those occasions.

"Ataan, is something wrong?" Iliana asked as she took the seat opposite him.

Now he was avoiding even making eye contact. "Of course not, Intendant."

Iliana sighed and sat back in the chair beside Ataan's. "This is about Ashalla, isn't it?"

There it was, a flicker of reaction on the otherwise

hard and emotionless face. Although it disappeared as quickly as it had come, there was no mistaking the man's grief.

"I know you spent a number of years on Bajor, but—"

"Me?" Ataan said sharply, looking at her for the first time since he'd entered the office. "Intendant, those are *your* people down there."

"That's where you're mistaken, Ataan," Iliana said. "They aren't *my* people. Not really. Not yet. But they will be soon."

"How can you believe that?"

"They same way that I know you're going to help me find the dissidents now," she said. "Faith."

"*This* again? I've told you I don't—"

She interrupted him. "If you *really* don't know anything about the Bajoran dissident movement, then why did a confessed member of that group implicate you?"

"I can think of any number of reasons a traitor to the Alliance might lie about being a traitor," he said, seeming to take her accusation wholly in stride. "Can't you, Intendant?"

"Perhaps that's something both of us should remember," Iliana said. "Why are you protecting them? What are these dissidents to you anyway?"

Ataan stared at her. "You talk about them as if they're aliens."

"And you talk about them as if they were not," she said sharply. "As if you weren't a Cardassian. As if you weren't an agent of the Obsidian Order. As if you weren't trained to abandon childish sentiment to better serve the state in the eternal struggle against its enemies."

Ataan leaned forward in his chair. "You know who you remind me of right now?" he asked quietly. "You remind me of Tekeny Ghemor, just before—"

Iliana backhanded him across the face, knocking him out of his chair. She'd connected with his left orbital ridge, and the impact tore the skin of her knuckles. The pain was blinding, and as it slowly passed she saw the blood streaking the back of her hand.

Ataan was on the floor, propped up on an elbow, his legs still draped over his overturned chair. He rubbed the side of his face with his free hand.

Iliana was shaking. "What hold could they possibly have over you?"

"Kurn to Kira."

"What?" she shouted.

"Forgive the interruption, Intendant, but my tactical officer has detected readings of the type you told him to search for."

Not now!

"Why didn't that fool know about it sooner?"

"He claims they were exceedingly difficult to detect, Intendant, and that only his diligence permitted their discovery at all."

Iliana cursed and marched out of the office and into ops. Kurn and his tactical officer were standing inside the narrow triangle of the sciences station.

"So . . . agents from the other universe have invaded Bajor." She looked accusingly at Kurn. "The static field was not so effective after all, it seems. Where is the source of the readings?"

The tactical officer rechecked his displays. "The northern hemisphere. Kendra Province. A mining operation known as Vekobet. I have the coordinates."

Kurn looked at her. "Do you wish the camp targeted for destruction?"

Before Iliana could give her answer, a strangled "No!" erupted from her office. Iliana looked up toward the cry and saw Ataan standing in the office's open doorway, fear contorting his face. "Please, Intendant, I'm begging you. I'll tell you anything you want to know, I'll *do* anything. Just please spare . . ."

"Spare who?" Iliana asked.

Ataan bowed his head. "My wife."

In spite of herself, that revelation took her aback. *Wife? But Ataan's file indicated he was unmarried. How could that fact be omitted from— Oh. Of course. Why didn't I see that?*

"You mean a Bajoran wife, don't you?" Iliana said.

Ataan nodded, and into the ensuing silence Kurn started laughing.

"Shut up!" Iliana snapped. "Ataan, listen to me. What can you offer me for her life?"

"Intendant, what are you doing?" Kurn asked.

"Answer me, Ataan," Iliana pressed, ignoring the general. "Validate my faith in you. What will you give me if I save her?"

Ataan looked down at her, his gray-complected face a portrait of pleading and devastation.

"I'll give you dissidents," he said.

"How?"

"Vekobet is home to one of their enclaves. Their leaders can give you the location of every other enclave on the planet, and the names of their secret supporters. All I ask in return is that you spare Vaas."

"Vaas," Iliana repeated quietly, the name seeming to echo inside her skull. "Dakahna Vaas."

Ataan swallowed, obviously surprised that she knew the name. "Yes."

For long seconds, Iliana couldn't bring herself to move or speak, despite being acutely aware that every Klingon in ops was watching her intently.

"General Kurn," she said at last. "Have this man escorted back to his quarters. Keep him under guard."

Kurn gave the order, and two soldiers immediately ascended to the office level and moved in to grab Ataan's arms in an immobilizing grip.

"Intendant, wait!" the Cardassian cried as he was hustled toward the turbolift. "I've kept my end of our bargain. Please tell me you intend to keep yours."

Iliana turned her back on him. "Get him out of here," she told Kurn.

"Intendant! Please!"

Ataan's entreaties echoed from the turboshaft, and seemed to linger in the air long after the Klingons had dragged him away.

"That was . . . diverting," Kurn ventured. "Now, if we can return to the matter of the invaders from the other universe . . ." The general trailed off portentously.

Iliana felt the hand she had bloodied striking Ataan begin to shake; not wishing to call attention to it, she discreetly placed it flat against the bulkhead at her back.

"Send your six *Chutok* assault craft down to the surface, General," she said to Kurn. "Have them surround the camp. Instruct your men to move in on foot."

Kurn sounded confused. "Why should we do that? We could simply beam down—"

"You heard our guest."

"I heard a weakling tell you what he thought you wanted to hear."

"That's where we differ, General. *I* heard a man who has everything to lose make a choice about what matters most to him. We're going to honor that choice.

"These are your orders: Your men will move in on foot, with a mission to capture the invaders from the other universe, the leaders of the enclave, and the woman Dakahna Vaas. But they're *not* to be killed. Am I understood?"

Kurn bared his snaggly teeth. "But if they are enemies of the Alliance—"

"I want them *alive*," Iliana said. Taking note of Kurn's frustration, she added, "And just to make sure there are no accidents this time, Taran'atar will lead the ground assault."

"What?" Kurn exclaimed. "My men will *never* allow that thing to lead—"

Iliana stepped directly onto his objection. "If your men have a problem with 'my Jem'Hadar pet,' then by all means, let them take the matter up with *him*." She allowed a thin smile to tug at the corners of her mouth. "The outcome of *that* should be quite amusing."

The general's frustration was becoming palpable, but to his credit he still seemed able to keep it in check, if only barely.

"Very well," Kurn growled. "But I urge you to reconsider deploying the *Chutok*s. If you're truly concerned about the invaders from the other universe, we should not give up the element of surprise. Why even bother landing ships when we could simply beam down troops!"

"Because, my dear General Kurn," Iliana said, beaming at the general, "I want them to see it coming."

PART FOUR

THE ALTERNATE UNIVERSE

13

With great reluctance, Vaughn opened his eyes, knowing that he needed to get past the identity of the messenger and focus instead on the message.

Ashalla's been destroyed. My God, the rebels have attacked Bajor. . . .

"Prynn, how do you know this?" Jaro asked.

For the first time since he'd met the man, Vaughn heard a tremor in Jaro's voice.

Prynn continued to weep, a sound he so often heard in his nightmares, her anguish a knife-thrust into his heart. *She's not your daughter*, Vaughn reminded himself. *Get hold of yourself.*

He thought he'd been sufficiently prepared for this encounter. Intellectually, he'd understood what he was getting into the moment Kira had allowed him to join her on the transporter platform. And when first Opaka, and then Jaro, had recognized him, he knew the possibility of meeting Prynn's double in this place had risen dramatically.

Still, it was all hitting him with the force of a hammer.

Ashalla's been destroyed.

"Prynn!" Jaro repeated, more forcefully this time. "How do you know?"

"Essa, please," Opaka said, still holding the young woman in her arms. "Give her a moment."

Very slowly, Prynn seemed to be regaining control of herself. Vaughn thought she would turn around and face the rest of them any second now.

Vaughn stood up. For some reason, he backed away from the table.

"It's all over the comnet," Prynn told Jaro. "The city was bombarded from orbit. They're estimating a death toll as high as two million people. First Minister Li and at least half the Parliament were in the capital during the bombardment. The whole planet's in chaos."

"O'Brien," Winn said through gritted teeth.

Opaka seemed to sag within herself. "It was supposed to be a bluff," she said. "He gave me his word that he would never actually—"

"A Terran's word," Winn said with undisguised bitterness.

Prynn opened her mouth to speak, looking as if she wanted to protest vehemently Winn's condemnation of her entire species, but didn't know how.

"Let it go, child," Opaka counseled her as she shot Winn a hostile glare. "Adami is just upset, as we all are."

"What of the fleet?" Jaro wanted to know. "What of the space station?"

Prynn swallowed. "The Alliance is confirming that the Intendant has retaken Terok Nor. She's assuming control over planetary affairs from the station for the duration of the current state of emergency."

The Bajorans looked at one another, all color draining from their faces.

"Go, child," Opaka told Prynn. "See what else you can learn."

"But I—"

"Sshh," Opaka said gently. "Go. I'll call on you later."

Prynn nodded and turned to leave while the Bajorans started arguing among themselves. Her hair was longer than his daughter's, Vaughn noted, tied back from her face, much the way Ruriko had sometimes worn it.

Ruriko. My God, what if she's alive here?

Suddenly Prynn noticed him. She stopped. She stared. And while Vaughn doubted she was over the devastation she'd clearly felt over Ashalla, it seemed that for those few seconds, at least, she'd forgotten it.

Not knowing what else to do, he simply nodded to her.

A moment later, she nodded back, and then she proceeded out the door.

"—unconscionable!" Winn was shouting. "You heard her, Sulan! Two million people are dead! Once again, the Terrans stand revealed for what they truly are."

"We should have done more," Opaka muttered, shaking her head dejectedly. "If we had tried harder to turn Bajor against the Alliance sooner—"

"They might well have turned their fleet against us," Winn said.

"How are we to go on after this?" said Opaka.

"We cannot! Our movement's alignment with the

Terran rebellion is finished. Vekobet must be shut down immediately. If anyone learns we've been aiding and abetting the rebellion—"

"What of the Shards?" said Opaka.

Winn seemed buoyed, at least somewhat, by a renewed sense of purpose. "We created the emergency tunnel in the reliquary for eventualities such as this one, Sulan. Essa can take a few of the guards, escape the valley, and move the artifacts downriver to the enclave in Mylea."

Opaka shook her head. "But we cannot simply—"

"Enough!" Jaro shouted. "It's done!"

Both Winn and Opaka were shocked into silence. Jaro fell back into his chair, holding his head in his hands.

"It's over," he whispered to no one and everyone.

"The *kosst* it is," Kira said, suddenly grabbing the edge of the table with both hands and toppling it over. The other Bajorans jumped back as food and furniture crashed. But at least she had their full attention.

"How *dare* you?" Jaro said through his teeth.

"No. How dare *you*?" the captain shot back, accusing all three of them in one sweeping arm gesture. "After all your talk about the risk to your *pagh* if you did nothing to further your cause, you're ready to shrivel up and fade away."

"I see what you are trying to do, Captain," Jaro said. "You think you can shame us into moving beyond our grief . . . that we can somehow convince ourselves that those two million deaths can be made to mean something. But nothing we do will bring those people back.

Nothing we do will make their sacrifice worthwhile. It's too much. It's too much!"

Kira grabbed the doctor by the shoulders and shook him roughly. "Listen to me. I understand what you're feeling now."

"You can't possibly—"

"I *do*," Kira said. "I've known death and devastation on a scale that I, too, thought was incomprehensible. But it was during those times, when things were at their darkest, that I clung most fiercely to my faith—when I sought out the virtues the Prophets revealed to us. Qualities that empowered me to keep on fighting, to keep trying to do whatever good I could accomplish for my people.

"We can't help the poor souls of Ashalla now," the captain continued. "But you people were in this because you wanted to bring about the renewal of Bajor. Well, there are billions of still-living Bajorans out there who need something to believe in, now more than ever, and your time to step up and offer them the strength and wisdom and hope to change their world is *now*. It's time for the enclaves to do what the Bajoran faith was *meant* to do: bring the people together and guide them closer to the Prophets."

"If that were enough, Captain, then I would shepherd this flock myself," Jaro said, his eyes glistening with unshed tears. "But our hope of stopping this madwoman from your continuum is gone now. Even if our so-called contingency plan to reach Terok Nor were still an option, I do not believe the Intendant will be viewed as anything but a hero after this. And when she opens the Temple Gates, and is recognized as the Emissary . . . Bajor will follow her on whatever ruinous path she sets, and no rabble of outlaw religious scholars will be able to stand in her way."

"What if someone else beats her to it?" Vaughn asked. They all looked at him, and he continued, "If the mantle of Emissary is defined by the discovery of the wormhole, then it seems to me the matter is pretty straightforward. Captain Kira and I should be able to find the wormhole of this universe, based on the knowledge we have of ours. If we can get off planet quickly and into the De-norios Belt, then someone else can claim the title before the Intendant does."

Opaka exchanged an uneasy glance with her fellow enclave leaders. "It was our hope from the start that someone would have already done so by now," she admitted.

"So where is he?" Vaughn demanded.

Opaka frowned. "*She*. You left her behind in your continuum."

What?

"Wait a second," Kira said. "You're telling us you expected *Ghemor* to become your Emissary?"

"I can't say it comes as a surprise that she didn't tell you, Captain," Winn said. "Iliana rejected most of the revelation that was imparted to her by the Shard of Prophecy and Change, fixating instead on what she learned about her counterpart—the threat that the other Iliana presented. She thought she could stop her without claiming her rightful destiny."

Kira looked as if she was still trying to process what she was hearing. "You chose *her*—?"

"We chose no one," Opaka said emphatically. "But when she came to us, we each felt her *pagh*. We recognized her for who she is meant to be, despite her protests to the contrary." She gazed into the middle distance, her eyes glazing with memory. "Ironic. One who did not wish to be among us was to be the Emissary."

"I'm so sorry," Kira said quietly. "If I had only known—"

"You're not at fault, Captain," Jaro said.

"There must be someone else," Vaughn prompted.

"This is not a political election, Commander," Winn said. "This is fate. We cannot simply turn to the next most favorable candidate—"

"Then why are we all worried about the other Iliana opening the Temple Gates? Why was *your* Iliana able to refuse her so-called fate?" Vaughn asked. "I'll tell you why. It's because free will *does* make a difference."

He looked at Jaro and continued. "Look, I can't pretend to be an expert on the Bajoran religion, but you said it yourself: This isn't about guarantees. It's about choices. If the new Intendant is the one to open the wormhole in this universe, then it's *Bajor* that will anoint her, and it's *Bajor* that will follow her—no matter *what* the Prophets may have really intended."

Silence fell over the table, broken a few moments later by Kira. "It has to be one of you."

"Blasphemy," Winn said.

Jaro reached out to take his wife's hand. "Adami . . ."

"I will not be silent about this, Essa!" Winn said, pulling away from him. "Nor will I be party to the arrogance and folly of claiming that holiest of responsibilities for one of us!"

"Overseer Winn," Kira said gently, "consider the alternative."

Yes, do that, please, Vaughn thought. But while their hosts might not be willing to speak about it openly, Vaughn already knew the alternative. *What I don't understand is why they seem to be protecting him.*

"Can you get us off this planet?" Kira pressed Opaka.

"It may be possible," Opaka said. "I'll need to contact some friends."

"Captain," Vaughn said. "With your permission, I'd like to accompany the Lady Opaka while you and the others sort the rest of this out."

"Why?" Winn asked.

"Because, respectfully, Chief Overseer, emotions on your world are running pretty high right now, and I want to be there in the event a calmer voice is needed." Vaughn consoled himself with the thought that the reason he'd given was at least partly true.

"It's all right, Adami," Opaka said as she left the table. "Commander Vaughn may keep me company, if that is his wish."

"Captain?" Vaughn asked.

Kira nodded her assent. "Good luck."

Vaughn followed Opaka out the refectory's back door. The sky outside had turned overcast, but Vaughn welcomed the fresher air after having been cooped up for so long in the dining hall. Opaka led him along a narrow alley between the refectory and another building, and he decided that there might be no better time to pose the question he had been waiting to ask her.

"Lady Opaka, wait."

She stopped and faced him. "'Lady Opaka,'" she echoed with grim amusement. "Tell me, Commander, did you come up with that yourself, or are all the Terrans on your side as extravagant in their courtesies?"

Vaughn resisted the impulse to point out that in his universe, only humans from Earth—as opposed to those born on, say, Berengaria VII—referred to themselves as "Terrans."

"I know that Benjamin Sisko is here," he said without preamble. "I need you to take me to him."

Opaka looked startled. "How did you—?"

"It wasn't hard to figure out," Vaughn said. "You said that you and he fought together before you came to Vekobet, and I know he's the one who's supposed to be your Emissary. If you take me to him, I may be able to persuade him to do what he was supposed to have done a long time ago, for all your sakes."

Opaka stared at him what for seemed like an eternity before saying, "You cannot persuade him, Commander."

"Let me try," he implored her. "Please. This is what I was sent here to do."

Opaka's eyes narrowed. "Sent? By whom?"

Vaughn sighed. "By his counterpart. The Emissary of *my* Bajor."

"I see," Opaka said, her frown deepening. "Very well, then. Follow me."

They continued down the alley, past a door in the other building. The door was marked with a glyph Vaughn recognized as the Bajoran symbol for healing. They passed it and the roof-access ladder beside it before coming to a stop at another door, whose Bajoran signage read MEDICAL REFUSE. Opaka gained them entrance with a thumbscan, and once they were both inside she re-sealed the door behind them and turned on a light.

Biohazard containers of various sizes were stacked all around the small chamber, which had little space in which to move except for a large open area at the room's far end.

But other than Vaughn and Opaka, the place was deserted.

He was about to demand an explanation when she drew a small device from her pocket and aimed it at the open area. The bare fusionstone floor immediately faded into nonexistence, allowing a narrow stairwell to emerge from holographic concealment.

Vaughn's brow furrowed in puzzlement as he followed Opaka down the steps. Going to such elaborate lengths to hide from one's responsibilities seemed a bit over the top to his mind, but it wasn't until the musty smell accosted his senses that he realized he wasn't going to find the object of his quest—at least, not in the manner he had expected.

Opaka paused to light several candles on the shelves that lined the walls, and the room gradually revealed itself: it was the enclave's reliquary. He saw several icon paintings on the walls, hooks from which hung a number of elaborate Bajoran earrings, stacks of ancient books and scrolls, even some broken statuary.

Along another wall, a meter-high brick shelf rose from the simple concrete floor. On it were arranged eight ornate oval boxes—with space set aside for a ninth—each of them no larger than his hand. In the corner of the room was a narrow metal hatch that Vaughn guessed was the emergency tunnel Winn had mentioned earlier.

On the opposite wall he saw the crypt.

"This is where Dava hid the Shards," Opaka said. "Along with some other items we've come to revere. Winn and Jaro unearthed it after they first came to Vekobet, and they took the steps necessary to conceal it. This is the most sacred place we have, and therefore offers the most fitting interment for the bones of my friend . . . the man who *should* have been our Emissary."

He strode toward the crypt until he could touch the Bajoran characters chiseled into the stone. He felt them with his fingers, read the Terran name that they spelled out.

BENJAMIN SISKO

And in the swelling silence of the musty reliquary, Vaughn felt his entire world unraveling.

14

This can't be right, Vaughn thought. *This isn't what I was supposed to find.*

"When did it happen?" he asked.

"Five years ago," Opaka said. "Less than a year after he started the rebellion. I became Benjamin Sisko's confidant and the first mate of his ship during the last six months of his life. I looked into his *pagh*, and I saw the promise he was meant to fulfill. I tried to explain what I'd seen in him, what it could mean to Bajor and to the rebels if he would open his mind and seek out the Temple, but he never believed me. We argued about it many times, until he finally forbade me to speak of it again. When we talked about forging a partnership with the dissident movement on Bajor, I thought perhaps I might have another chance to convince him of what I knew to be true, once I got him to stop risking his life on raids against the Alliance.

"But the Cardassians ambushed us. Many died, and Benjamin was mortally wounded. I got him aboard the emergency shuttle along with a handful of survivors just before his ship exploded. But he was dead by the time we managed to reach Bajor."

A mistake, Vaughn told himself, still incredulous. *This is a mistake, that's all. . . .*

Captain Sisko's counterpart was still alive—that's what Ben had told him when he'd asked Vaughn to make the crossover with Kira. He'd even told Vaughn that Kira couldn't be allowed to know what he'd come along to do. And although Vaughn had not understood the need for secrecy and hated keeping it from her, he had gone along with it because he trusted Sisko implicitly.

It's a mistake, his mind repeated. *But it was* Sisko's *mistake.*

Suddenly wanting nothing more than to get out of this place, Vaughn turned his back to the crypt. He saw that Opaka was watching him closely.

"Commander," she said, holding out her hand toward his left ear, "would I be presuming too much if I . . . ?"

He wanted to refuse. She wasn't the Opaka Sulan he'd come to know, to respect, to care for. But she *was* still Opaka, and he found that it simply wasn't in him to deny her request.

He nodded. Her touch was familiar, and he relaxed, opening himself up to her perceptions.

When she withdrew her hand, her expression had changed. "I think I understand, Commander."

"What is it you understand?"

"That there's something you need to see. Come with me."

They returned to the surface, and after Opaka had reactivated the security hologram and locked the room behind her, she led him back down the alley to the infirmary.

They walked into a long patient recovery room. Less than a third of the twenty cots had patients, and most of these were Bajorans. All of them appeared to have sustained superficial injuries, and they were all listening attentively to a comnet feed coming over a speaker embedded in the ceiling. News about Ashalla was holding their attention, and none of them seemed to have noticed Vaughn and Opaka's entrance.

On the other side of the room, an open doorway led down another corridor.

"What are we doing here?" he whispered, suddenly apprehensive without understanding why.

"Sulan?" someone called.

Vaughn looked up to see a black-haired Bajoran woman, perhaps a few years older than Kira, carrying a box of what looked like medical supplies as she walked out of a side room.

She stared at Vaughn for a lingering moment before focusing her attention on Opaka. "I heard we had visitors."

Opaka answered the woman with quiet but firm calmness. "Vaas, I need you to begin packing up the reliquary."

"I suspected you might," the other woman said with a grim nod as she finger-combed her lustrous black hair away from her eyes. "I'll get a team together and get started right away. Do you want me to contact Mylea?"

"No, I'll take care of that myself. Hurry along now." As Vaas set her box down on the floor and headed outside, Opaka turned to face Vaughn. "There's a secure communications unit in Jaro's office, at the end of this hallway. You can join me there when you're . . . finished." Then she moved quickly down the corridor without another word.

"Wait, finished with *what*?" Vaughn demanded as he started to follow.

That was when he heard Prynn's voice. It halted him in his tracks.

She was singing softly, a melancholy tune that he didn't recognize. He followed the sound, which was coming from one of several small curtained rooms that ran along both sides of the wide corridor.

Opaka had already moved on and disappeared into the office. He stood alone in the hallway.

The singing continued, and it tugged at him. Trying not to make any noise, he found the room from which the song was emanating—the only one of the private rooms that was currently occupied, it seemed—and peered through a narrow gap in the curtains that demarcated it. Prynn was sitting in a wooden chair beside a computer screen that displayed what he assumed to be the main portal of this world's public comnet.

Her chair faced the side of a bed, and lying there next to her was a dying man.

Prynn was holding one of his bony, translucent hands in her own, his thin arm looking impossibly fragile. The hospital gown he wore did little to hide the fact that he was emaciated, his narrow chest rising and falling almost imperceptibly with his slow, labored breathing. His white hair was unkempt, his beard neglected, and his milky eyes stared sightlessly at the ancient ceiling.

Prynn looked up, halting in midsong, startled to see Vaughn watching her from the corridor.

"Prynn," rasped the dying man, his voice pitifully weak. "What's wrong?"

The young woman opened her mouth to speak, but hesitated when Vaughn held up an index finger in front of his lips.

"Prynn . . . ?" the old man said.

"You have a visitor, Dad," Prynn told him, her eyes still on Vaughn, who shook his head reproachfully.

"Who?"

"I'm not really sure. I just know he comes from far away. I think he's a friend." Prynn released her father's hand and stood up. "I'll let the two of you talk. I'll be back in a few minutes."

"You should get some sleep," her father said.

"Later, I promise," she said, gently kissing his forehead before moving toward the doorway. She said nothing to Vaughn as she walked past him.

Vaughn sighed and stepped through the curtain. At first he simply stood there, more than a meter from the foot of the bed, his revulsion toward the invalid's utter decrepitude making him reluctant to approach.

"Hello . . . ?" the blind man said. "Are you there . . . ?"

"Yes, I'm here," Vaughn said quietly as he moved to take Prynn's vacated chair.

The man in the bed didn't answer right away. Was it because Vaughn spoke with a stranger's voice . . . or because he *didn't*?

"Who are you?"

Vaughn considered evading the question, but only for a moment. "My name is Elias," he said. "Just like yours."

Silence again. "I think I understand," said the other man. "I've heard stories . . ." His voice faded. His lips were parched; his tongue gray and dry.

"Do you need water?" Vaughn looked around and found a sipping bulb on a nearby table. He touched it to his counterpart's lips and allowed him to drink, hoping he wouldn't choke.

"Thank you," the other Elias breathed after he had finished swallowing. His voice sounded clearer now, but was still feeble.

Vaughn set the bulb back down.

"Why did you come here?" Elias asked.

Again, Vaughn didn't answer immediately. "Someone sent me. But it hasn't gone the way it was supposed to."

"What in life ever does?"

Vaughn bowed his head, his eyes clenched shut against the torrent of confused thoughts and conflicting emotions rising up inside him. "What happened to you?" he whispered.

"I got old," his frail alternate told him, as if nothing else needed to be said.

"But why are you on Bajor, in Vekobet?"

Elias turned his head toward Vaughn as if he could actually see him. But the rheumy eyes were still blank. "Where else should I be? I was one of the last generation of Imperial Terrans. When I was a young man, I watched our civilization transform and weaken, until it was too vulnerable to defend itself from the wolves that came scratching at our door. Overnight, I went from being a prince and an officer in Starfleet to being a slave. Eventually I wound up on Bajor, sold to the Jaro clan."

"Jaro? You're the doctor's servant?"

"I'm his *friend*," Elias said, and weak though he was, his anger as he corrected Vaughn was unmistakable. "Essa has protected my family from the beginning, taking us with him wherever he went. He's great man, with great vision, and I've tried my best to help him in his labors."

Tears formed in the old man's eyes. "But now, I fear I've become a burden to him. And to my daughter." His voice faded until Vaughn could barely hear him say, "To everyone."

"You never expected to live this long," Vaughn realized.

Elias shook his head, his tears finally brimming over and streaming onto his sunken cheeks. "I can tell that surprises you. Maybe where you come from it's normal for our kind to live to a ripe old age. But here, Terrans almost never make it past seventy. Most of us die from sickness or violence long before we ever get a chance to become . . . *old*. Essa thinks I've hung on this long because I'm so damned stubborn."

Vaughn smiled in spite of himself. "Is that what you think?"

"Once, maybe. Now . . . I'm not sure what I'm waiting for. You, perhaps."

"Me?"

"You think it's an *accident* that we're here together now?" Elias asked.

Vaughn blinked. "I told you, someone sent me."

"But it hasn't gone the way you thought it would. And now . . . here you are."

Vaughn considered what his counterpart seemed to be telling him, and it troubled him greatly. He'd tried to convince himself that his fool's errand to the alternate universe was a mistake, but an entirely different possibility was taking root in his mind instead. As much as he tried not to think about it, he kept coming back to the same unpleasant but impossible-to-ignore question.

Had Sisko lied to him?

Was *this* the real reason he'd sent Vaughn here, to meet this ruined husk of a man who shared his name? And if that was true, then *why*?

Vaughn studied Elias's pale, craggy, withered face, the thin neck that didn't seem strong enough to support the weight of his head. So much he saw was familiar, but so much was not. There wasn't even—

There's no scar, he realized.

Vaughn automatically reached beneath the neck of his Bajoran topcoat, felt inside the high collar of his uniform until he touched the raised line of flesh that had been a part of him since his youth. The scar ran all the way up his neck to just behind his left ear. It was a very old injury, one he seldom thought about anymore.

"How much do you remember about Berengaria?" he asked quietly.

A strange look passed across his counterpart's face. "Why would you need me to tell you about that?"

"I . . . I'm guessing it must have been very different from the one I knew."

"What I remember most is that it was a wonderful place to be a boy," Elias told him. "Wasn't it that way for you?"

Vaughn closed his eyes. "For a while, yes."

"Then maybe our birth worlds aren't so different after all."

"Maybe," Vaughn said, opening his eyes again. "I want to ask you . . . When you lived there, had you ever been to the Vale of Mists?"

"No," Elias said. "The creatures there, they don't tolerate intrusion. Why?"

Vaughn tried not to sound disappointed. "It's not important," he decided. "I just hoped you might be able to help me remember something that happened to me there a long time ago."

There was a rumble outside. Vaughn's chair vibrated beneath him. The water bulb rattled on the table.

"I hear thunder," Elias said.

Vaughn stood up, listening. "It isn't thunder," he said. He moved to the curtain, saw Opaka and Prynn heading toward him from Jaro's office. Prynn went immediately to check on her father, while the older woman spoke quickly to Vaughn.

"My friends in Singha can make offworld transport available to a small number of us. We can head there as soon as we relocate our artifacts to the Mylean enclave."

The building vibrated again. "You may not have enough time," he told her. "Does this place have a basement?"

Opaka shook her head.

"Then keep everyone away from the windows," Vaughn told her. "I'll be back as soon as I can."

Vaughn ran out of the infirmary. The rumbling sounded much louder outside, and it seemed to be coming from all directions. He searched for something he thought he'd seen when Opaka had first led him through the alley, and quickly found it: an alcove with a narrow metal ladder that led straight up the side of the infirmary. He grabbed hold of a rung and started to climb.

The roof was a short square wall surrounding a fusionstone dome. Judging from the access panels along the dome's base and the low vibration he felt through the stone, Vaughn guessed it housed a dedicated power supply for the infirmary, as well as the facility's climate-control equipment. He kept low as he drew his phaser and crept around the dome's perimeter.

Once he'd reached the north wall, his view opened up. From here Vaughn could see over the rooftop of the refectory, as well as those of the other nearby buildings. From this vantage point, he had a fairly decent overview of the entire camp.

All around Vekobet, touching down on clouds of dust set swirling by their thrusters, were Klingon ships.

They've come for Kira and me, he realized. *But how would they have known—?*

His combadge chirped. *"Kira to Vaughn."*

"Vaughn here. I see them, Captain."

"Assessment?"

"An invasion force of six *Chutok*-class assault ships

completely surrounding the labor camp. I see soldiers disembarking. If they're like the *Chutoks* of our universe, we can expect a minimum combined troop strength in excess of nine hundred, backed by ship-based armaments. I don't think there's any question why they're here. We've screwed these people but good, Captain."

"Anything else?"

"Use of infantry suggests that the Klingons want to keep collateral damage to a minimum, or that they're planning to take prisoners, or both. The camp's 'work-force' is already moving into defensive positions. They look pretty good, but at three-to-one odds, the most they'll do is slow the Klingons down a bit."

"Recommendations?"

"We should attempt to keep the Klingons' attention on us so we can cover our hosts' escape."

"Agreed. Meet me back in the refectory as soon as you can. That's where we'll make our stand."

"I'll be there as soon as I can. Vaughn out."

Vaughn hurried down the ladder and back into the infirmary, even as the first sounds of disruptor fire rang out in the distance. Opaka had retrieved a cache of weapons from somewhere and was handing them out to the half-dozen patients in the main room, all of whom were quickly getting dressed and preparing to head out the door.

"Wait," Vaughn said to them, blocking their exit. They halted but were clearly impatient to get outside, before they even knew what awaited them. "Your camp is surrounded. You're outnumbered and outgunned. What do you intend to do?"

"We intend to fight," one of the Bajorans declared, and the others voiced sentiments of agreement.

"Then you're all going to die," Vaughn told them. "This isn't a fight you can win."

More disruptor fire rang out. Anger seeped into the first Bajoran's face and he tried to push Vaughn out of his way, but he stopped short of doing so when Vaughn suddenly drew his phaser and raised it to the man's face.

"You have to listen to me, all of you," Vaughn said.

Opaka was looking at him in shock. The other patients raised their weapons and aimed them straight at Vaughn.

"Who the *kosst* do you think you are?" the first Bajoran asked.

"Just tell me one thing," Vaughn said quickly. He nodded toward Opaka. "What do you owe the leaders of this enclave?"

The patients looked at Opaka, then one of them turned back to Vaughn. "Everything."

Vaughn lowered his weapon. "Then you need to help them get out of Vekobet," he said. Opaka tried to protest, but Vaughn pushed ahead. "This place is about to be overrun by overwhelming Alliance forces. None of you stands a chance against them. But you *can* save Opaka. You *can* save the Shards of the Prophets."

The assembled Bajorans began grumbling loudly, prompting Vaughn to raise his voice. "The six of you can escort Opaka through the escape tunnel, take whatever artifacts you can carry, and help her to reach another enclave. But your only chance is to do it *now*. Before the Klingons discover the reliquary and overrun it."

"Commander, my people are under attack," Opaka said angrily. "I have no intention of—"

"Listen to me," Vaughn said to her. "Bajor needs you *alive*. It needs the hope that those Shards represent. You have to get away, *now*, before the Klingons get past your soldiers."

"I will *not* abandon my followers!"

"It's we who will not abandon *you*, Mistress," the first Bajoran said, and Opaka stared at him as he gestured at Vaughn. "This man is right. We cannot afford to lose you, especially now, after what happened to Ashalla. Our people need the guidance of the enclaves. And *this* enclave must survive, even if Vekobet does not."

"My captain and I will try to keep the Klingons busy while you get away," Vaughn said. "We'll send Winn and Jaro after you. If you have explosives, you'll need to use them to seal up the tunnel behind you. If you can, try to force the parts of the building directly over the tunnel to collapse, so that the Klingons never find your escape route."

"Wait," Opaka said. "Elias and Prynn—"

"I'll see to them as well." Vaughn looked at the first Bajoran. "Take three of your men and Opaka out of here, now. The rest of you, follow me." He started back toward Elias's room.

"Commander," Opaka called after him.

He turned to look at her.

"Thank you," she said.

Vaughn nodded and marched on to Elias's room, followed by the two remaining armed Bajorans. Prynn looked up expectantly and Vaughn said, "You two need to be evacuated immediately. Opaka will be waiting for you in the reliquary."

"My father can't walk," Prynn said.

"We'll carry him," said one of the two armed Bajorans as the pair moved to either side of Elias's bed.

"No," the old man said, waving off the hands that reached for him.

"Dad, please, there's no time for this," Prynn said.

"I said *no*," Elias said with as much force as his feeble voice could muster. "I can't do this, Prynn . . . I would only slow you down . . . and I wouldn't survive the journey anyway."

"You don't know what you're saying."

"Prynn," Elias rasped. "Don't be foolish. You have to leave me and go with Sulan. Now."

"No!" Prynn cried. "I'm not going to—"

"Elias . . . tell her," the dying man said.

Vaughn looked down at his counterpart. The disruptor fire outside was getting louder, more insistent. He knew they didn't have much time.

"He's right, Prynn," he said. "He can't do this."

"Shut up!" Prynn shouted. "I'm not leaving my father here to be slaughtered."

"Prynn, look at me!" her father said. "I'm dying . . . and I've had enough. I love you with all my heart . . . but it's over. You need to let me go."

"I can't! Dad, please, *get up!*"

"Elias," the old man said. "She'll never be safe while I'm alive."

Vaughn's eyes narrowed. There was no misunderstanding what the other Elias was asking of him.

Vaughn drew his phaser and turned to the others. "Get her out of here."

"What? No!" Prynn screamed as the two armed Bajorans moved in quickly to pull her out of the room. "Don't do this! Dad, please—"

Vaughn gripped Elias's arm and leaned in close to his withered face. "I'll make it quick," he whispered.

"Thank you," the dying man said. He clutched Vaughn's forearm with unexpected force, his blind eyes jerking wildly back and forth as if he could catch one last glimpse of something, anything—

"Dad!"

Vaughn aimed the phaser and gently squeezed the firing stud. He saw the weapon's flash through his closed eyelids.

When Vaughn opened his eyes he saw that all light and life had vanished from those of his counterpart.

Prynn broke away from the others and threw herself at Vaughn. *"Damn you!"* she screamed, pounding her fists against his face. *"Damn you, damn you, damn you!"*

Vaughn deflected the worst of the blows, but he found himself savoring the pain of the ones that connected. Perhaps they would shake loose the tears that refused to come.

"Take her," he said quietly to the Bajorans. "Keep her safe."

Vaughn drew a bedsheet over Elias's still form. Prynn's screams continued to echo, even after the two Bajorans had dragged her out of the infirmary.

15

"Winn, look out!" Kira shouted, pulling the other woman down and just barely out of the path of a slashing *bat'leth*. She raised her phaser and fired three quick bursts, striking down the entire trio of Klingons who had spotted them emerging from the refectory's back door.

Vaughn was overdue, and with the sounds of fighting drawing ever closer to the refectory, Kira knew she could wait no longer to get the enclave's leaders to safety. They had protested, of course, believing they should be leading their followers in defense of the camp. Kira had kept her arguments brief: they simply didn't have the right to throw their lives away, or to waste the sacrifices of their followers. Not when they could keep their cause alive and escape with the Shards.

From her position at the refectory's open back door, Kira swept her eyes around the alley for any sign of more Klingons. She raised her phaser again when a door about twenty meters away in the adjacent building burst open, and a screaming Prynn was dragged out by two of Vekobet's fighters.

"Hold your fire," Winn told Kira as Jaro went to learn what was going on. Kira couldn't make out what they were saying, though she gathered that a tragedy of some sort had just occurred, for Prynn seemed inconsolable, and Jaro himself seemed ready to fall apart after hearing whatever the soldiers had to tell him.

Opaka . . . ?

Another Klingon suddenly stepped into the alley, no doubt drawn by the sounds of Prynn's screaming. Kira and Winn raised their weapons in tandem, and both their beams struck the Alliance soldier squarely in the chest, dropping him instantly.

"Go," Kira told Winn. "Get them out of here, before more of them come!"

Winn looked at her gravely. "Walk with the Prophets, Kira Nerys."

"You too," Kira said. "Now *go!*"

Kira kept her weapon ready as the group hurried down the alley to another door near the far end. She held her breath, watching as Winn herded her charges inside before slamming the door shut behind her. Only then did Kira permit herself to exhale.

Vaughn stepped into the alley about a heartbeat later, passing through the same door from which Prynn had emerged. He saw Kira standing on the threshold of the refectory and started running toward her.

About five paces into his sprint, perhaps six more Klingons turned into the alley behind him.

She froze for a split second as she saw that a Jem'Hadar was leading their advance.

"*Down!*" Kira shouted, and sprayed the alley with

phaser fire. Vaughn responded automatically by throwing himself the rest of the way forward, twisting as he fell and firing his own phaser back in the direction from which he had come.

Three of the Klingons went down immediately, while the remainder went for cover.

The Jem'Hadar had already vanished.

Kira pulled Vaughn inside the refectory and slammed the door behind him. She quickly led him to a hastily fashioned barricade behind the serving stations, a stopgap reinforced with propped-up tables and benches for additional shielding. She wasn't sure what she hoped to accomplish with it when Jaro and Winn had assisted her in its construction, other than to keep the Klingons occupied for a few precious extra seconds before they inevitably killed her. But she also knew that those seconds might make all the difference for the enclave's leaders.

Now she wondered if she would die today instead by Taran'atar's hand.

"Thanks for the assist," Vaughn panted, rubbing the shoulder on which he'd landed when he'd completed his desperate lunge down the alley.

"Did you see him?" Kira asked, her weapon raised as she peered past the tables at the back door.

"See who?"

"He's here," Kira said. "Taran'atar."

Vaughn cursed. "Did he shroud?"

"I think so."

Kira's eyes panned across the windows. She could still hear the sounds of fighting in the distance, but it was strangely quiet near the refectory. *Where did they go?*

After a moment she said, "We're going to have to kill him, Elias."

Vaughn nodded slowly. "I understand."

"Do you?" Kira asked. "Because I want you to know I'm not talking about taking revenge against him, or exacting justice. Or even self-defense."

"What *are* you talking about, then?"

"If we can't cure him of his programming, then we should at least try to set him free. Snap his chains."

Vaughn seemed almost to wince at that. "You mean . . . put him out of his misery."

Kira hesitated. "I think he'd want that. Wouldn't you? If you had no control over your life?"

Vaughn didn't answer right away. "Maybe," he said finally, in a surprisingly quiet voice.

"I didn't see Opaka out there," Kira said. "Is she—?"

"I made sure she got to safety."

"Good." Comforted to hear that, Kira took a deep breath. She felt a deep surge of gratitude toward him. Perhaps she'd have enough time to let him know how much she appreciated everything he'd done, before . . .

"Look," she said. "About my relieving you of duty . . ."

He shook his head. "Captain, you don't have to—"

The ceiling creaked. Kira and Vaughn both shifted their positions, taking aim at the sagging rafters.

"I don't think we have a lot of time left, Elias," she said. "So please shut up and listen to me. I think maybe I was feeling a lot like Taran'atar—as if nothing was within my control anymore. It made me feel weak. Ineffectual. I felt like everything was going to hell, and that it was all my fault because I wasn't a strong enough captain. I was wrong to take my frustrations out on you."

"For whatever it's worth, Nerys . . . you may just be the strongest captain I've ever known."

"That's worth a great deal to me," Kira said. "I wish to hell we weren't in this mess, but I'm glad you've got my back."

Silence settled between them, broken only by the sounds of combat beyond the dense nyawood walls and the small creaks and groans of the refectory's damaged ceiling. The approaching sounds of small arms fire and explosions mingled with shouting and screaming, and it was all Kira could do not to abandon their position and join the fight outside. It went against every instinct she had to sit around waiting for a strike force to storm the doors while the people outside were laying down their lives just to slow the Klingons down.

Stick to the plan, she told herself. *Jaro and the others need time to get away. . . .*

"Captain, I need to ask you something," Vaughn said suddenly. "It's about Ben Sisko."

"What is it?"

Vaughn turned to face her. "Have you ever known him to lie?"

Kira's eyebrows shot up in bemusement. "Why are you asking me that?"

"Has he changed much over the years you've known him?"

"Of course," Kira said. "Everybody changes. You know th—"

Vaughn shook his head. "What I guess I mean is, since he returned from living among the Prophets . . . is he still the same man you used to know?"

Kira considered the question for a moment before answering. "I guess the honest answer is 'yes and no.' In some ways he's exactly the same. But in others, well . . . I suppose being among Them changes you."

"Have you?"

"Have I what?"

"Have you been among the Prophets?"

Kira hesitated again before saying, "I don't really feel comfortable talking about this, Elias."

"I'm sorry," Vaughn said. "I realize that was an inappropriate question. I'm just trying to wrap my head around something, and the more I try, the more I—" He stopped, distracted by a heavy thud overhead, and a renewed groaning from the nyawood timbers overhead.

Uh-oh.

The roof exploded.

Kira and Vaughn took cover as broken beams and splintered wood rained down, crashing everywhere. Dark figures descended through the rising dust cloud on lines, at least a dozen of them. Vaughn and Kira shot through the haze, felling the closest of the Klingons while drawing fire from others. Disruptor blasts shattered portions of the barricade, sending shards of wood flying in every direction.

Kira looked at Vaughn, who was bleeding profusely from a gash in his forehead. She saw the question in his face, and she nodded. Neither of them was willing to remain pinned down. If this was to be their end, they were going to give the Klingons a moment to remember.

They ran out from behind the barricade together, heading in separate directions, their phasers singing as they set the dust cloud aglow in orange light. Disruptor fire answered them from two of the Klingons, but it went wild as both warriors were suddenly felled by a fast-moving shadow that vanished as quickly as it had appeared.

Kira spotted another Klingon setting his sights on Vaughn and she swept her phaser around, her shot knocking the warrior off his feet.

Vaughn broke into a run toward his next nearest attacker, but something unseen knocked her XO's legs out from under him, forcing him to the floor before it slashed open the Klingon's chest.

Kira searched in vain for their invisible opponent. She saw instead that one more Klingon was moving in her direction, his *bat'leth* sweeping inexorably toward her—

The Klingon rose suddenly into the air, tumbling over Kira's head and crashing insensate against the barricade's broken remains.

An excruciating silence descended over the half-demolished refectory.

She stared into the dissipating dust cloud, desperately searching it for some sign of movement not consistent with the settling haze.

There.

He was directly in front of her, less than a meter away, a partial outline of his distinctive silhouette suddenly discernible in the grit-laden air. She brought up her phaser . . . and he slapped it out of her hand.

Invisible fingers clamped around her neck, and Taran'atar unshrouded, staring coolly into her eyes.

His expression, as usual, was unreadable.

"You saved us from the Klingons," she croaked.

"They would have killed you," he said in a voice utterly devoid of emotion. "We were ordered to capture you alive. Obedience brings victory."

"No," Kira gasped. She knew he was cutting off her oxygen. The world was rapidly becoming edged in black. *Not much time left.*

"It doesn't have to be that way," she said, each word a mortal struggle. "You're stronger than that. You're stronger than *her*. You can break the cycle. You can *choose*. . . . Finish your battle, once and for all, Taran'atar. . . . Reclaim your life."

He pulled her toward him until his cobbled face completely filled the narrow, dimly illuminated tunnel that was all that remained of her dying vision.

"I already have," he said.

Then the gathering darkness enclosed her entirely.

PART FIVE

THE ALTERNATE UNIVERSE

16

"What have you *done*?" Iliana hissed.

She scowled at Taran'atar in the privacy of her chosen quarters aboard Terok Nor, a relatively spacious cabin that had once been shared by O'Brien and his lover. Too many artifacts of their life together were still here—a few framed photographs, a chipped porcelain cup, a blanket that still reeked of sex—and Iliana's failure to have gotten rid of them by now only served to darken her mood even further.

Taran'atar answered her anger impassively, standing at ease in the middle of the main room, his uneven gray skin and black coverall stained with dirt and dust.

"I did exactly as you commanded," he told her. "Five designated targets were identified and captured."

"But you personally killed nine of Kurn's men!" Iliana was pacing back and forth between the Jem'Hadar and the cabin's viewport. "The general is furious!"

"The fatalities were justified," Taran'atar said. "The first five were about to use lethal force against Kira and Vaughn. This was in direct violation of your orders."

"What about the rest?"

"Fatalities six and seven occurred after the three Bajorans were captured. One of the enclave's leaders—Winn—provoked her guards. It was necessary for me to intervene to prevent her death."

"*How* did she provoke them?"

"She spat on them."

Iliana rolled her eyes. "And the two Klingons you killed aboard the ship during the return flight?"

"They attacked me in retaliation for the deaths of the first seven. I merely defended myself."

Naturally.

"Was I at fault?" Taran'atar asked.

Iliana sighed and rubbed her temples. "No," she said at length. "No, you weren't at fault. You did well, Taran'atar. Now go get cleaned up and wait for my next summons. When you're not in your quarters, it'll be best if you stay shrouded. At least until I can smooth things over with Kurn."

"Understood," Taran'atar said, and he immediately took his leave of her, shimmering into invisibility as he marched out into the corridor.

As the door closed behind him, Iliana reflected that Kurn's newest call for Taran'atar's head was actually a minor inconvenience in the larger scheme of things, one she would gladly endure as her endgame approached. But first she needed to deal with her new guests.

The first one would be the hardest.

It was a brief ride by turbolift to the appropriate level of the Habitat Ring, followed by a short walk to the correct cabin, but the journey furnished her with an eternity in which to reflect upon and curse herself, yet again, for her weakness and overemotionality. She never should have allowed herself the pointless indulgence of looking for the Ataan of this universe—and when that excess had nearly brought disaster upon her, she should have simply left him to rot on Letau. And now, after he had revealed the thing that had driven her to such distraction over the last half-day, she knew she should not be going to visit the focus of her latest crime of sentiment: this continuum's Dakahna Vaas.

Ataan's wife.

"I was hoping we could talk," was how Iliana began a moment after entering Vaas's cabin. To the dismay of the Klingons, she was keeping Vaas under minimum security: two guards outside a single-occupant stateroom, just like Ataan.

At least the Klingons could take some comfort in the fact that the station's *other* rebel prisoners were faring far less well than these two.

"I won't betray my people, Intendant," Vaas said immediately. "So whatever you think you're going to accomplish here, the Pah-wraiths can take you and anyone who follows you."

Iliana was suddenly overcome with the desire to embrace the other woman, which she barely suppressed. Vaas's defiance was genuine and fearless. *Just like* my *Vaas.* She was older and more careworn, of course, and she had undoubtedly lived a life that had been far different from that of the beloved friend Iliana recalled from Kira's years in the resistance. *But the fire is the same.*

"I'm not here to ask you to betray your people, Vaas,"

Iliana said. "I strongly suspect you would willingly die before you ever did such a thing."

That seemed to catch Vaas off guard, but the belligerence remained. "That's right. I would."

"So it's just as well that I've come to see you for another reason," Iliana said, settling into a chair while Vaas remained standing. "I'm here because of your husband."

The other woman began to offer her the obligatory denial. "I don't have a—"

"Ataan is here, Vaas. He's on Terok Nor."

That silenced her, if only for a moment. Iliana took the time to admire the long black hair that had always been her friend's single most distinguishing physical feature.

The Bajoran's body had not vanished with the rest of the simulation. Nor had the knife that protruded from the back of her adversary's neck. Blood was pooling beneath the black hair.

"What have you done to him?" Vaas demanded.

Iliana shook off the memory. "Nothing he won't recover from, I promise you. Especially now that I've kept my end of our bargain."

Vaas looked at her suspiciously. "What bargain?"

"Later," Iliana said, waving away Vaas's question. "First I want to ask you something. If you answer truthfully, then I promise to return him to you unharmed."

"I already told you, I won't betray my people."

"My question has nothing to do with the dissidents."

"I don't trust you, Intendant."

Iliana nodded. "Fair enough. But you can trust this: If you don't cooperate, you'll never see Ataan again."

One of Vaas's hands curled into a fist, then slowly relaxed. She took a chair opposite Kira, spun it around, and straddled it.

"Ask."

"How did you and Ataan fall in love?"

Vaas scoffed. "Is this a joke?"

"No," Iliana said. "It isn't."

"You want to know how my husband and I fell in love? That's *it*?"

"That's it."

"What meaning could that possibly have for you?"

Iliana shrugged. "Think of it as a test of your honesty."

Vaas hesitated, shaking her head at what undoubtedly seemed like the greatest absurdity she'd ever heard. Then, with a small shrug, she began her tale.

"Twenty years ago Ataan was assigned to Bajor as part of an exchange program between the Obsidian Order and Bajoran Intelligence."

"You were with BI?" Iliana asked.

"Back then, yes. I was an analyst, and I was curious about our young visitor from the Order. The exchange program was ostensibly to foster trust between our two organizations, but in practice it was all for show. Both BI and the Order isolated their visitors from anything they considered truly relevant. My superiors seemed content to allow me to baby-sit Ataan—that's how they saw it—and they tasked us with minor and irrelevant assignments, which were very obviously chosen to waste Ataan's time for the duration of his stay on Bajor. We didn't care. He grew to love Bajor over the next five years. And he grew to love me.

"When his assignment was over, Ataan was recalled to Cardassia, as we both knew he would be eventually—but not before we wed, quietly and in secret."

"Because mixed marriages are forbidden among Cardassians," Iliana said.

"Premarital dalliances outside one's species are one thing," Vaas said. "But a mixed marriage is seen as a threat to the sanctity and purity of what Cardassia values the most highly."

"Family."

"Yes."

"That must have been difficult for you both."

"Ataan always returned to me as often as his duties permitted over the years. Love endures."

Vaas fell silent, and Iliana replayed the tale in her mind, sifting through the words chosen, the details given and omitted, her changes in inflection, the movements of Vaas's eyes, face, and hands, and the subtle shift in posture as she spoke. Iliana parsed it all, individually and collectively, and quietly reached her verdict.

"That's not the whole story."

Vaas shrugged. "It's all you need to hear."

"Not if you want to be reunited with your husband." Iliana rose to leave.

Vaas grabbed her arm and forced her to turn around. "I did as you asked!"

"Let go of me," Iliana warned.

"I told you the truth about how we fell in love!"

Iliana delivered a sharp blow to Vaas's sternum with the heel of her palm. The other woman fell backward, winded, and dropped to a sitting position on the floor.

"No," Iliana said. "You told me things that were true, but you weren't honest. Lies of omission are still lies, Vaas. And the truth, I now believe, is that you were already a dissident when Ataan was assigned to Bajor. Perhaps you were born into the movement, or perhaps you weren't. But you were its inside operative at Bajoran Intelligence, and when the dissident leaders learned about Ataan, he became your assignment. Your task was to seduce him, to make him fall in love with you, with Bajor, and eventually, when he was sufficiently ensnared, with the dissident movement itself. All so that when he returned to Cardassia, *he would be one of you*. A believer. A double agent in the service of sedition."

"I love my husband!"

"Perhaps you do. But that wasn't something that happened immediately. It came later. It was something you learned over time."

Vaas glared at her as she finished catching her breath. "You have . . . an impressive imagination, Intendant."

"Only because I've known . . . others like you, Dakahna Vaas. You put your world and your people before everything else, and you make whatever sacrifices are necessary in their service." Iliana unsealed the door and stepped through it. "I have no intention of allowing that cycle of misery to continue."

"You sadistic, lying filth!" Vaas roared, lunging toward the door as it closed in her face. Iliana could hear her pounding her fists against it while she screamed. *"Is this how you gratify yourself? With mind games? Why are you doing this? Give me back my husband! Ataan!"*

Iliana couldn't get to the turbolift fast enough.

Of all the inversions she had encountered since learning of the alternate universe, this one had been the most . . . what? Shocking? Distressing? Unbelievable? What word could possibly be sufficient to describe the raw emotional upheaval of learning not only that both Vaas and Ataan were still alive in this universe, but also that they were joined together?

Happy. It made you happy.

She recoiled from the thought as quickly as it came, suddenly understanding why she had sabotaged any chance she had of earning the love of either of them. That, after all, was what she had wanted all along, wasn't it? To somehow win them over to her, these alternates of the people she remembered having loved and murdered—as if she could atone for what she had done to them, and thereby recover some semblance of the happiness she'd always believed she had lost forever.

But to accept the possibility that she might find a source of joy outside of the revenge she so craved introduced an intolerable element of doubt—one that she knew she had to crush at any cost if she was ever to know what it was to be whole again. Ataan and Vaas were the source of that doubt, a challenge to her resolve that she had to overcome.

Even if it meant killing them both.

Again.

"Murderer! Terran monster!"

Vaughn found it difficult to argue with Winn Adami as she lunged at Ashalla's destroyer.

He'd been conscious since his capture—unlike Kira, who had been out cold when more Klingon troops had moved into the demolished refectory in the aftermath of Taran'atar's rampage and taken her and Vaughn back to one of their ships.

He'd felt fortunate to be able to walk under his own power; the Jem'Hadar may have dealt him a nonlethal blow in knocking his legs out from under him, but they still ached—as did his left scapula ever since it had struck the dining hall's hardwood floor. That Vaughn had no broken bones—only a minor laceration on his forehead and a wound from a finger-length shard of wood that had become embedded in his right forearm—was certainly as much a product of luck as anything else.

But it wasn't until after he'd been marched outside and across the smoking, corpse-strewn desolation of Vekobet that he realized Kira had been the lucky one; she'd been spared having to see the carnage that she and Vaughn had unintentionally brought down on this place by crossing over and drawing Iliana's lightning down on those around them.

Stow that kind of thinking, Mister, he told himself sternly. *You didn't provoke any of this insanity. Get your head right, and do it* now!

Once he and Kira had been beamed up to Terok Nor, the Klingons immediately separated them; they placed Vaughn alone in a bare cargo hold, leaving him to wonder whether his captain had been transferred to someplace similar, or if she had simply been sent directly to her death.

I said, stow it!

Vaughn tested his prison. All the access panels and ventilation shafts had been welded shut, and recently from the hasty look of the workmanship. He had no tools with which to engineer an escape; the Klingons had taken his combadge almost immediately, and the bay was utterly empty.

All he could do now was wait.

Forty minutes after his arrival, a group of Klingon guards tossed Jaro and Winn into the cargo bay with him. Both of them were beaten and bruised, and their rumpled, torn clothing was covered in particulate rock, as if they'd been dug out of a cave-in just prior to their capture.

"I guess Kira and I didn't buy you quite enough time to get away after all," Vaughn said, regret sitting in his belly like an inert, indigestible lump of stone. "The Klingons must have discovered the escape tunnel."

Jaro nodded sadly. "They did."

"But you mustn't blame yourself, Elias," Winn said. "I know that you and Kira did everything you could."

"But the Klingons got what they came for anyway," Vaughn said glumly, despite the stern voice of experience that continued to insist that he belay that sort of negative self-talk. "And right now that adds up to Kira, both of you, and probably everybody and everything else we were trying to get safely out of Vekobet."

Winn shook her head vigorously, a motion that caused a small cloud of dust to rise from her hair. "No, Elias. The only other captive we know of besides Kira and the three of us is Dakahna Vaas."

Vaas. Vaughn recalled the name, and quickly associated it with the black-haired Bajoran woman he'd seen at the camp infirmary.

Vaughn allowed himself to grasp at a slender reed of hope. "Opaka and the artifacts?"

And Prynn?

"They got away," Winn said.

Staring off into the middle distance, Jaro said, "Once we realized that the Klingons had found the tunnel, we doubled back with Vaas, hoping to stall our pursuers just a little longer."

"That gave Opaka, Prynn, and the others just enough time to reach the Yolja River with the artifacts," Winn said. "One of the other enclaves was to pick them up there."

Prynn did *make it out of there. Thank God*, Vaughn thought. He felt an enormous sense of relief as the Bajorans went on to tell him how confident they were that their gambit had worked—a turn of luck they both insisted would never have come to pass but for Kira and Vaughn's having engaged the Klingons, thereby slowing down their eventual discovery of the escape tunnel.

Unfortunately, the worry that both Bajorans felt for Dakahna, from whom the Klingons had separated them immediately after their arrival on the station, was as palpable as either their confidence or their gratitude.

After Vaughn explained what he knew of their improvised holding pen, both Bajorans by mutual decision knelt together and began to pray. They invited Vaughn to join him, but he politely declined.

Even if I were a believer, he thought, *I'm really not sure I could continue to be one after what I've learned today.*

Though his inner turmoil remained unspoken during the prayers, the Bajorans seemed to sense it nevertheless. Maybe they could read it in his face, for when they concluded their communion, they both walked toward him and regarded him with grave expressions.

"We know about what you did at the infirmary," Jaro said, though there was no accusation in his tone. The doctor looked down at the deck as he spoke, as though uncomfortable gazing into the eyes of the living doppelganger of his dead friend—the man who had also killed that friend.

"Yes," Winn said. "It was a tragic choice."

And a choice that Vaughn knew he could neither unmake nor justify.

Just as he couldn't imagine making any other choice, given the same circumstances.

It's a good thing I don't believe in hell, he thought. *Otherwise it'd be my next long-term posting, sure as gravity.*

Winn reached toward Vaughn's face. He resisted the urge to flinch as she gently grasped his earlobe between her thumb and forefinger.

"We know why you had to do it, Elias," she said, closing her eyes as she read his *pagh*. "Just as we know what the deed must have cost you."

"I suspect that the cost would have been far higher," Jaro said, tears standing in his eyes, "had you allowed Elias's suffering to continue."

"Or had you left him and Prynn to the tender mercies of the Klingons," said Winn, releasing her hold on Vaughn.

He took an unsteady step backward, collecting his

scattered thoughts and emotions. Their forgiveness both shamed and relieved him, though he doubted that Prynn would be this understanding any time soon.

Some three hours into their captivity, the room shuddered—a low, momentary vibration that seemed to Vaughn almost familiar. It felt like a greatly amplified version of the slight sensation of acceleration caused by Deep Space 9's maneuvering thrusters, as though they were being fired at full burn.

Not long after the persistent and slightly disorienting acceleration effect began, the door to their cage opened again, and a group of Klingon guards delivered another eight weary and dejected rebels to the cargo bay. As soon as Winn noticed that Miles O'Brien was among them, she underwent an abrupt and total transformation.

She went berserk, screaming accusations and epithets as she pushed against the rebels in her naked desire to commit violence against their leader.

"Back off!" Keiko Ishikawa shouted back, placing her body squarely in Winn's path. "It wasn't him!"

"He cannot escape responsibility for this!" Winn roared.

"He didn't *do* it!" Tigan shouted from behind Ishikawa.

"Who, then?" Winn demanded. "Who among you was responsible for carrying out the atrocity at Ashalla? For slaughtering two million people?"

"None of us!" Ishikawa shot back. "It was the Intendant!"

Winn's grief finally caught up with her anger, and

she broke down. Jaro caught her as she fell to her knees, and the two of them wept as Ishikawa described what had happened, how the Intendant had called their bluff and carried out the very act that the rebels had only threatened.

"She said she would bomb another city if Miles didn't surrender immediately," Ishikawa said, now weeping as well. "We had no choice but to stand down."

O'Brien came forward to meet the Bajorans, their grief reflected plainly in his eyes.

"I'm sorry," he told them. "I'm so very sorry. I never meant for any of this to happen."

As Winn continued to sob, she reached out to touch O'Brien's ear, grasping the lobe in her trembling hand. For some time after that, Vaughn watched a catharsis unfold as the rebels and Bajorans together began to work through the worst of their shared anguish.

And finally, once much of the initial emotional storm had passed, he started asking questions.

"O'Brien . . . what's going on aboard the station?"

The haggard rebel leader looked at Vaughn as if he had just noticed him for the first time. "You're from the other side," he realized, noting Vaughn's distressed Starfleet uniform.

"Commander Elias Vaughn of Deep Space 9. After we lost our comlink with you, Captain Kira and I crossed over to Bajor, hoping we might be of some help."

"Only two of you?" Tigan asked.

"It was all we could manage," Vaughn said. "Some kind of scattering field is shielding local space from interdimensional transport. There was no time to do anything else."

"We appreciate the effort, Commander," O'Brien said. "It's just too bad you wound up in the same mess as the rest of us."

"I felt the station vibrate a short while before you were put in here. Can you tell me what's happening?"

"The Intendant," O'Brien said, shaking his head. "She had us make some insane modifications to the deflector generators and the maneuvering thrusters. The whole station is now moving at speed toward the Denorios Belt."

The wormhole.

Jaro looked at Vaughn. "Is that where she expects to open the Temple Gates?"

"Temple Gates?" asked another of the rebels, Sloan. "That's that crazy thing Ghemor warned us about, right? The religious thing? She was *serious* about that?"

"Yes," Vaughn said, cutting off whatever explanation Winn and Jaro seemed poised to offer. "Think of it as a dangerous hazard the Intendant wants to exploit. It's imperative that we stop her."

"Commander, you'll get no argument from us," O'Brien said. "But this station is swarming with Klingons, and all my people have been penned up in cargo bays just like this one."

"Then we'll just have to be ready to act when the opportunity finally presents itself," Vaughn said.

"Opportunity?" O'Brien said. "*What* opportunity? Look, Commander, with all due respect, I don't know how they handle situations like this where you come from, but in *this* universe, you can't simply fake an illness and expect the Klingons to open the door for you!"

"That isn't exactly what I had in mind," Vaughn said.

"What, then? If we have a hope in hell, I'm not seeing it!"

Vaughn allowed himself a small smile. "We have one."

17

Kira gasped for air as consciousness returned to her, accompanied by an eye-searing blast of light.

She felt hyperaware of everything, a side effect of the stimulant that had undoubtedly been used to force her awake. She was in a holding cell back on Deep Space 9.

No, she quickly realized. *This is Terok Nor.*

She stood flat against one wall of the cell, her hands encased in shackles that looked as though they had recently been welded into the bulkhead. She was missing her combadge, and Vaughn was nowhere to be seen.

Kira's double stood in front of her, dressed in the familiar black garb of the Intendant, watching her with interest.

"I really have to hand it to you, Captain," she said. "Beaming to the alternate Bajor before the Klingons' static field could fully envelop the planet was a crafty bit of quick thinking. Apparently I wasn't being paranoid after all when I ordered the Klingons to scan the planet for anomalous quantum signatures. But what did you think you were going to accomplish in that rebel stronghold? Did you honestly believe those thugs masquerading as slaves were going to be of any use to you?"

Kira said nothing.

"That's all right," Iliana told her. "It was more of a rhetorical question, anyway. And it's not that I mind your being here—quite the opposite, actually. You've saved me the trouble of going back for you."

"Why?" Kira asked, tugging uselessly at her shackles. "So you can talk me to death?"

"Oh, good," Iliana laughed. "You're not completely demoralized yet. There's still a little defiance left in you. That makes it all *so* much sweeter. Now I can't wait to see your face when this Bajor names me its Emissary."

"So *that's* why I'm still alive?" Kira asked. "To give you an audience?"

"Of course not, Captain. An audience I already have. Klingons, rebels, even your geriatric friend . . . but best of all, I have two of the religious leaders behind the Bajoran dissident movement." She held up her hand, displaying the Shard of Souls. "And with me in possession of a sacred artifact native to this continuum, they'll be here to bear witness when I open the Temple Gates.

"So, no, Captain. You aren't here to give me an audience. You're here to suffer what I'm about to do."

Kira finally decided she'd had enough. "What the *kosst* has happened to you? What can you possibly think all this is going to get you?"

"I thought that would be obvious to someone as devout as you, Captain," Iliana said. "I'm going to get back my life."

"What are you talking about?"

"Trakor's prophecy, of course," her double said, speaking to Kira as if she were a small child. "Not to mention a dozen other visions about the coming of the Emissary, all of which cite the same three criteria by which all Bajor would know its deliverer: the one called by the Prophets; the who opens the Temple Gates; and the one to whom the Prophets will give back her life."

"And exactly how does killing the Kira Nerys of one universe after another fit into your getting your life back?"

If Iliana was taken aback by Kira's knowledge of her broader plan, she gave no sign of it. "I don't fault you for not seeing the big picture, Captain. After what was done to me, it took me a while to understand what I needed to do so that I could be whole again. But when I meet the Prophets, they'll see inside me, just as they did with *your* Emissary. They'll understand what I need to get my life back. And I'll use the Soul Key"—she raised the Shard again—"to find every other Kira that has laid claim to a piece of my soul."

"And what about Iliana Ghemor's soul?" Kira asked.

Iliana said nothing at first, then abruptly broke eye contact with Kira for the first time since she had begun speaking.

"You don't understand. I'm going to be whole. For the first time in my life I'll finally be *whole!*"

"Are you trying to convince me of that . . . or yourself?"

Iliana suddenly grabbed Kira by the hair and slammed

her head back against the wall. The impact sent a sharp pain into Kira's eyes. "Don't push me, Captain. There are others here I could make suffer along with you."

"Yeah, you could," Kira said. "You could do the same to everyone I care about, and extend that cruelty to every Kira in creation. But it won't make you whole, Iliana. It'll *never* make you whole. You're chasing a sick, twisted idea of who you're supposed to be. And in the end, you're going to crash and burn."

Iliana smiled. "Bravely spoken. But a lot has happened since you were captured, Captain. You see, after I retook Terok Nor, I decided to borrow a page from your own book, and I coerced Smiley into doing the very thing you commanded of *your* O'Brien, on the day that *your* wormhole was discovered: propel the station toward the Denorios Belt. It has a pleasant symmetry, don't you think? And if my calculations are correct, we should arrive at the Temple Gates within the hour. So you see, I'm already well on my way to becoming whole again."

With an almost carefree stride, Iliana exited Kira's cell. At once one of the two Klingon guards activated the force field barrier that sealed the tiny room.

"But don't worry," Iliana finished as she left the holding area. "I'll be sure to give the Prophets your warmest regards."

18

"We have arrived," Kurn announced.

Iliana turned away from the starfield displayed on the ops holoframe and smiled. "All stop," she commanded. "Hold this position, and have your men bring Winn and Jaro to operations immediately."

From where he stood at the situation table, Kurn issued the orders, then returned to the task of checking the readings that were coming in. In a displeased tone he told Iliana, "There is little out here but charged plasma and cometary ice."

"Open your mind, General," Iliana said, grinning as she gestured toward the starry expanse displayed on the holoframe. "Some of the greatest treasures of the universe are those we can't even see."

"An enlightened perspective, I'm sure, Intendant," Kurn mocked, showing her the points of his filed teeth. "But I prefer the tangible. You assured me that the effort of moving this space station would be worthwhile."

"It will be," Iliana assured him. "Come, Kurn. We've

come this far together. Surely you wouldn't turn back now, this close to the prize?"

"Very well," said Kurn, the expression on his face leaving no doubt that his patience was nearing its end. "How do you wish to proceed?"

"The next part is for me alone," Iliana said. "Is the *River of Blood* ready?"

"My personal craft was transferred from the *Negh'Var* before we broke orbit, as you requested," the general said. "It is standing by at shuttle pad three."

"Good. It'll be necessary to conduct the final phase of the search by ship, since the stresses created by the wormhole will rip the station apart if we venture too close."

"We should not have left our fleet in orbit of Bajor," Kurn grumbled. "They might have been able to pinpoint exactly where—"

"Your fleet was left in orbit to provide needed assistance while Bajor recovers from the destruction of Ashalla," Iliana reminded him. "Don't make the mistake of underestimating the value of such goodwill. The Bajorans will remember who helped them during this time of crisis."

"Bajor will remember who is *responsible* for that crisis, Intendant!" a voice shouted across ops.

Iliana greeted Winn Adami and her husband with a smile as two guards escorted them off the turbolift. "And well they should, Winn. But when I return to Bajor, I promise you the rebels will know justice for the massacre they committed."

Winn and Jaro both glared at her in undisguised contempt as the Klingon guards brought them before her.

"We know who was really responsible for Ashalla, Intendant," the doctor said. "Just as we know who you really are."

Iliana scoffed. She showed them the *Paghvaram*. "Do you also know what *this* is? And what I'm about to do with it?"

Anger blazed in Winn's eyes. "Yes," she grated.

"Then I'm certain you both must realize why I've brought you here now. The hour for which your movement has waited all these years is finally upon you. You'll be Bajor's witnesses to the opening of the Temple Gates. And you'll both affirm the coming of the Emissary. "

"You will *never* be the Emissary," Winn said.

"There's no one left to block my Path, Winn," Iliana said.

"General!" the officer manning sciences called out. "I'm picking up unusually high proton concentrations, as well as a localized presence of verteron particles."

Iliana's head snapped toward to the holoframe. *So soon? But we shouldn't be close enough to trigger—*

And suddenly there it was, flowering before her eyes as if it sensed she was near; the cerulean bloom that had been the object of her quest opened to her, its petals of shimmering brilliance spiraling rapturously outward, beautiful and beckoning—

Yes! Yes, I've done it! I'VE DONE IT!

—and something came out of the maelstrom's glowing center.

"Sensor contact, dead ahead!" Kurn shouted. "Intendant—it's *Defiant*!"

And as the first salvo of pulse phasers slammed

against Terok Nor's shields, Iliana screamed in outraged surprise.

"Attack Pattern Delta! Give it all you've got, Prynn!" Ezri Dax shouted as she leaned forward in the command chair. "Sam, target their shield emitters! Fire at will!"

Behind her at tactical, Sam Bowers let fly with continuous salvos of pulse-phaser fire while Tenmei maneuvered *Defiant* for its close-quarters attack upon Terok Nor.

Dax quickly tapped her right-hand command console. "We're in the thick of it now, Nog. Make sure your team keeps up."

"Understood, Captain. We'll keep her together."

"I'm counting on it, Nog. Bridge out. Sam, what's the word on the hostiles?"

Defiant was jolted by a disruptor strike. "Other than the station? I read a dozen Klingon ships in orbit of Bajor, too far away to be a problem any time soon, but it looks as if they've already started to break orbit. ETA two hours."

Their ship shook again. "Keep up the attack," Dax ordered. "We need to get those shields down!"

"Their shield strength is down to sixty-eight percent," Bowers reported. "A few more minutes and—"

"Not fast enough," Dax said. "Arm a quantum torpedo. Target the zenith of their shield envelope, above the upper pylons. It's our best chance of punching a hole with minimal risk to the station."

"Right. . . . Torpedo armed. . . . Target acquired."

"Fire!"

Her eyes locked on the viewscreen, Ezri brought up her hand to shield her eyes as Terok Nor's invisible shell of force flared to near-blinding brightness before blowing out.

"Their shields are down," Bowers said, unable to hide his own astonishment.

"I'm in the room, Sam." Dax said. "Try not to sound so surprised." The ship buckled beneath her as it took another hit.

"Readings coming in from the station," Ensign Tariq Rahim reported from sciences. "Approximately seven hundred distinct life signs, mostly human and Klingon, with a small percentage of other species present as well. The Klingons seem to be the only ones with any degree of mobility, and are scattered throughout the station. The rest are confined to the Docking Ring."

"Prisoners?" Dax asked.

"That would be my guess, Captain. I'm also picking up Captain Kira and Commander Vaughn's combadges."

They're on the station? That makes things a little less complicated, Dax thought. "Can you confirm their location?"

"Operations. The station commander's office. But there are no human or Bajoran life signs in close proximity to the combadges."

Dax cursed. *So either they're dead, or their badges were removed and they're somewhere else.* "Any luck pinpointing a Jem'Hadar life sign?"

"Negative," Rahim said.

"Keep trying." She tapped her combadge. "Dax to Bashir."

"*Go ahead,*" came the reply from sickbay.

"How's our guest doing, Julian?"

"*She's with Chief Chao, and ready to go when you give word.*"

"Stand by. Prynn, we need a window of time to lower our shields and beam over Ghemor. Recommendations?"

Tenmei didn't hesitate. "Our best option is to make a run at the station from the ventral side, move up toward the fusion core, and slip between the Habitat Ring and the Docking Ring. We'll be most vulnerable as we pass the defense sails on that arc of the Habitat Ring, but we may be able to knock them out on approach."

Dax managed not to laugh. "You up for that, Prynn?"

"Hell, yes," Tenmei said.

"Sam?"

"You're not serious."

Dax was knocked back against her chair as *Defiant* took another hit. "If you have a better suggestion, now's the time to make it."

"You don't pick the easy ones, do you?"

"Where's the fun in that?" Dax asked. "Can you do it?"

"Take out the defense sails? Maybe the lower one. The upper one could be a problem, since it'll be partially obscured by the Habitat Ring during our approach. But if Prynn can manage a straight pass, there's at least a chance I could hit both of them."

"No promises," Tenmei said.

"All right, enough chatter," Dax snapped. "Tariq, where's Taran'atar?"

"Still no confirmed biosigns," Rahim said, shaking his

head. "And I can't get a reliable reading on any quantum resonance signatures."

Ezri cursed. "Dax to Chao."

"Go ahead."

"We can't locate Taran'atar, Jeanette. We need to move on to Plan B. But stay on your toes. It's likely to be a bumpy ride."

"Understood."

"Iliana, can you hear me?"

"Yes, Lieutenant."

"I just wanted to say . . . good luck."

"To you as well."

Dax got up from her chair and moved to stand behind Tenmei's seat at the conn station. "Let's do this, then. Prynn, commence run."

The roughly spherical shape of Terok Nor seemed to rotate as they swept beneath it. The station's spiral wave disruptors tracked with them, hammering their shields as the ship moved from one cone of fire to another until she was looking directly up at the fusion core. Completing its arc, *Defiant* swiftly straightened out and shot forward.

"Bowers, drop shields and fire at will!" Dax ordered. "Chao, you're on! Energize!"

Subjectively, *Defiant*'s passage seemed to take forever. In actuality, it took precious few seconds for Tenmei to execute her run as Dax fought panic at the sight of the station's glowing red fusion core rushing toward her. It veered away at the last moment, replaced by a near miss with a crossover bridge while the first approaching defense sail lashed out at her with disruptor fire. Bolts of energy from *Defiant*'s pulse phasers rained on the weapons array, finding their mark as the clawlike tower tore free of the Habitat Ring in a cloud of tumbling debris.

The phasers missed the upper sail.

Struck point-blank by spiral-wave disruptors, the entire vessel seemed to scream with the impact as unshielded ablative armor vaporized on *Defiant*'s ventral side, exposing the naked hull beneath as she continued forward, narrowly avoiding a collision with one of the upper pylons.

Then there was only black space and stars on the viewer, and *Defiant* was clear of the station.

"Raise shields!" Dax ordered. "Damage reports!"

The news wasn't terrible. Despite the beating she'd taken, *Defiant* was still in prime fighting shape. Terok Nor was a wounded giant; it still had teeth, but it couldn't pursue them.

"Dax to Chao. Report."

"Transport successful. Package is away."

Dax allowed herself a small sigh of relief, thinking that the only problems that remained now were subduing Taran'atar, capturing Ghemor's counterpart, ascertaining whether or not her commanding officers were alive, and safely returning home . . . all before those Klingon ships on their way from Bajor arrived in less than two hours.

"Easy-peasy," she muttered to herself.

19

"We've lost shields!" Kurn shouted. "Intendant, what are your orders?"

Iliana stood frozen as Terok Nor quaked around her. *This can't be happening. My Path leads here. I'm fated to be the—*

"Fire reported in Upper Pylon Two, near the emergency oxygen tanks," one of the Klingons called out. "Suppression system offline."

"Blow the emergency ports," Kurn ordered. "Vent the pylon, before those tanks explode!"

"General, we have personnel inside the—"

"Do as I command!" Kurn roared. "Weapons, target that ship and fire at will!"

Another jolt shook the station. Beside her, the Klingon at engineering struck his head against a bulkhead and fell to the deck, either unconscious or dead. The station sustained still another resounding strike, which flung Iliana hard against the engineering console; she grunted as she fought to prevent herself from toppling over it.

Engineering. Thruster controls. Navigation.

"Lower Defense Sail one has been destroyed," someone reported behind her. "Turbolifts are offline stationwide. Habitat Ring has sustained heavy damage to Sections Four through Nine, Levels Five and Six. Several compartments have opened to space."

The Habitat Ring. No. Oh, no . . .

"General, thrusters have fired—the station is moving again!"

"What? On whose authority—?" Kurn shouted. He turned toward the engineering station, where he saw Iliana hunched over the console. "What are you *doing*?"

"They aren't going to stop us," she vowed. "We're too close now for that."

"General, she's put us on a course for the wormhole!" the weapons officer said.

Kurn moved up the steps toward her. "Are you *insane*?"

"Keep your place, General!"

"No," Kurn said, drawing his *d'k tahg*. "I've had enough of your madness. No more. This farce ends now."

Iliana's eyes narrowed. She backed away, forcing Kurn to follow, allowing his large frame to eclipse her view of the other five Klingons in the ops center. Then she stopped and gave him an opening.

He took the bait, thrusting his knife as she brought up her hand and captured his wrist. Kurn continued to grin, pushing his blade toward her neck as if he were only toying with her. With her other hand she reached for her disruptor, and of course he caught her arm with his free hand and kept her weapon angled well away from him.

Of course, that meant he now had both hands full, and she had armed herself.

Kurn leaned in, clearly savoring the slow, incremental progress his knife was making toward Iliana's skin. His grinning face was aligned alongside the hilt of his *d'k tahg*—and, not coincidentally, right beside Iliana's gripping hand.

A subtle motion of her wrist was all it took. The spring-mounted blade hidden in her sleeve deployed, biting deep into Kurn's neck. The general's eyes went wide as her blade abruptly sliced through artery and bone and spinal cord as though they were made of paper. The general's dying, twitching body slumped heavily against her much smaller frame.

Using Kurn's body as a shield, Iliana raised her disruptor and fired on the remaining Klingons in ops. Three of them got off shots of their own before they fell; two of those were rendered harmless by Kurn's broad back, which now sizzled under the thermal onslaught, while the third shot missed her entirely.

A few heartbeats later, she was the last one standing in ops—or at least the last one standing under her own power.

Her nose twitching in disgust, Iliana shoved Kurn's partly roasted corpse away from her. It landed with a moist thud on the steps that led to the engineering station and rolled to a halt on the deck. Panting at the exertion, she took a moment to recover her wind.

I'm running out of time, she realized as she glanced at her chronometer. She touched her communicator patch and spoke breathlessly into it. "Kira to Taran'atar."

No answer came back.

"Taran'atar, this is the Intendant. Come in."

Still nothing. *Damn him, where is he?*

"Taran'atar, this is a direct command," Iliana said as she recovered a couple of extra disruptors from the nearest fallen Klingons. "Go immediately to Airlock One, on the Docking Ring. Wait for me there."

With no more time to spare, Iliana looked for her two Bajoran rebel guests. She found them cowering behind the sciences station.

"Wait here," she told them as she quickly programmed the console's transporter controls. "And be sure to keep watching the holoscreen. This is far from over."

But first . . . the Habitat Ring.

Leaving them where they were, Iliana hurried toward the transporter stage, whose shimmering curtain of light took her a moment after she reached it.

20

Taran'atar moved through the docking bay, a Jem'Hadar at war.

He stalked his targets invisibly, cutting down Klingon after Klingon with stealth and speed. Necks snapped. Throats were cut. Hearts were punctured. With each kill he claimed their sidearms, and when the trail of corpses began to attract attention, he waited in ambush, emerging from his shroud at intervals, becoming visible long enough to spray the passageways with disruptor fire.

The bay he sought was close now. A few more meters . . .

"Kira to Taran'atar."

Her voice. He unshrouded.

"Taran'atar, this is the Intendant. Come in."

It no longer carried its former power, but still it tugged at him. Insistent. Demanding.

"Taran'atar, this is a direct command. Go immediately to Airlock One, on the Docking Ring. Wait for me there."

Obedience brought victory. But his vow was already broken. So *much* was broken now. Even before L'Haan had reached into his mind with that final, dying effort to undo the damage Iliana Ghemor had done to him, his existence had become a farce. L'Haan's meld had been slow to heal him, snapping his bonds one coppery tendril at a time, allowing him to assert more of his own will with each passing hour.

He had in the days since stared into the eyes of his false god, knowing even as he continued to acknowledge her every word and carry out her every command, that he was coming ever closer to exacting his revenge for what she had done to him.

Now as he heard her voice calling to him, Taran'atar knew that he was free at last to act.

Airlock 1. Halfway around the Docking Ring—

The cargo bays.

No. The false god would have to wait. He had another task to finish, another vow to keep.

Taran'atar continued down the passageway, crossing the final meters to the door he wanted. The guards had abandoned their posts. He shot out the keypad, ripped open the manual release, and pulled the level down. Forcing his fingertips into the hatchway's edge, he shoved the door aside, pushing it into its wall pocket.

He looked inside. Vaughn stood on the other side of the doorway, flanked by eight of this station's former masters.

"It's good to see you, Taran'atar," Vaughn said. "Thanks for keeping your promise."

VEKOBET, EIGHT HOURS EARLIER

Captain Kira blacked out, and Taran'atar dropped her unconscious form at his feet.

There was not much time. He had succeeded in delaying both her capture and Vaughn's, but more Klingons would soon be coming. Their release from captivity would have to wait until they were back aboard Terok Nor, where it might be possible to tip the odds more forcefully in his favor.

He stepped away from Kira and hurried toward Vaughn, who was still on the ground where Taran'atar had left him, lying on his back several meters away.

Vaughn became more alert when he saw the Jem'Hadar's face over him. He tried to attack, but Taran'atar held him down with a firm hand over his chest.

"Commander, listen to me. I'm trying to help. This is very difficult, because I'm still not entirely myself. Klingons will be here soon to take you and Captain Kira prisoner. Don't resist. They'll take you to Terok Nor. Once I get there, I'll find you."

"How can I possibly trust you?" Vaughn asked.

"You can't," Taran'atar answered. "Nevertheless, I give you my word."

And with that, he shrouded and left.

TEROK NOR, NOW

Taran'atar dropped his cache of weapons on the deck. While the rebels got busy arming themselves, he turned to Vaughn. "I surrender to your authority."

Vaughn grabbed a weapon and checked its charge. "Good to know. What's the tactical situation?"

"Unclear," Tarna'atar said. "Within the last thirty minutes, this station came under attack by *Defiant*. The Intendant has reactivated the station's maneuvering thrusters and has put Terok Nor on a collision course with the wormhole. I chose that moment to make my move, and I am personally responsible for the deaths of thirty-two enemy combatants in the Docking Ring. That leaves potentially as many as three hundred twenty-eight other Klingons scattered throughout the station."

"What about *my* people?" asked O'Brien, the rebel leader.

"Presumably they're still in confinement along this corridor," Taran'atar said. "Freeing them should not be difficult."

"Arming them will be a different matter altogether," O'Brien said.

"One of the armories is close by," said the counterpart of Ezri Dax.

"Go," O'Brien told her. "Vendiki, go with her. The rest of us need to get down to engineering and pull this station off its present course."

"I'll come with you," Vaughn said. "Maybe I can help." He turned to face Taran'atar. "Where's Kira?"

"In a holding cell on the Promenade."

"I want you to release her. Tell her what's going on. Tell her you've already freed the rest of us and that we're working to correct the station's course."

"She will not trust me," Taran'atar said.

"No, she won't," Vaughn agreed. "So you need to give her a message from me."

Iliana was intensely relieved to discover that the damage to the Habitat Ring had not extended all the way to Vaas's cabin. The Klingon guards assigned to watch Vaas's quarters were gone, having been redeployed to more vital areas when the station had come under attack.

Her weapon drawn and ready, Iliana unlocked the door and stepped cautiously inside. "Let's go," she told Vaas at gunpoint.

"No," the other woman answered, folding her arms defiantly.

"Idiot! We don't have time for this!" Iliana said. "Do you want to see your husband again or not?"

"Another mind game?"

"No games. This is your last chance. If you don't take it, you'll never see Ataan again."

Vaas swallowed. Finally she followed Iliana back across the cabin's threshold. Iliana grabbed her by the arm and pulled her down the curve of the corridor.

"The station's under attack, isn't it?" Vaas asked.

Iliana scoffed. "What gave it away?"

"So why are you taking the time to bother with Ataan and me? Especially after what you said about—"

"I want you to understand something, Vaas. I told you before that your husband and I struck a bargain. I was ready to bombard Vekobet from orbit, because I knew it harbored agents from the other universe. Ataan pleaded with me to save you, because he knew you were down there, and in exchange for your life he told me what Vekobet really is."

"He betrayed the enclave?"

"That's one way of looking at it."

"Why are you telling me this?"

They stopped in front of a door, and Iliana answered, "Because after everything he's done to advance the cause of revolution, every selfless act and every sacrifice and every crime he's committed against his own people— when he faced the very real possibility of losing you, he chose to turn his back on all of it.

"That's how much he loves you, Vaas. I just wanted you to understand that."

Iliana keyed the cabin open. Ataan looked up from his bunk, and when he saw his wife, he launched himself toward her. Vaas went to him, and the two met in an embrace that looked unbreakable.

"Come on," Iliana prompted. "You need to hurry."

"Hurry? I don't understand," Ataan said.

Iliana pointed down the corridor. "Follow the curve until you reach an emergency stairwell. Go up to the top deck and follow the passageway to Shuttle Pad Three. There's a Klingon ship there. Take it and go."

"Go where?" Vaas asked.

"Anywhere you want. Just get out of here." She handed them each a disruptor. "The ship may be guarded. I imagine you both know how to handle these."

They took the weapons. "Why?" Ataan asked.

"Go *now*," Iliana said as she backed away, heading in the opposite direction. When the couple had nearly receded from view, Iliana saw them start to run.

21

Terok Nor was in chaos.

Ghemor had beamed herself to an isolated corner of the Promenade, an alcove tucked away behind one of the old, defunct shops. She could see now that she needn't have bothered with her act of concealment. Peeking out at the mad rush of Klingons that swarmed in all directions, she thought she could have transported directly into their midst without anyone even taking notice.

Taking a deep breath, she bounced a few times on her toes before breaking into a purposeful run, blending in at once with the flurry of activity that now surrounded her.

Those who saw her coming quickly got out of her way, giving her a wide berth.

She might have guessed that one clumsy oaf would be the first to put to the test the crazy idea she'd had on Deep Space 9. That near collision had forced her to stop while the soldier met her eyes, then quickly lowered them.

"Intendant, please forgive me," he stammered. "I had no idea—"

"Out of my way, you idiot!" Ghemor snapped, shoving the soldier aside as she raced on.

Slowing as she neared the security office, Ghemor caught her reflection in the transparent window of the door just before it opened to admit her. The face of Kira Nerys, complete with the silver headpiece and black garment of the Intendant, stared back at her. She had to hand it to Doctor Bashir; she'd suspected Federation doctors had the capacity for such transformations, but the results had far exceeded her expectations—easily on a par with anything the Obsidian Order could have done.

The Klingon who sat behind the desk rose respectfully when she entered, and she answered the gesture with a quick phaser strike to his chest. If anyone in the corridor had noticed, they would simply think Intendant Kira was in another one of her unfortunate moods.

At least, she hoped so.

Pushing aside the stunned Klingon, she moved behind the security console and checked the list of prisoners being held inside. She found only one: Kira.

Well, it's a start.

Marching into the holding area, she dispatched the two guards who were watching over the captain with the same economy of action she had brought to bear against the one in the outer office.

Obviously stunned by the sight of the Intendant effecting a rescue, Kira could only stare as Ghemor recovered a small object from one of the corpses, quickly deactivated the force field barrier, and waved the device over each of Kira's shackles, which promptly snapped open.

"Sorry that took so long, Captain. We got here as soon as we could."

"Ghemor?" the captain asked, clearly reluctant to believe her own conclusion. "Is that really you?"

"I know you'd probably appreciate a long explanation," Ghemor told them, "and I wish I could give you one, but I'm afraid we just don't have the time. *Defiant* has taken out most of Terok Nor's defenses—"

"*Defiant?*" Kira asked. "*My Defiant?*"

Ghemor nodded. "There's a fleet of Klingon ships due here soon, so if we—" Ghemor stopped as an ominous vibration passed through the soles of her shoes. "What was that?"

"The station's moving again," Kira realized. "Something's wrong."

An unexpected voice answered her with chilling clarity. "Terok Nor is on a collision course with the wormhole."

Ghemor spun around, her phaser aimed directly at Taran'atar's head as he unshrouded in front of her and Kira. With movements almost too fast to follow, the Jem'Hadar grabbed her wrist and spun her around, slamming her hand hard against the bulkhead so that she released the phaser.

Then he slowly turned her back around, studying her face. "You aren't her."

He released her, and she stepped away from him quickly, finally having the presence of mind to slap the neuropulse device, which was disguised as the Alliance emblem in the middle of her chest.

But she saw no apparent change in Taran'atar. *Oh, no.*

Ghemor saw the look in Kira's eyes. She was angry. Angry enough to launch herself against Taran'atar, even though to do so was to risk her life.

For Taran'atar's part, the Jem'Hadar made no further threatening moves. He remained armed, but his hands were free and open at his sides.

Then he spoke directly to Kira.

"I came to help."

Kira stared at Taran'atar for a long moment before she managed to find her voice. "What are you telling me? That you're no longer under her control?"

"I'm no longer under *anyone's* control," Taran'atar answered. Despite his characteristically flat affect, the hard fact of the statement almost seemed to cause him pain.

"Why should I believe that?"

"I saved your life on Vekobet," Taran'atar said. "Yours and Vaughn's."

"You said you were following orders to capture us alive!"

"I did indeed receive those orders," the Jem'Hadar said. "But that isn't why I followed them, Captain. I've freed Commander Vaughn and the rebels. Even now, they're attempting to correct the station's course."

"How do I know that anything you're telling me is true?" Kira demanded.

"In the event you doubted me, Commander Vaughn asked me to give you a message."

"What message?"

"He still has your back."

Kira blinked, but allowed herself to relax somewhat.

"Captain, please tell me you aren't going to trust him," Ghemor said.

Kira ignored her. "Where is she, Taran'atar?"

"The Intendant is on her way to the Docking Ring, Port One."

"Why there?"

"She is positioning herself at the leading edge of the station—the section that will reach the event horizon first."

"She's still bent on fulfilling the prophecy," Kira realized. "Even if she has to destroy the station to do it."

"So what do we do now?" Ghemor asked, sounding frustrated.

"We go after her." Kira looked at Taran'atar. "You still want to make yourself useful?"

"Yes."

"Then get down to engineering and see what you can do to help Vaughn and the rebels."

Taran'atar inclined his head in a silent gesture of assent, then exited the holding area, shrouding as he passed through the door.

Ghemor paused to grab a weapon from one of the fallen Klingons, then handed her Starfleet phaser to Kira. "You'd better take this. I feel a lot more comfortable with a disruptor."

"Thanks," Kira said, checking the weapon's charge.

Ghemor likewise readied her disruptor before looking up at Kira, expectation in her eyes. "You ready?"

Concealing her phaser inside her uniform jacket, Kira nodded. "Let's move."

Letting Ghemor drag her by the arm to keep up appearances, the two women rushed out of security and straight toward the nearest emergency stairwell. As before, the Klingons rushed to get out of Ghemor's way. Once they were clear of unwelcome eyes, they broke into a run for the Docking Ring.

At first they moved together in silence, but by the time they reached the first crossover bridge, Kira could no longer hold back the question she'd been waiting to ask.

"So were you ever going to tell me that *you're* the one who was supposed to become the Emissary?"

"Let's be clear about something, Captain," Ghemor said as she continued to run alongside Kira. "I'm doing what I was trained to do: trying to neutralize a threat, nothing more. And no offense, but I'm not even overly fond of Bajor. Let somebody else usher in the new age."

Someone who doesn't wish to be among us is to be the Emissary.

"I'm not sure it's possible to accept one part of a prophecy while denying the rest, Ghemor," Kira said. "It tends to be all or nothing."

"Great. *Now* you tell me," Ghemor muttered, but Kira thought she heard wry amusement in the other woman's voice.

Just as they reached the second crossover bridge, the station lurched, and its artificial gravity and inertial compensation systems offset the unexpected motion only incompletely.

Kira permitted herself a shred of optimism; the rebels must be making some progress in trying to regain control of the station. At least, that what she *hoped* was happening.

And if that's true, it means that Taran'atar kept his word.

Ghemor suddenly downshifted to a brisk, silent walk. Kira fell in step beside her, seeing that they'd nearly reached their destination. The inner door of Docking Port 1's airlock was open, and the two women stopped at the port's edge. Kira took the point and peered around the circular lip of the tunnel as the station jolted and shuddered again.

Iliana was standing there, her back to the corridor, the hand that held the Shard of Souls pressed against the transparent aluminum of the outer door as she gazed out into the plasma-streaked blackness of the Denorios Belt. Waiting.

Her other hand was holding a disruptor pistol.

Kira nodded to Ghemor, and the two of them entered the tunnel, their weapons raised.

"It's over, Iliana," Kira said. "The station's course is being altered as we speak. Drop your weapon and step out of the airlock. Now."

Iliana didn't move, and quite suddenly, the wormhole opened beyond her.

It filled the space beyond the airlock, bright and blue and churning—a roiling maelstrom against which the figure of Iliana became shadowy, almost a silhouette. And for the first time in the eight years since she'd become a witness to the majesty of the Celestial Temple, the sight of it filled Kira with fear.

The station shook, but the destruction Kira had expected didn't come.

The rebels must have done it—they must have altered the station's course enough to just brush the event horizon before veering away from it! Any second now the wormhole will close and—

Iliana glanced over her shoulder at Kira and Ghemor and smiled.

"You're too late," she said.

Lifting her weapon to the airlock, Iliana fired.

The portal shattered outward. Swept into the hurricane rush of atmosphere that exploded from Terok Nor, Kira heard the roar of the wind and the deafening silence that followed it as she and the two women who shared her face plummeted across the gap of icy space and into the gaping maw of the unknown.

INTERLUDE

She fell through the Temple Gates, down into the gullet of infinite possibilities. And as the wormhole consumed her, the world she knew receded behind an infinite vista of radiant white, until all that remained was the beating of her heart—the steady rhythm that kept her anchored to her life on the linear plane. She found her hand, pale fingers flexing above her open palm, and slowly she came to understand that she was not alone.

"I'm here!" Iliana announced. "Can you hear me? I've opened the Temple Gates! I've fulfilled the prophecy of the Emissary! Show yourselves!"

"Corporeal entities," noted Tekeny Ghemor. Her father stood before her, aglow in a strange light that made him indistinct around the edges. "They come from the Broken Line."

"No," said Corbin Entek, his face as strangely diffused as her father's. "Only one of them is from the Broken. The others other are from the Penitent."

Suddenly Iliana saw that her counterpart and Kira were present as well, not glowing like the others, but seeming more tangible. The three of them formed the points of a triangle in the whiteness through which the others—the Prophets, Iliana realized—circled and weaved.

"Broken?" asked Kira. "Penitent? What does that mean? Is that how you refer to our two universes?"

"They are intrusive," said Skrain Dukat as he approached Kira. "Aggressive. Adversarial."

"One is the Hand," interceded Kira Taban, suddenly standing between Kira and Dukat. He turned toward the two Ilianas. "One is the Voice. One is the Fire."

"But only one was meant to come to us," said Ataan Rhukal.

"Then send these others away!" Iliana said. "You don't need them!"

"Why do you need *any* of us?" her counterpart asked the Prophets. "Why must you interfere with our worlds?"

"*You* interfere," Dakahna Vaas said. "*You* come to *us.*"

"*I'm* the one!" Iliana cried. "*I* can fill the vacuum that Sisko left when he died."

"This one is conflicted," Entek said, studying Iliana's face. "It speaks with two voices."

"*I* opened the Gates!" Iliana insisted. "*I'm* the Emissary. Please! You must help me—"

"Help?" asked Shakaar Edon. "What is this?"

"Give me back my *life*," Iliana screamed.

The Prophets looked at one another, but whether they were conferring among themselves in some way she couldn't perceive, or were merely puzzled by her demand, Iliana had no way of knowing.

Finally the Prophet wearing Kaleen Ghemor's face turned toward her. "Which life?" she asked.

Iliana opened her mouth, but no answer came.

"Conflicted," repeated Entek. "Broken."

"Her existence is entwined with that of our Hand," observed Kira Meru. "It is no longer linear."

"An anomaly," Dukat said as he slowly approached her. "We should examine it more closely."

Without warning, the past of Iliana Ghemor exploded. Faces and events were yanked from her soul like pages ripped from a book. And as the tatters of her exposed lifescape were laid bare before the beings arrayed around her, she began to understand just how small she truly was.

22

"Here she comes!" Dax shouted. "Helm, hard to port! Weapons, target their impulse drive!"

"Incoming fire!" Bowers announced. "Ahead one-ten mark two."

They came under attack much sooner than expected. The *Negh'Var,* a monstrous Klingon warship, had somehow managed to pull ahead of the rest of the Klingon fleet that was still speeding toward them from Bajor.

She was coming in with every weapons tube blazing.

Dax instinctively reached for her armrests. "All hands, brace for impact!"

Defiant's bridge rocked as a spread of photon torpedoes pummeled the ship's shields. Men and women all around were tossed away from their stations as instrument panels cracked and erupted in flames.

The fire suppression system kicked in as Tenmei clawed her way back to her seat and fought to right the wounded vessel, aligning inertia with *Defiant*'s artificial gravity. Portside instruments became coated in a fine mist of flame retardant that quickly doused the fires.

"Damage report," Dax called out.

"Power outage on deck two, section three," Leishman reported from the engineering console. "Hull breach on deck four, section three. Force field in place and holding. Impulse power reduced by twelve percent."

"Several injuries reported, Captain," Bowers said. "Doctor Bashir is on it."

Dax hit the comm to engineering. "Nog, how's it going down there?"

"You want the good news first, or the bad?"

Dax sighed. "Give me the bad."

"You're about to lose another fifteen percent of impulse efficiency."

"What's the good?"

"You're only going to lose another ten percent shield strength."

"Your way of looking at the bright side never ceases to amaze me, Nog," Dax said. "How much time do you need to crank up those numbers?"

"Ten minutes, minimum," the engineer said.

"Take your time. You've got five. Bridge out."

"Negh'Var coming about on an intercept course," Bowers said.

"How long until the rest of the fleet gets here?"

"Nineteen minutes."

Dax watched the screen, the hawkish forward profile of the *Negh'Var* resembling an ungainly raptor descending on its prey.

She rose from the command chair. "Prynn, can you get us under the belly of that thing, inside their shield envelope?"

Tenmei turned to look at her. "We'll take a hell of a

pounding if I do," she warned. "And with the shields and impulse drive both getting weaker, we could easily lose one or both by the time we're through."

"I have a thought about that," Dax said, and proceeded to describe what she had in mind. Prynn listened, her eyes widening only once as Dax outlined her plan.

"I'll need a few extra seconds to plot that," she said.

"Get started," said Dax. "Sam, I want pulse phasers and shields at full strength for this. Get the power from wherever you have to, but get it done." She turned to Leishman. "Mikaela, call engineering and let Mister Bright Side down there know what's going to be expected of him."

"The *Negh'Var* is closing fast," Bowers said. "Phasers at full. Shield strength up to ninety percent and climbing...."

"Prynn, have you got that maneuver plotted yet?" Dax said, hearing the tension in her own voice, willing herself back to calmness. *Easy-peasy.*

Prynn didn't respond, her hands continuing to fly across her console.

"Prynn!"

"Done!" she said.

"On my mark," said Dax, returning to her chair. "Execute!"

"*Negh'Var* firing forward disruptors," Bowers said.

Defiant dived on approach, corkscrewing as she passed below the *Negh'Var*'s command pod, putting her ventral hull toward that of her adversary. *Defiant*'s shields glowed with terrifying brilliance as the Klingons' particle beams sought to slice them open and sink deep into the remaining ablative armor that protected the starship's exposed belly.

As the *Negh'Var* streaked past, *Defiant* rotated on her lateral axis, her nose angling toward the Klingons, freeing her pulse phaser cannons to target the aft section of the *Negh'Var*'s impulse drive.

"Fire!"

Massive sections of drive plating ripped apart as multiple phaser bolts tore through them, exposing the glowing fusion plants within as the two ships pulled away from each other. *Defiant* poured on the acceleration as the Klingon power cores burst behind her, the entire back half of the *Negh'Var* blowing apart as it began to tumble out of control toward the charged plasma fields of the Denorios Belt.

It didn't take long for Dax and her command crew to assess that the victory had been a costly one, however. *Defiant*'s shields were gone, and her ablative armor was now severely compromised. Impulse power was functioning well below optimal levels. EPS conduits and isolinear optical cable had been exposed by fallen ceiling plates, and now hung over the bridge crew like rainforest vines.

"Klingon attack fleet closing in," Bowers reported. "ETA now three minutes."

"Nog," Dax called, breathing heavily. "Can you give me shields?"

"Not in three minutes, I can't. Sorry, Captain."

Dax pushed the hair out of her eyes. "Prynn, how long can we evade them?"

Prynn turned and simply shook her head.

"Oh, damn," Dax muttered. "Status of warp drive?"

"Online," Leishman told her.

"Prepare to withdraw," Dax ordered, her own words

stabbing her in the throat like knives. "We'll return and reengage as soon as—"

"Captain, the Klingons are veering off," Bowers said, sounding nonplussed. "*All* of them. They're now taking a heading of two-nine-three mark fourteen."

Dax opened her mouth to ask why, but Rahim saved her the trouble. "I have multiple contacts coming out of warp," Rahim said. "Thirty—no, *forty* ships, heading two-nine-three mark fourteen."

Dax's heart sank, and she sagged into the command chair. "More Alliance forces?"

Rahim took a second look at his instruments, as if he couldn't quite believe what he was seeing. "No, sir. They're Talarian."

"Talarian?" Dax said. "Confirm."

"They're definitely Talarian, Captain. And there's now a ship decloaking directly in front of them, taking the point."

Rahim turned to look at Dax with eyes like deflector dishes. "It's *Defiant*!"

"The Klingons are heading straight for us," Shar said, his antennae taut with tension as battle approached. "They've forgotten the other *Defiant* completely. Just as you guessed, Leeta. They'll be in firing range in six minutes."

Leeta smirked. Klingons just never knew when to pack up and go home. She turned toward the broad-bodied man who stood next to her command chair.

"Once again, I want to thank you for your assistance during this crisis, Minister Endar," she said.

"You can thank me *after* the battle is won, Captain." the Talarian said. "The Alliance has threatened my people long enough. We are eager to join swords with whoever else may share our enmity."

Leeta nodded toward Pennak, who was manning communications. "Raise the other *Defiant*."

"They're answering," Pennak said a few moments later. "On screen."

The face of the other ship's captain filled the forward viewer. To Leeta's surprise, it was Ezri Tigan's counterpart.

Okay, now that's just plain weird, she thought.

"Leeta, isn't it?" the other woman asked.

Leeta grinned, wondering if her counterpart and this Ezri were married, too. "It is. Pleased to make your acquaintance, Captain Tigan."

"It's Dax, actually."

Oh, right. The worm. Zee told me about that.

"Thank you for your timely assistance," the other Ezri said. *"As soon as we've effected some necessary repairs, we'll join—"*

"From what I've been able to see," Leeta said, interrupting, "you and your people have done plenty already. Do what you need to do. But my new friends and I can take it from here."

Ezri Dax nodded. *"Good hunting, Captain. Defiant out."*

"Shar," Leeta said. "Begin attack run. Weapons, target the lead ships and fire on my mark. Prennak, send word throughout the fleet . . .

"It's showtime."

INTERLUDE

Kira witnessed the life of Iliana Ghemor unfolding, and felt pity.

The terrible things Iliana had described to her in Kira's holding cell on Terok Nor had seemed intolerable. Now Kira knew they'd merely been a glimpse into the depths of the loss, misery, heartache, and betrayal that had defined this woman's life.

And the tragic, winding path that had led her to this moment.

"It speaks with two voices," she'd heard the Prophets say. And so it was. She really was as much Kira Nerys as she was Iliana Ghemor, and it was a sobering thing to understand—that Kira's life had played such a part in shaping such a dark and damaged creature.

She looked at Iliana and saw tears flowing freely down her cheeks, saw her spreading her hands toward the nonexistent sky, soundlessly pleading to those whom she had so fervently sought.

And, at last, she was answered.

A radiant white light enveloped Iliana, permeated her,

and mingled with her. Her features became indistinct as the light steadily escalated in magnitude, but Kira saw her expression change just before she vanished completely. It was a look that Kira recognized, though she had but rarely been sufficiently blessed to experience its cause.

Clarity.

Iliana disappeared.

And then there were two, Kira thought.

"What happened to her?" she asked aloud.

The image of Opaka Sulan answered: "She is the fire."

"What does that *mean*?" Ghemor demanded. "What does *any* of this have to do with *my* universe? What is the Voice?"

"*You* are the Voice," a spectral Winn Adami told her. Kira suddenly noticed that Ghemor's left hand was encircled by the Paghvaram.

"Does that mean I'm the Emissary?"

"You are not the Sisko," Jaro Essa's image proclaimed, as if he were offering clarification. "But you will do."

And like her counterpart, Ghemor also vanished, leaving Kira alone to face her gods.

23

Ezri Dax stood on the bridge, watching the wormhole open yet again as she considered everything that had transpired aboard *Defiant* during the past few tumultuous hours—as well as the recent developments from Deep Space 9's mirror image.

According to the reports that had just come in—and the evidence of Dax's own eyes—O'Brien and his people had successfully beaten back the Klingons who had seized Terok Nor, and had succeeded in steering the station away from the wormhole's event horizon. The station appeared to have sustained only minor structural damage from the tremendous shearing forces of the wormhole's mouth, and had already been settled into a stable parking orbit that corresponded—coincidentally?—to Deep Space 9's position back home.

Thanks to the Talarian fleet and the two *Defiant*s, the Klingon fleet had been entirely routed from the B'hava'el system, at least for the present.

Vaughn had beamed to *Defiant* with Taran'atar in custody, and the Jem'Hadar offered no resistance as Lieutenant McCallum and Ensign Gordimer escorted him straight to the brig.

Dax turned as Vaughn stepped out of the turbolift and onto the bridge, where he cast an appreciative glance at the damage that surrounded him, as well as the organized mayhem of the crew hustling to make final repairs.

He offered Dax a knowing smile. "You've never really captained a starship until you've wrecked the bridge at least once," he said before moving on to a mutual debriefing, each bringing the other quickly up to speed about recent events.

Together, Dax and Vaughn soon reached the conclusion that the only important question that remained unanswered was what had happened to Kira and the two Ilianas. If Taran'atar was to be believed—and Vaughn seemed to think that he was—then Kira and Ghemor had gone after the Intendant alone, and all three were unaccounted for in the aftermath of the explosion that had destroyed Terok Nor's primary airlock.

If they'd been blown out into space, it seemed impossible to think that any of them could have survived.

And then Ezri saw the wormhole open again.

No ship entered or emerged, but Rahim reported detecting two unknown energy emissions: one aimed at Terok Nor, the other at Deep Space 9's *Defiant*.

A moment later a blinding flash appeared on the bridge, smack between the flight control station and the main viewscreen. At the center of the intensifying brilliance, for just an instant, Dax thought she saw the familiar shape of a Bajoran Orb, before the light coalesced into the familiar form of Captain Kira.

Dax allowed a broad grin to escape. "Captain on the bridge!" she cried.

The bridge became a party after that. And as word spread, the jubilation spread throughout the entire ship. Nerys was peppered with questions, naturally, but she kept saying, "Later." She said she was beyond tired, and frankly looked it. All she wanted now, she said, was for the crew to finish making preparations to get under way for the journey home.

"Captain," Sam said suddenly. "We're getting a hail from Terok Nor."

"On screen," Kira said, turning to face the transmission.

It was Ghemor. Or, at least, Ezri *thought* it was Ghemor. She looked like herself again—Cardassian. But her visage carried a strange serenity now that Ezri could recall having seen only once before.

On Benjamin's face.

Ghemor was in ops. Beside her stood O'Brien and Keiko Ishikawa, along with two Bajorans that she recognized as Jaro and Winn.

"We just wanted to thank you and your crew for everything you've done, Captain," Ghemor said to Kira. *"But if you don't mind, everybody here has agreed that it's time that the people of this universe got back to handling their own affairs."*

What a nice way to tell us to get lost, Ezri thought, suppressing a grin.

"So what happens next?" Kira asked.

Ghemor grinned. *"What happens is that things really start to change around here."*

"For the better?" Kira asked.

"We'll see," Ghemor said, and the transmission ceased.

Dax watched as Kira took the command chair, sighing as she settled into it. The captain took one final look at the image of Terok Nor before she spoke the words Ezri had been waiting to hear.

"Set a course for the wormhole, Ensign Tenmei. Take us home."

PART SIX

DEEP SPACE 9

24

Kira leaned forward in the straight-backed chair she had brought with her to security, her elbows resting on her knees, her eyes fixed upon laced fingers. She was less than a meter from the force field barrier that separated her from Taran'atar, but not a word had passed between them during the entire ninety minutes that had elapsed since she'd seated herself in front of his holding cell.

Finally she lifted her head. "What am I going to do with you?"

On the other side of the invisible barrier, Taran'atar answered her only with silence. But she refused to let that silence dissuade her. On some level, she suspected she was doing this more for herself than for him.

Can that be true? Has it become more about me than about him?

She considered the feel of her heartbeat beneath her breast, the steady rhythm of the artificial organ upon which her life had depended ever since the Jem'Hadar had destroyed the original one. Perhaps Sisko had been right when he'd suggested that Taran'atar had been too confused and too conflicted by Iliana's control to distinguish friend from foe when his new god had summoned him to her side. Something inside him had simply broken in that moment, and he really was not to blame for the lethal violence he had unleashed upon her and Ro.

"I think . . ." Kira began, and then immediately lapsed back into silence. *Why is this so hard? He's himself again. Julian confirmed that there's no longer any trace of Iliana's control.*

So why can't I simply do what I came here to do?

She looked into his hard, cobbled face. It was unreadable. And she knew that was the problem, right there: she couldn't tell what he wanted. In fact, the very idea of wanting anything was alien to him. For all of Odo's good intentions, when you got right down to it Taran'atar was little more than the test subject in an ambitious social experiment—one designed to test the possibility of breaking the patterns that the Founders had engineered into him.

An experiment aimed at enabling weaponized sentient beings, creatures familiar only with obedience and violence, to live in peace by choice.

The problem with such test subjects, unfortunately, was that they were sometimes tested to destruction.

So how can this possibly end for him?

She bowed her head and tried again, speaking slowly. "I think I've finally come to terms with the fact that what happened—the things you've done—weren't your fault."

"But it was."

Kira looked up. They were the first words Taran'atar had uttered since he'd surrendered.

"I'm guilty," he said.

Kira sat up straight. "Of what?"

"Of being weak," Taran'atar told her. "Of being vulnerable. Of being a liability to you and those for whom you are responsible. In the Dominion, such crimes are irredeemable."

"That doesn't surprise me," Kira said. "But you aren't in the Dominion. You're in the Federation, where we have far more shades of gray to our lives."

"So I have seen."

"There's something I want to ask you. . . ."

The Jem'Hadar nodded slowly. "Ask."

"All right. If I were to release you from your service to me, what would you do with your freedom?"

"I would return to the Dominion," came an answer that sounded almost like a reflex to Kira's ear. "I would report on my actions, and then accept the judgment of those who understand what it means when a Jem'Hadar soldier breaks his oath."

"You don't want to be judged," Kira said quietly. "You want to be punished."

"I *deserve* to be punished."

But Kira wasn't satisfied with that. And she wasn't certain that he was, either.

"If you're so convinced of your own guilt, then why haven't you simply taken your own life?" she said. "After all, other Jem'Hadar have done the same thing for far less."

Taran'atar didn't answer her that time.

"You see?" Kira said at length. "Shades of gray. I can appreciate your preference for a black-and-white existence. It's a lot simpler—binary: yes or no, on or off, live or die.

"The problem for you, as I see it, is that you've already crossed over into a world that's a lot more complicated than that. You've started questioning the order of things. I honestly don't know if there's any going back for you once you've crossed that line."

Again Taran'atar answered only with silence. Kira sighed and stood up, coming to within a few centimeters of the security force field.

"You once told me that the faith we both had in Odo could be our common ground," she said.

"I remember."

"I'm going to honor that faith for both of us. So there are two things I want you to know. The first thing is that there's a decommissioned Bajoran scoutship at Port Four on the Docking Ring. It's been disarmed and it won't do better than warp five.

"The second thing is that we've repaired the damage you did to your quarters. It's exactly as it was before.

"What I'm telling you is, you have a choice. You can return to the life you had before you were compromised, try to move beyond it, and rebuild what you have here. Or you can leave. Go where you want. As I said, the choice is yours. I'm setting you free. . . . What you do with your freedom is up to you."

Kira reached toward the control pad on the holding cell's outer wall, and the force field snapped off. Then she turned away from him and started to leave.

"I was not meant to be free," Taran'atar said.

Kira stopped at the exit, and answered him over her shoulder. "Maybe. But I'm afraid you're going to have to find a way to deal with freedom, just the same. The strings have been cut. All of them. For better or worse, Taran'atar, you have to make your own choices now. But whatever you decide to do from this moment on, you won't be able to hide behind your genes anymore."

Kira walked out, not waiting on his decision.

With a gentle upward push, Sisko tossed the baseball a rough meter into the air. By the time the small sphere reached the apex of its ascent, he had completed his back-swing, and he was now following through as the ball fell to the level of his heart. The crack of wood against tightly stitched pseudoleather echoed across Kendra Valley as the ball rocketed into the clear sky, sailing over the line of trees that defined the western edge of his and Kasidy's home on Bajor.

In the shade of his favorite *nya* tree, Sisko lowered his bat and scowled as he watched the ball disappear from sight. It was still arcing too far to the right. Never in his life had he seemed to have so much trouble keeping his aim true.

He stooped to retrieve another ball from the half-empty bucket at the base of the tree. As he straightened, he caught sight of a familiar figure marching toward him across the meadow that led back to the house: Vaughn.

Like Sisko, the commander was in civilian clothes—black turtleneck shirt and matching trousers under a light brown jacket. But this informal attire did little to mask the tension in the older man's bearing as Vaughn closed the distance between them. Ben saw what was coming, and he let the bat and ball slip from his fingers, keeping his hands at his sides.

Vaughn came at him and swung, striking Sisko hard across the jaw.

Sisko stumbled back a half step and breathed, letting the pain do its work, waiting as his vision blurred for a moment and then cleared. From the instant he'd learned about Vaughn's return to Deep Space 9, he'd expected this, and the commander's choice to come to him in civvies had merely clinched it; Vaughn simply wasn't the type to strike a superior officer while wearing the uniform. And they both knew Sisko had it coming.

"You son of a bitch," Vaughn snarled. "I trusted you."

"I know," Sisko answered quietly. "And I'm sorry."

"You're sorry?" Vaughn repeated the words as if they'd been spoken in an unfamiliar language. "Do you have any idea what I did over there? *Do you?*"

"Yes. I do," said Sisko. "You ended one person's suffering so that others could be saved."

"*Why?* Why did you lie to me?"

"I didn't have a choice."

"Oh, the hell you didn't," Vaughn said. "The hell you didn't! You played on my trust, you told me everything you knew I'd need to hear to get me to play your game. You even convinced me to lie to my own CO—your friend! You planned all that very carefully, Captain, so don't you dare stand there and tell me to my face that you didn't have a choice! *Everyone* has a choice!"

"It was necessary."

"Necessary for *whom*?" Vaughn demanded.

Sisko sighed. "You know Who, Elias."

Vaughn stared at him. When he found his voice again, it seemed on the verge of cracking. "Was it supposed to be me? Did you send me over to——" He stopped, as if afraid to ask the question, then tried again. "Did I have to go through all that because They meant for me to become the other side's Emissary?"

"Would you really believe any answer I gave you at this point?"

That seemed to surprise Vaughn. "I don't know. . . . Probably not."

"Then maybe you should let it go for now."

Vaughn shook his head. "Don't do that! Don't talk to me as if there's some dire secret you're protecting me from."

"It isn't for your protection, Elias," Sisko said. "It's for everyone else's. It was never about you. It was about making sure that when events do finally come to a head, all the right players are on the field, exactly where they need to be in order to win."

"Are you listening to yourself?" Vaughn asked. "Do you have any idea what you sound like? What the hell has happened to you?"

Sisko abruptly turned away and recovered his bat. "You haven't known me long enough to ask me that."

Vaughn yanked the bat out of his grasp, forcing Sisko to look at him. "Maybe not. But I know what the people who served under Captain Benjamin Sisko think about him. I know he earned their respect, their admiration, and their loyalty. And with all due respect, sir—that

doesn't sound like a man who would manipulate someone as callously as you manipulated me."

"Maybe I'm just not deserving of my sterling reputation," Sisko said, the bitterness of his words ringing in
his own ears.

"Or maybe you've simply gotten in too deep with this
whole Emissary thing," Vaughn said. "You aren't living
by *your* rules anymore. You're living by *Theirs*."

Sisko had no answer.

The commander's knuckles were white around the
slender end of Sisko's bat. Then, as if fearing what he
might do next, Vaughn broke it against the trunk of the
nya tree.

"Find someone else to play your games, Captain,"
Vaughn said as he walked away. "I'm done with them."

Ro hobbled off the turbolift on her cane and stepped into
the Habitat Ring. She would need to hurry if she was
going to have time to shower before her next physical
therapy appointment with Kol. Now that the station was
starting to settle back into some semblance of normalcy,
she found that she couldn't wait to be free of her damned
exoframe. Subjecting herself regularly to Kol's sadistic
ministrations was the only way she had to keep her recovery time to a tolerable minimum.

Sweat beaded on her forehead as she rounded the
curve of the deck that led to the sector of the ring that
housed her quarters. She could see her door.

Almost there.

As she got closer, she noticed that someone had stuck
a small envelope to the external keypad.

That's odd, she thought. *Who would— Oh. Quark. Of course.*

She shook her head as she grabbed the envelope and keyed the door open with her thumb. *He just won't give up*, she thought, letting her cane drop as she reached her sofa. She settled into the cushions and unsealed the envelope. *What'll it be this time? Another holosuite invitation? Dinner in his quarters? A weekend getaway in Ashalla?* Despite the fact that she and Quark had, by mutual agreement, decided a few weeks ago to keep things casual between them, he was still an incorrigible flirt.

Ro took out the piece of hardcopy and unfolded it.

It wasn't from Quark.

The note bore a few handwritten Bajoran characters, including the Bajoran analog for the sender's initial. The message was brief:

> *I'm sorry.*
> T.

Ro stared at the note for a moment until she took it in and comprehended it. Suddenly, she found it difficult to breathe. Her emotions seethed. She wasn't even sure which emotions they were, only that they were coming too fast and threatened to overwhelm her. She closed her eyes against her conflicted feelings and crumpled the note in her fist.

She tried to relax, and after her breathing had finally settled down she read the note again.

This time tears welled up in her eyes.

"Computer," she called out, reaching for her cane. "Locate Taran'atar."

"Taran'atar is not aboard the station."

Ro blinked. "Repeat."

"Taran'atar is not aboard the station."

The cane fell from Ro's fingers, landing on the carpet, along with her tears. She didn't answer the door when Kol came calling a short while later, and she wept long into the night.

25

The Anomaly opened, and he was back in the Gamma Quadrant.

The old Bajoran warp vessel vibrated noticeably when its sublight drive was engaged. More than once during his brief passage through the wormhole, he had doubted his ability to maintain the ship's structural integrity. He could only hope that the FTL propulsion system would offer a smoother flight; at warp five, it would be a long voyage back to the Dominion.

Through his starboard viewport shone the star Idran, which cast yellow-orange shafts of light into his control cabin. Pivoting the scoutship away from the star, he plotted his course and entered it into the autopilot. The onboard computer acknowledged his navigational instructions, then prompted him to confirm the ship's heading. After a final tap of his gray finger on the flight control console, the vessel jumped to warp.

The Dominion.

Knowing he was returning home to the ordered, disciplined life he understood so well felt decidedly agreeable. It had been too long since he'd led true soldiers into combat, too long since he'd carried out the will of the Founders.

Too long since he'd acted according to his design.

More than likely a swift death awaited him, as with all deviant Jem'Hadar. The flaw of his nondependency on ketracel-white had been identified before his exile, after all, and that alone would have merited his termination, had it not been a precondition for his assignment to Deep Space 9. But when it became known that this defect had since been compounded—his body's occasional need to eat, sleep, and dream, as well as all the damage done to his mind by Iliana Ghemor and L'Haan—he doubted that even Odo would have any further use for him, especially once he learned what Taran'atar had done to Kira Nerys.

It was acceptable. Better to die a Jem'Hadar than to live as a deviant.

An alert flashed on his console. The communications system had picked up a faint subspace signal from several parsecs distant. He ignored it.

Moments later, he looked at his console again. *An audio transmission.*

Taran'atar put it on the control cabin's speakers, and was rewarded with a burst of static . . . and something else as well. He fine-tuned the reception, boosting the gain.

"*. . . anyone . . .*"

Taran'atar activated a filter, hoping it would reduce the white noise until the voice being drowned out beneath it emerged.

"... *attack. Please* ..."

He tried another filter, then another. Eventually the message resolved as much as he thought it would given its signal strength and the limitations of his equipment; a tinny, digitally distorted voice emerged.

"... *This is the independent courier* Even Odds, *calling anyone within range of this transmission. Our ship is under attack. Repeat, we are under attack. Please, if anyone is receiving this, we request immediate assistance.* ..."

The message repeated. A loop.

After the eighth iteration, the signal began to break up, despite every signal enhancement he had brought to bear on it. His ship was moving out of the signal's range.

By the twenty-first iteration, it had dissolved completely.

He turned off the speakers, and his ship continued in silence toward Dominion space. He contemplated the signal for the next nine minutes.

Then Taran'atar made a choice.

He altered course and set out to find the distress call's source.

EPILOGUE

For the first time in millennia, the Ascendants were gathering.

Raiq felt the heat of her soul rise as more and more Archquesters strode over the lip of the crater on the barren planet to which they had been summoned. Slowly and with purpose they descended its slopes to join the rings of tall, gleaming knights that had already begun forming within the caldera of black volcanic glass. With each new arrival, the crude fire at the center of the assemblage seemed to burn more brightly, its dancing flames mirrored in the reflective surfaces of the Archquesters' organic armor, and in every mercurial face.

Raiq's fluted, luminous eyes turned toward the watching stars above; whatever transpired here this night, it pleased her to know that the Unnameable would witness it.

Never in all her long cycles of life had Raiq dared hope to take part in such a congregation. She'd held to her faith that the Fortress of the True would be found in her lifetime . . . but untold generations of Questers had come and gone believing theirs would be the time when the Unnameable and their chosen people would be reunited—when the Ascendants would be judged, and burned, and join with their elusive gods once and for all. It was the longing of every knight: that they would live to see their faith rewarded. But the long centuries had seen their numbers dwindle, and had scattered them ever more thinly across the vast reaches of space. In their neverending quest to achieve the Final Ascension, theirs had become a race of nomads, proud and solitary, so that now even the pairings necessary to propagate their kind were few and far between. Not since they had last united for war, ages ago when the heretical Eav'oq had been driven into hiding, had there been a cause great enough to call the leaders of the Orders together.

Raiq knew this was not a call to new action, however; it was, rather, one of desperation. Many knights, she among them, had reported receiving signs that the Unnameable had returned, and that a new breed of heretics had risen to claim kinship with Them. Raiq herself believed she had recently encountered a shaman of the false worshippers. But because of the lifedebt she owed that priestess, Raiq had stayed her swift and vengeful hand, issuing only a thinly veiled warning to Opaka Sulan that she would do well to fear any future contact between them.

Other signs had been just as telling—none more so than the realignment of stars in the very vicinity of Raiq's encounter with Opaka, and the rumored return of the Eav'oq that had followed it. Yet despite the power of these omens, the Ascendants still had failed as yet to reach the Fortress of the True, finding instead that they were divided by doubt and uncertainty about the Path they were to take, and sidetracked still further by a conflict with one of this region's newer empires, the so-called Dominion and the shape-shifting false gods who ruled it.

To answer that growing discord, the Archquesters of the Ascendants were now, by mutual agreement, convening to debate the conflicting interpretations of the signs. Raiq approved; divisions among the Orders at such a critical moment would be their undoing. Unity was the only acceptable course—even if it meant resorting to another civil war in order to achieve it. Better that one side should annihilate the other than both be held back from the True by internal strife. For just as each knight was responsible for seeking the destruction of those who worshiped falsely, so too were the Ascendants avowed to cleanse their ranks of heterodoxy.

As the last of the Archquesters filled the caldera, one knight detached himself from the innermost circle and quelled the central fire with a wave of his long silver hand. As the light died, a dark tetrahedron was revealed within, unblemished by the flames. Raiq held her breath as a ritual she had previously known only through scripture played out before her eyes. The knight's voice rang out across the crater, calling on the Unnameable to reveal themselves and sanctify this gathering of their faithful soldiers.

At the conclusion of his prayer, the knight silently brought his palms together, then spread his hands wide. In response, the triangular sides of the tetrahedron flowered open, and in the dim starlight Raiq could make out the faceted shape within: a crude crystal cylinder, narrow in the middle, flaring at the top and bottom—the last of the revered Eyes of Fire.

Once there had been nine. It was said that in ancient times, the Eyes burned with inner Fire of the True, and through them the Unnameable had watched their followers, and sometimes spoke to them by imparting dreams. But that was before the crusade against the Eav'oq had turned knight against knight, devastating the Ascendants' homeworld but purifying its survivors. Eight of the Eyes had been lost in the conflagration, and the last one—this one—had been dark ever since.

With the ritual concluded, the knight turned to address the gathering. As he did so, Raiq's mouth dropped open—along with that of every other Ascendant in the crater.

Within the Eye, a light had begun to burn.

Seeing the shocked expressions of his fellow Archquesters, the officiating knight turned in time to see the light of the Eye flare to blinding intensity. Raiq instinctively brought up her hands to shield her eyes, but it was too late: her vision whited out, the heat of the lightburst warming her armor before quickly dissipating. Slowly her sight cleared, and she could make out the officiating knight standing before the Eye, manually closing the walls of its casket.

Then Raiq realized her mistake.

The officiating knight, having been closest to the burst, had fallen to his knees, and he was still there, covering his head with his hands. But the figure standing before the Eye casket was no Ascendant. She was smaller, unarmored, her dull gray skin punctuated with prominent ridges that defined the edges of her face—a face framed in long black hair.

The Archquesters stared in stunned silence until one of them—Raiq could not tell who—asked the question that surely burned in the mind of every gathered knight.

"Who . . . are . . . you?"

The stranger looked out over the congregation, and she answered with the words the Ascendants had waited millennia to hear.

"I am the Fire," she told them.

ACKNOWLEDGMENTS

As it was with *Fearful Symmetry*, I'm indebted to a small army of folks who paved my way, including the talented producers of *Star Trek: Deep Space Nine*—but most especially Robert Hewitt Wolfe, who introduced Iliana Ghemor in the episode "Second Skin."

To all the DS9 novelists who came before me, especially S. D. Perry for *Rising Son*; J. Noah Kym for *Fragments and Omens*; David R. George III for *Olympus Descending*; and David Mack for *Warpath*.

To my editors: Marco Palmieri for starting me off, and Margaret Clark for seeing me through.

And finally, to Paula Block, for an idea I simply couldn't resist.

ABOUT THE AUTHOR

Olivia Woods was born in Cape Town, South Africa, where she also spent her early childhood before moving with her parents to Ireland. At the age of fourteen she came to live with her extended family in the United States and began her torrid and enduring love affair with all things *Star Trek*. She currently resides in upstate New York with her spouse and daughter.

Star Trek: Deep Space Nine

The Never-Ending Sacrifice

by Uma McCormack

Coming in September 2009

One

While he was still a young man, Rugal Pa'Dar experienced loss, separation, a brutal frontier war, and the attempted destruction of his species. Yet, if asked, he would say without hesitation that the worst moment of his life was when he realized he would not be returning to Bajor with his father. All the rest of it, that was simply the Cardassian experience. The Cardassian lot. Practically everyone else he knew had gone through it too, and at least Rugal was one of the survivors. But being taken away—not wanting it, but being unable to do anything to prevent it—that was the defining moment of his life. He was sixteen when it happened. The shock of it propelled him forward for the best part of a decade, before he came to rest.

Rugal and Proka Migdal had come to Deep Space 9 for the same reason that many people go on a journey: they were hoping to make a fresh start. Migdal—Rugal would always think of him first as *Father*—had, as a young man, been a policeman in a city that the Cardassians had chosen to obliterate. In the years that followed, oppression, poverty, and a regrettable tendency to end up in the middle of whatever fistfight was going on around him had left their mark on Migdal. He had lost his only child when Korto City had been destroyed, and he had lost his most recent job when a fellow construction worker had made a sly comment about his adopted son. Migdal had thumped him. The other man thumped him back, very hard, and Migdal, who was not a young man, fell unceremoniously to the floor. After he had been patched up, he was shown the door.

Neither his wife, Etra, nor his son was greatly surprised to see him back home so early. In all the burgeoning city of Ashalla, which seemed daily to be expanding as the Bajoran people woke up to their freedom and the opportunities it was bringing them, it seemed that only Proka Migdal regularly found himself out of work. His problem, Etra said, was that there was no going home for him. Some people were like that about a place. They could never settle down anywhere else. But Korto was gone for good. So they'd have to make the best of all that Ashalla had to offer.

"I've finished with this city," Migdal said.

Etra and Rugal exchanged long-suffering looks.

"It's turning into a bad place. Everybody's on the make. Nobody has time for anyone else. It's nothing like it used to be on Bajor. I blame the Circle, setting us all against each other like that."

Proka Etra was a sensible woman who had humored her husband's diffuse and not always well-informed monologues for many years. She was a seamstress—properly talented, Migdal liked to say; her grandparents had all been *Ih'valla* caste, although that was something else that had changed on Bajor now, and not necessarily for the better—and she made good money from piece work.

All these new arrivals in the city needed something to wear. Right now, Etra was barely on schedule and her mouth was full of pins. She made a soothing noise and carried on with her work.

"I was talking to Reco outside the temple last night," Migdal went on, "and he was saying that the place to be these days is that big space station the spoonheads put up . . . Prophets, what are they calling it these days?" He snapped his fingers, trying to recall the new name. "Why do they have to keep on changing everything?"

"Deep Space 9," Rugal offered, without looking up from his lessonpadd. He rubbed the ridge above his right eye and tried to concentrate again. He was studying for a school test on the causes of the Occupation and he did not find the subject easy reading.

"That's it! Deep Space 9! That's the place to be! More and more people passing through there every day, Reco said. I bet they could do with a good seamstress up there, Etra. What do you think? We've never lived on a space station."

Etra made what Migdal took to be an encouraging sound.

"I could go up, take a look round, see whether we'd like it. Rugal could come too, it'd get us both out of your way while you get all that finished." He was as excited as a boy with a *jumja* stick the size of his head. "What do you think, Rugal? A fresh start? Isn't that what we need?"

Rugal had reached a section in the text that was supposed to detail the role played by the Obsidian Order in the conquest of Bajor, but was in fact a series of lurid vignettes. "What we really need, Father," he replied, "is for you not to lose your temper once we've made it."

Migdal frowned. Etra stopped her work and gave her

husband a fierce look. And since nothing was ever done in that small household that would make Etra truly unhappy, Migdal relaxed and laughed. Rugal put aside his books—truth be told, he wasn't all that enthusiastic about school work—and he and Migdal cooked supper while Etra worked.

Father and son were in high spirits when they went over to the spaceport the next day. Migdal was upbeat and optimistic, as he always was at the start of a new chapter. Rugal was glad to be getting out of school and grateful his father was so cheerful. Whenever they ended up moving on, Migdal always made it seem like an adventure rather than Rugal's fault. They enjoyed the journey out to Deep Space 9, and if anyone remarked upon a Bajoran man traveling with a Cardassian boy, they managed not to hear it.

Both Migdal and Rugal took to the station immediately. True, Bajorans were in the majority here, and Cardassians a very marked minority, but with all the other strange people passing through, it did seem that this was the kind of place where their odd little family could live in peace and without the constant comment about Migdal's Cardassian son that tended to result in his losing first his temper and then his job. Within a couple of hours, father and son were sure they would come to Deep Space 9. They went into the Ferengi's bar to celebrate their decision. It was a measure of Migdal's cosmically appalling luck, Rugal would later reflect, that almost the first person they ran into was Elim Garak.